The Honeymoon

TINA SESKIS

PENGUIN BOOKS

PENGUIN BOOKS

UK | USA | Canada | Ireland | Australia
India | New Zealand | South Africa

Penguin Books is part of the Penguin Random House group of companies
whose addresses can be found at global.penguinrandomhouse.com.

Penguin
Random House
UK

First published in Penguin Books 2017
001

Text copyright © Tina Seskis, 2017

The moral right of the author has been asserted

Set in 12.5/14.75 pt Garamond MT Std
Typeset by Jouve (UK), Milton Keynes
Printed in Great Britain by Clays Ltd, St Ives plc

A CIP catalogue record for this book is available from the British Library

ISBN: 978–1–405–91797–1

FT
Pbk

PART ONE
Missing

The ᵣ.

ABOUT THE AUTHOR

Tina Seskis grew up in Hampshire, and after graduating from the University of Bath spent over twenty years working in marketing and advertising. She is the author of two other novels, *One Step Too Far* and *When We Were Friends*. Tina lives in North London with her husband and son.

I

Now

I gaze at the sea, and it is a wondrous, ever-shifting patchwork of paint-box blues, the likes of which I've never seen before, and I wonder if he's out there. I strain my eyes to look for a snorkel, a flash of yellow, but the glow of the indigo further out is so deep and dominant I'm not sure I would even notice. I wait forever, but still there is nothing. A bat flaps lazily above my head, and then it turns and heads back into the trees.

My feet can feel the silken scratch of the sand, and it grates against my fractured nerves. My head throbs, almost to the point of nausea. Nothing feels right. He will come back, I am sure of it. Everyone has rows, even in paradise. I just have to wait for him.

I sink down on to the beach and sit cross-legged. I let the sand sift through my fingers, soft like dust. It makes me think of ashes, the urn on the mantelpiece at home, and I wonder if he is dead. The thought drifts into my mind so calmly it borders on trauma.

Time passes. The sun continues its inexorable rise into the whisper-thin sky as the heat settles on my skull, and my arms and legs begin to burn, even at this hour. My bones feel spongy and useless. But I cannot leave. I have to wait for him. The moment I turn away will be when he comes back. After all, it's happened before.

Watching for him becomes all-encompassing, like a mantra. My eyes strain with the effort, and my brain aches, and then, minutes or hours later, finally it is too much. I bow my head, and I can't look any more. I can't look out at nothing forever – it will be the undoing of me.

I stand up. The beach is empty. I walk across the soft white sand towards our bungalow, which is set back in the palm trees, nearly invisible from the beach. The sunlight freckles through the lush green canopy, and the heat is sultry. The brightness can't burn off the foreboding, though. It seems to permeate the island now, insidious and subtle. I stall, at the slightest noise from the bush, and I wonder who is there. I call his name, and I can hear the fear in my voice.

Nothing.

Perhaps it was just a lizard, or a bird. My mind is piled high with crazy theories and demonic premonitions, and the longer I wait the more the absence of my husband grows, like a monster puppet shadow over this most utopian of places.

I return to the bungalow and search, just in case, but he's not in the bedroom, nor in the lounge. I check in the bathroom, and even in these circumstances I acknowledge that there will never be another bathroom like

4

this. It is outdoors, enclosed by large-leaved exotic plants shielding tall white walls, and it has its own infinity plunge pool, a free-standing bath, an outside jungle shower, matching his-and-hers sinks. At night, the lamps light up the fronds of the palms and make the geckos glow, and it's almost as beautiful as the beach itself.

But he's not to be found here either, which of course I knew, and it's at this point I decide that I can't wait any longer. I have to report that he's gone.

2

Seven-and-a-half years earlier

The evening Jemma met Dan was bitter and stormy, and the weather had only added to her reluctance to go. She'd even tried to compose a text politely cancelling, but she'd prevaricated over its precise wording for so long that in the end she'd decided it was too late, and far too rude, to send it. Yet sometimes being a woman of her word did Jemma no favours, and her subsequent journey to meet Dan took her through London at its worst. The rush-hour Tube had been halted in a tunnel, without explanation, for just a minute or two too long for the passengers' potential-terrorism-frazzled nerves, and unease had crept through the carriage from human to human, spreading and growing like a malevolent virus, infecting everyone. And then, when the lights had *finally* come back on and the train had lurched into the station, a tall well-dressed man had physically barged past her on the platform, as casually as if she'd been a swing door, without even looking back. She was still fuming when she reached the top of the escalator, where the warm atmosphere of below ground was replaced by a fierce, freezing rush of air that came at her so viciously it nearly knocked her backwards. The final insult was that it was raining, hard and horizontal, and completely appearance-ruining.

The only saving grace was that the pub her date had suggested was right opposite the Tube station, as he had promised. Its fascia was newly painted, and even through the deluge Jemma could see a dim, upmarket glow coming from the hanging industrial-style lamps inside. It looked inviting, and safe; a welcome respite from the foulness of the evening. She checked her watch. Despite her journey, she was seven minutes early, and the thought of having to hang around only made her feel more stressed somehow. But at least it gave her plenty of time to dry off, compose herself, make herself look presentable. And, who knew, the evening might even be fun – and even if it wasn't, she had nothing to lose. She never had to see him again.

Jemma put her leather handbag over her head as ineffectual protection from the rain and sprinted diagonally across the road, dodging cars and buses and puddles with the expertise of a true Londoner. As she burst into the pub, someone familiar turned from the bar and looked over quizzically. *Oh shit*. Was he early too? It was a strange feeling – as if they already knew each other, which she supposed they sort of did, seeing as they'd read each other's online dating profiles and had emailed each other a couple of times. He was a little taller than she'd imagined, but still instantly recognizable; and, if anything, better-looking than his photo. Jemma realized she had no choice but to brazen it out. She marched across the dull wooden boards, her head held high, despite being completely drenched.

'Hi – Dan?' she said, trying to keep the question in her voice as discreet as she could manage, but still making the cute barman immediately look over.

'Hi, yes. Jemma?'

'Hello,' she said, and she wondered just how bad she looked, although she supposed it didn't matter. It wasn't as if she was ever going to marry the guy.

'Good to meet you.' He said it quietly, and shuffled awkwardly, making no attempt to kiss her or even shake her hand. He looked dubiously at the rain dripping off her. 'Er, would you like a drink?'

'In a minute,' she said. 'I think I'd better go and stick my head under the hairdryer first.' She flashed him a smile that she hoped was full of bravado. 'And then I'll have a glass of red, thanks.'

'Of course.'

'I won't be long.' As Jemma walked across the half-empty room, she could hear the tap-tapping of her ankle boots, and she could feel eyes watching her. When she reached the toilets she went straight to the mirror and was relieved to see that she didn't look quite as bad as she'd imagined. Just soaked through, and a bit flushed, perhaps. She could feel the rhythm of her heart, though: quick and insistent, definitely edgy somehow. Or maybe it was simply that she was still out of breath. She took a couple of deep gulps of air as she grabbed some paper towels and rubbed her hair with them, wiped the water off her coat sleeves. She rummaged in her handbag, found her one item of make-up and smudged it on to her lips, rendering them pink and pale. In the absence of a comb she ruffled her pixie hair with her fingers, and decided she quite liked the wet look. Her eyes glowed, feisty yet startled, like a rambunctious tiger cub's. She'd looked worse.

When Jemma got back to the bar she could tell that the barman had sussed that she and Dan were on some kind of blind date, and she blushed. Dan picked up their drinks and led her towards the back of the pub, but even as Jemma slid into an old-fashioned booth in the corner, she still felt on show. 'Would you like to get anything to eat?' Dan asked, as his opening gambit. 'They do good tapas-type stuff.'

'No, I'm fine, thanks.' There was an awkward, self-conscious silence. She took in his khaki jacket, which looked new, and the blue shirt beneath it. She'd noticed earlier that he was wearing dark narrow-leg jeans, although she couldn't see them now, and some kind of suede boots, which she'd liked. His eyes were bark-coloured.

'Have you had to come far?' he asked.

'Oh, just from work. It was only four stops on the Tube. It would have been easy – apart from the crowds, the rain, a nerve-jangling blackout in the tunnel . . .' She smiled, to show she was joking, and picked up her drink. Her hand was shaking a little, and she wondered what was wrong with her. She felt weird in a way she hadn't expected, and that she couldn't quite put a name to. He was attractive, she had to give him that, but not at all her type – which was probably because her best friend had picked him out in the first place, saying he looked perfect for her. *Bloody Sasha*, Jemma thought now, always thinking she should play Cupid. Why did she listen to her?

Jemma watched as Dan picked up his pint. She assumed it was real ale rather than lager, as it was rich and dark-golden, with a pale foam on the top, like spittle. His hands were rough, and although his nails were neatly clipped, they had thin lines of dirt deep under them.

'So, you're an interior designer, Jemma?' Dan was looking straight at her, unblinking. There was an intensity to his gaze which felt almost intrusive.

'Yes.'

'And what does that involve?'

'Oh, you know. Nothing remotely glamorous, like people think. Just normal office life, really . . .' She paused, and Dan didn't step in to rescue her. Instead he was still staring, waiting for her to speak. 'Er, so you're a garden designer?' she managed at last. 'That sounds exciting.' She almost sounded rude – her jokes had a tendency to come out wrong when she was nervous.

'Hardly,' Dan said. 'Mostly I dig holes and shift dirt about.'

'Oh.' What was she meant to say to that? Was he joking? Or just deliberately making it hard for her? But it didn't matter anyway, she reminded herself. The way things were going, there was no way they'd have a second date. She just needed to get through tonight. She decided she preferred her normal method of meeting guys, which was almost always whilst drunk.

A group of men in suits entered the bar, and their blokeish banter breathed welcome life into the atmosphere, enabled Jemma and Dan's conversation to be more private at last.

'Have you done this many times before?' Dan asked now.

'No. You?'

'A few. Nothing has really taken off.'

'Oh,' she said. And then the conversation fizzled out again. When she dared another look at him, his eyes were brooding, perhaps slightly tormented, and so she turned her gaze down, studied the table, the deep grooves in the dark wood, noticed how Dan's hands seemed to meld in with it. When she imagined them touching her face she experienced an odd jolt, and almost felt like asking him if he wanted to cut the crap and just go home and have sex with her, but of course she didn't. Besides, she knew *nothing* about him. He could be anyone. He could be a stalker – or even a murderer. The thought appalled her. She'd had enough. Why were they wasting each other's time?

'Look, I'm sorry,' she said. 'I think I'm going to have

to go in a minute . . . I, er, I've got a bit of a headache coming on.'

'Oh,' said Dan. Was he disappointed? It was hard to tell. He unnerved her somehow.

'I'm sorry,' she said. She couldn't look at him. 'I'm not usually like this. Honest.' She muttered goodbye and virtually ran across the bar, ignoring the doe-eyed barman, who was still looking far too interested in proceedings, and out into the rain. And then when Sasha called later to ask her how it had gone, Jemma was far too pissed off with her best friend to pick up.

3

Now

It should be the fifth morning of our honeymoon, and even though I swore just a minute ago that I would report my husband missing, I still pray that maybe, miraculously, he'll turn up. Surely he must be on the island somewhere, I tell myself – sunbathing on one of the secluded beaches, perhaps. Despite the ominous feeling that hovers like an unseen hand at my throat, it seems I'm still not ready to face the idea of the outcome being anything else. The island is too big to navigate quickly on foot, and so I take one of the sand bikes they've given us to whizz around on, for when we don't want to walk (heaven forbid) or be chauffeured by our butler in a golf buggy. I find myself doing a lap of the island, calling for him, which wastes another twenty minutes or so that other people could have been looking for him too.

And yet still I delay. I don't want to raise a false alarm, or, perhaps more pertinently, attract any unnecessary attention. Instead I head to the main restaurant. Maybe he slept on the beach somewhere, and now has come here for breakfast? It's possible. A swift

13

glance around the mostly empty tables assures me he hasn't, but I go inside to scout out the buffet anyway. Perhaps he's skulking in one of the corners, waiting for a cheese-and-mushroom omelette, his favourite.

As I search amongst the various serving stations, with their gleaming silver domes, I feel a growing sense of despair. At home I usually just eat toast for breakfast, and the mountains of food here overwhelm me – even more so today, now that I feel sick to my stomach with champagne and fear. I find I don't want pork dumplings, or bacon and eggs, or pancakes, or beef enchiladas, or chicken curry. I don't want fried fish, or sushi, or cold meat and cheeses, or yoghurt, or muesli. I really don't want doughnuts. The sight of crispy duck turns my stomach. I just want to know where my husband is.

'Yes, ma'am?' a voice says now. I realize I've been standing still, as if rooted to the spot by the profligacy of the offerings. It is Chati, my favourite chef, in a tall white hat, and he has a wide, wicked smile and teeth as sparkling as a toddler's. As I stare forlornly at him, my sense of despair grows at his inability to help me. I don't have the heart to tell him that I'm not hungry, and in a hurry, so I let him serve me an unidentifiable curry that under normal circumstances might be lovely for dinner, but that I know I won't eat, and certainly not for breakfast. He hands me the plate like it's treasure.

I hurry outside, to our usual table, intending to put down my food and scarper. 'Morning, ma'am,' says our breakfast waiter, Bobbi, who appears from nowhere and helps me into my chair. I feel I have no choice but to sit down. 'Would you like tea or coffee this morning?'

The question stumps me. *Of course* I don't want either. I don't want to be here in the restaurant, with a plateful of food. I need to go and report my husband missing, like I said I would. I'm just wasting time here, time that could make all the difference. *What the hell am I doing?* I jump up, my chair scraping discordantly in this most serene of settings.

'I'm sorry,' I mumble. 'Have you seen my husband?'

'No, ma'am, not this morning, ma'am.'

'I have to go and find him.'

Bobbi doesn't miss a beat. 'OK, ma'am,' he says. He is smiley, like all the staff, so lovely and accommodating, even to apparent capriciousness. 'You have a good day, ma'am.'

The path to Reception, on the other side of the island, is idyllic, palm-fringed. I take my bike, and the fat, soft wheels swish through the sand, setting my teeth on edge. On the way, I decide to make yet another detour to look for him, just in case – I really don't want to make a fuss unless I absolutely have to. I cycle past the tennis courts, and when I see they are empty, a single errant ball abandoned by the nearest net, I feel my panic rising. I am shouting his name now, as though I don't care who hears me. Maybe I want them to hear.

I carry on to the far end of the island, jump off my

bike and run into the dive centre. There I find Pascal, the resident marine biologist, who is French and slim and deeply tanned, and who usually makes me blush – but today I bound up to him, distraught and jabbering, and he just looks blank, as though he doesn't even know who I mean.

I get back on my bike, and when I reach the beauty spa with its treehouse treatment rooms I even decide to stop there, just in case, but it's not open yet. My last hope is the resort pool. He could be having a swim, or be laid out on a lounger. You never know. I'm aware that I'm panting now, and the breaths reverberate through my skull, and when I arrive to see that he's not here either, I swallow down sweet bitter vomit, and it burns the back of my throat.

There's only one other couple in the resort that we've befriended, but of course we didn't come here to be sociable, seeing as we were meant to be on honeymoon. Chrissy and Kenny are at the pool already, although sadly my husband is not. They are laid out on sun loungers, apparently asleep, and I'm loath to wake them. I park my bike and hover uncertainly, until one of the pool staff rushes over to give me a towel, which causes Kenny to stir. When he finally acknowledges me his eyes are bluer than I've ever seen them, like the water – and it's as if the world has been beefed up, has had the contrast and colour turned up to maximum. He gives me a brief nod, but his smile is forced, as though he's not particularly pleased to see me, and I'm suddenly too afraid to ask him if he knows where my husband is.

'Oh, morning, Jemma,' says Chrissy, lazily opening her eyes and noticing me at last. She seems slightly awkward too, or have I just become suspicious of everything? 'You all right? I feel rotten myself, just having a bit of kip.' She waves vaguely, and then shuts her eyes again, and I think it might even be deliberate, so she doesn't have to talk to me.

Kenny shifts on the sun lounger next to her. He jiggles his legs and lets out a theatrical sigh. I stay sitting across from the two of them, stiff and fearful, aware I'm wasting yet more time, wondering how it might end up looking to the staff, once they know. I desperately want to talk to Chrissy, but not in front of Kenny.

'You want another drink?' Kenny says to Chrissy, even though the cocktail she has is still nearly full. He doesn't offer me one.

'Uh-uh,' Chrissy says. She arches her back and lifts her arms above her head and stretches. Her stomach concaves and her hip bones jut out from her £200 bikini bottoms. She looks like a Bond girl.

Kenny continues to fidget. He adjusts his sun bed, picks up his Sudoku book and promptly puts it down again, drums his fingers. I silently will him to leave.

'Kenny!' Chrissy says. She opens her eyes and giggles, but it seems he's annoying her too now. Doesn't he ever sit still? She leans over and picks up her drink, and the fresh lime and mint of what I can only presume is a Mojito is vivid against the ice. I almost ask for a sip.

Kenny seems to get the hint at last. He stands up and hobbles over to the beach, which is just a few yards away, beyond the infinity edge of the pool. He lumbers himself into the postcard hammock and swings his legs off either side. He looks muscular in his swim-shorts, but his stomach is livid against their bright yellow swirls. He really shouldn't be in the sun at all today – he's so burnt already, and it's too fierce for his pasty British skin, even at this hour. His bandaged leg gleams white in the sunshine. He starts humming 'The Girl from Ipanema', and his voice travels across the pool sloth-fully, low and perversely melodious. I'm pretty sure his wife finds it irritating.

Chrissy's eyes are hidden behind her sunglasses.

'Chrissy,' I say, quietly. 'I need to talk to you.'

'OK,' she says. I can't make out her tone. She lifts her glasses onto her head and stares at me. She is fully made up. 'You all right?'

'No. Not really.' I lean back on my sun lounger and stare straight ahead, so I don't have to look at her.

'Well, you were off your face last night.'

I feel myself going red. 'I know, I'm so sorry. But it's not that . . .'

'What's going on?'

'I'm not sure,' I say. 'Probably nothing.'

'Come on, tell me,' she says. She looks around. 'Where's yer hubby?'

'Well, that's just it,' I say. 'I don't know.' My voice breaks a little. I swivel my wedding ring on my finger, and it's too tight.

'What d'you mean, you don't know?'

'I haven't seen him since last night.'

'Oh.'

'Chrissy . . .' As I hear the distress in my voice, I acknowledge it at last. 'His snorkelling gear is gone.'

Chrissy pauses for a moment before she speaks. 'What are you saying?'

'Exactly that.'

'What, you think he might have . . .' She trails off.

'Yes. Maybe. I don't know.'

'Have you told anyone that he's missing?'

'No, not yet.'

'Why not? You must. Oh, flippin' hell, Jemma.' As Chrissy sits up at last, she almost bursts out of her orange bikini top. She takes another huge slug of her cocktail.

'I'm going to. I was on my way, but I thought he might have been here, that's why I came to check. I keep hoping he'll appear somewhere. I don't know what to do.' What a mess, I think as I say it. It's true, though – he could have just gone off on his own for a while, after what happened last night. He could be hidden away, somewhere on the island. It's big enough. But even so, I probably need to tell someone.

'D'you want me to come to Reception with you?' Chrissy says.

'Oh, yes, if you don't mind. Thank you.'

'OK.' She puts down her cocktail, plants her scarlet-painted toes onto the pool decking and stands up. When she puts on her beach dress, which is white and holey, like a sexy string vest, she positions it for maximum cleavage. She seems quite pissed already, or maybe she's still drunk from last night. As she approaches me, she smells of almonds.

'Come on,' says Chrissy. Her skin is smooth nut-brown all over. My supposedly doting husband never knew where to look, and my heart takes a dive as I find myself thinking of him in the past tense, and I'd do anything this morning to watch him gawping at her again.

'Let me just tell Kenny,' she says. She struts her way around the pool over to the beach, albeit a little less brightly than usual. She passes another couple that we see every day but who still look straight through her, as though just because she's from Essex she doesn't deserve to be here. I watch her brief exchange with her husband, and it's clear that Kenny seems shocked, but he nods and continues swinging in the hammock. Physically he's as brash as Chrissy, glittering with gold rings and Rolexes, and although he is currently pink, he is all-male and muscular, and they go well together. They look right together. The big man and his trophy. I wonder briefly how we must have looked. I dread to think.

As Chrissy and I leave, Kenny glances over at me, and there is a look in his eyes that unmasks me, as though he knows all my secrets, and for a moment I feel truly terrible. Yet I manage to walk steadily enough along the pristine white path that leads to Reception, still trying to convince myself that there's probably an innocent explanation. But the closer we get to making this official, the more I shiver and yearn to dawdle – and the more my apocalyptic dread grows.

4

Seven-and-a-half years earlier

'So . . . how did it go?' asked Sasha. 'You cannot keep me in suspense for *any* longer.' She was draped along the length of Jemma's sofa, like an artist's nude. A glass of wine was propped between her chin and the cool brown leather. The glass was in danger of tipping over or, worse, breaking at the stem, but Jemma was either too polite or couldn't be bothered – she wasn't sure which – to say anything. Leather was wipe-clean anyway, she told herself, and at least it wasn't red wine.

'It was a *total* disaster. I'm too embarrassed to even tell you.'

'Ooohh, do elaborate.'

'It's not funny, Sasha. Anyway, I am never doing it again, that's for sure. I would rather my eggs shrivel and die and I end my years being eaten by my cats than go on another date with someone off the Internet. I bloody hated it.'

'So what was the problem? Was he a weirdo?'

'No. He was nice enough.'

'Bad dress sense?'

'No.'

'Shorter than you?'

'Nooo. It was nothing to put your finger on.' How could she explain it to Sasha? She recalled the intense way Dan had looked at her and how uncomfortable she'd felt, yet also how oddly attractive it had been. There was something about him, but she couldn't work out what.

'I just wasn't in the mood,' Jemma said, at last. 'And then I acted like a complete prat.'

'How?'

'Oh, you know. I arrived soaking wet for a start. And then I couldn't look him in the eye, couldn't think of anything to say, had the personality of a plank – that kind of thing.'

'Hmmm. It sounds like you fancied him.'

'I did *not.*'

'Ha! Yes, you did! I can tell.'

'Sasha, I can assure you we didn't get far enough for me to have any feelings about him.' Jemma took a gulp of her wine, and then, shoving Sasha's legs out of the way, sank onto the far end of the sofa.

'But what was he like?'

'I've no idea, really. I didn't stay long enough to find out. He did have some nice boots on, though. That's about as much as I can say. Oh, and he had dirty fingernails.'

'Dirty fingernails? Eeugh. In that case all is forgiven.'

'Yes, but he's a gardener. He works with his hands.'

Even as Jemma said it, she wondered why she was making excuses for him now.

'I *knew* it. You do fancy him!'

'I *don't*.'

Sasha sighed. 'Is it to do with that tosser?'

'What d'you mean?'

'You know exactly what I mean.'

Jemma looked out of the window. Now she and her ex-boyfriend had split up, Sasha didn't hold back. 'Of course not,' she said.

'Oh God. Jem, you're not back with him, are you?'

Jemma decided to be honest. Sasha had the nose for these things, and would wheedle it out of her sooner or later. 'No, it's just he rang me last week.'

Sasha sat up and smacked her legs. 'Oh, bloody hell, I *knew* it.'

'He said he misses me.'

'He was obviously after a shag.'

'Thanks,' said Jemma. 'Sensitive as ever.'

'Sorry,' said Sasha.

Jemma ignored the apology. She picked up two remote controls and busied herself with switching on the TV. Her best friend might well be right, but she didn't need to be so obnoxious about it. It wasn't easy dating a succession of losers, not that Sasha would understand – she had Martin, who she'd been going out with ever since they were all at college together. Sasha had no idea what the dating scene was like these days.

After Jemma had spent an age pressing various

buttons, the TV finally flared into life in the middle of an episode of *Come Dine With Me*. A fight was breaking out over one guest's digestive inability, or else ornery unwillingness, to finish his starter, and that distracted Sasha for a few moments.

'So what are you going to do?' Sasha said, when the ad break came on.

'About what?'

'About Dan.'

'About *Dan*? Nothing.' A tell-tale flush spread up Jemma's neck, which she knew Sasha would have spotted.

'What's his surname again?'

'Armstrong.'

'Hmm, that's quite manly.' Sasha's tone turned casual. 'Why don't you contact him again? Give him a chance.'

'You have *got* to be joking. He thinks I'm an idiot. A rude, personality-free idiot.'

'What did he say when you left?'

'Nothing. Just goodbye.'

'Was he angry?'

Jemma paused. 'Not that I could tell. He was perfectly polite, in fact.'

Sasha said nothing, but Jemma knew her too well.

'Don't even start, Sasha.'

'What?'

'Trying to fix me up with anyone else. I know you're plotting something.'

Sasha expertly flicked her head, so her thick black fringe covered her eyes, hid her expression. 'I am *not*. You are so paranoid.'

'Hmmm. Anyway, I need to go and check on the dinner.'

Jemma got up and went to the kitchen. She was trying out a new recipe that she was unsure about – but seeing as Sasha was on another of her fad diets, it was the only qualifying dish Jemma had found that sounded even half edible.

When Jemma came back into the room a few minutes later, carrying a plate of pistachio-and-quinoa balls on a bed of radicchio in each hand, she paused, immediately aware that something was up. Sasha was still in her prone, potential-wine-spilling position, trying but failing to look nonchalant.

'What's that look on your face?' Jemma said.

'Nothing.'

Jemma shoved one of the plates at Sasha and perched on the arm of the sofa by Sasha's feet. 'What have you done?'

'Nothing.'

'I mean it, Sasha. I know you.'

Sasha didn't have time to answer as Jemma's phone pinged on the coffee table in front of them. Jemma leaned over and snatched it up. Her face turned blush-pink, the colour high on her cheekbones, clashing prettily with her hair. It was an email from Dan, responding to the one 'she' had just sent him.

'Hi Dan,' Sasha had written. 'I am so sorry for my rudeness the other day – I just wasn't myself at all. Of course I entirely understand if not, but if you'd like to give meeting up another go please do get in touch. Best wishes either way and sorry again, Jemma x.'

'You —' Jemma rushed at Sasha, swatted her head, slapped at her face, only half playfully.

'Owwww! That hurt, you nutter! What does it say?'

'I hate you. How did you guess my PIN?'

'Well, I know your birthday, so it was quite easy, actually. What's he said?'

'None of your business.'

'Oh, come *on.*'

Jemma stood up straight, and her face was serious. The room felt smaller suddenly, and she had a feeling that something significant was happening, and she wasn't sure whether she wanted it to, or whether she'd rather it all stopped right there. The guests on *Come Dine With Me* prattled on, indifferent to her plight. Jemma switched on the table lamp, and the light glowed orange as the corners of the room gained definition. It reminded her of old movies that had been retouched into colour, where the shades are not quite nuanced enough to seem real.

'He wants to take me up on "my" offer to meet up again.' Her fingers made speech marks. She pulled her mouth thin and straight, to stop herself saying anything further.

'I knew it! You're welcome.'

'I hate you.'

'You love me.'

'No, Sasha, I don't. You piss me off. And anyway, I'm changing my password. It's not fair on anyone.' Jemma headed back across the steel-grey rug, towards the kitchen. She turned at the door. 'And no, I'm not going,' she said. 'Before you even ask.'

5

Now

A slender, sheeny girl is behind Reception, smiling beatifically. She clasps her hands together and bows slightly
as Chrissy and I approach. She soon stops grinning,
though, as if her computer program has been updated
from 'well-meaning obsequiousness' to 'genuine alarm'.
I feel bad for ruining her morning.

'Oh, my goodness grief,' she says. She appears to
lose grip of her English. 'You think he in sea? When
this happen? You should have report.'

'I'm sorry,' I say. 'It's just I . . . I didn't want to cause
a fuss. I thought he might have gone off somewhere.'

'Mr Armstrong go off island?'

'Um . . . yes . . . no,' I say. 'I'm not sure.'

I don't know what I should say about anything, and
it's clear I'm not helping. But who knows where he
might be – it's pretty hard to hide for long on an island
this size. Yet if this turns out to be serious, I realize I
might be in trouble. In fact I may even be implicated –
I've no idea what the police are like here. I start to cry,
at first perhaps simply to stop the receptionist from
asking any more questions, but then I genuinely start

sobbing, until I can't stop. Chrissy puts her fragrant arm around my shoulder, and I lean into her. It's as if the scene isn't real, as though we're all acting. You're not meant to cry on your honeymoon. There again, you're not meant to sully luxury islands with the unfortunate matter of missing husbands either.

The receptionist – Leena, according to her shiny name badge – makes a phone call through her headset, and as she speaks rapidly in Maldivian, she flutters her hands up and down as if they are little caged birds with scarlet wing tips. I hunch my shoulders and try to calm down, while Chrissy pats my shoulder sympathetically.

'We call Security. We send rescue boat out,' says Leena as she comes off the phone. I can't say anything in reply. It's happening. It's real.

'OK, thanks,' says Chrissy. 'Should we keep looking on the island?'

'No, ma'am,' says Leena. 'The manager is coming.'

'OK, fine. Shall we wait here?'

'Yes, please, ma'am. He here soon.'

Chrissy helps me across the sandy floor of the reception area, as if I'm an invalid, and sits me down at one of the giant round podiums that pass as sofas. The back rests are positioned in a smaller circle in the centre, and they are so far away, it's almost impossible to sit back without lying down. In normal circumstances it would be heavenly, but it seems inappropriate to lounge around now. This whole place is geared to beauty and relaxation, not to drama and regrets and impossible vanishing acts. I know I should tell Chrissy to go back to the pool now that the hotel has been informed. It's not fair to get her caught up in all this, although I suppose she already is.

'I'm sorry, Chrissy,' I say. I'm aware I sound half-hearted, desperate even. 'You can leave me here if you like. I don't want to spoil your honeymoon.'

'Well, maybe I'd better go and tell Kenny what's going on,' she says. As she hauls herself up from the cushions, it seems she can't wait to escape, but then she adds that she'll come straight back, and I'm not sure whether it's because she feels bad for abandoning me, or because she wants to stay involved. It's hard to tell. She walks away, her head held high, her platinum hair blinding against the sun, her statuesque figure swaying with the breeze; and as I watch her leave I want to call after her, beg her to stay, but I can't, so I don't.

6

Seven-and-a-quarter years earlier

At times, Jemma was secretly grateful to Sasha that she'd sent Dan that email, and at others it put her in a quandary. Jemma had never felt able to admit that her friend had written it, as that would have been humiliating for him, and so she'd found herself going on a second date (in a different, busier pub, with a less nosy barman), and she'd finally found her tongue, and then later, outside the Tube station, so had Dan. And when he'd asked her to come to Kew Gardens with him at the weekend, she'd not had anything else on, and the day had felt comfortable, and yet romantic too. The next time they'd met was to see an art house movie that her previous boyfriend wouldn't have dreamed of watching, and as they'd parted ways afterwards, she'd found herself almost annoyed that she still hadn't slept with him – and so, before she'd had time to think, she'd invited him to hers the following week, for dinner.

Now here they were, nearly three months later, apparently boyfriend and girlfriend; and whenever he came round, she'd feel an odd thrill as she opened the door to see him standing there, tall and faintly embarrassed, and smelling of the earth. She and Dan continued to do simple things that she hadn't done with other lovers, such as getting up before dawn to watch the sun coming up over London; or going for a walk in the autumn woods where Dan would tell her what each fallen leaf was and, even more surprising, she'd find she was interested. One time they even took conkers home to bake in vinegar, and then tied strings onto them and had a fight, which Jemma won, of course. She grew to enjoy hanging out with Dan at his place, cooking together, watching box sets of the latest Scandinavian thriller as they cosied up on the sofa, and as the weeks passed, she found happiness creeping up on her, the roots of their relationship being laid down in simple decency, calm acceptance, stability. He became a secret pleasure that she kept to herself, and it suited her.

Yet now Sasha had gone and disrupted the equilibrium by inviting Jemma and Dan for dinner with a group of their other friends. Jemma wasn't exactly sure why she didn't want to go – whether it was because of Sasha's involvement in how she and Dan had got together, or the fact that Dan was shy, or (and she couldn't quite admit it to herself) because he wasn't as sophisticated as her previous boyfriends had been. It didn't help that Sasha could sometimes be a bit full-on, and Jemma didn't trust her not to drunkenly blurt out the truth about the email, which would be terrible. But anyway, whatever the reason, Jemma had decided she was going to tell Sasha that she and Dan were busy.

Jemma pulled on her coat, closed the door to her flat behind her, and started along the long, cold road towards the Tube. It was a Monday morning, and the day was one of those glum autumnal ones, without much to report: low clouds, colourless sky, an apathetic wind, slowly undressing trees revealing houses behind them in need of a paint. The summer was well and truly over, the mornings getting ever darker, and maybe it was that, on top of the unwanted dinner invitation, that was lowering Jemma's mood. She decided that she would call Sasha instead of replying to the email and make her excuses verbally. Sasha would only ring her up anyway and try to force her to come.

A horn tooted, and Jemma ignored it. The sky had begun to spit at her, and she kept her head down as she pulled her coat tighter and put the collar up. The sound repeated, beside her this time, and when she finally looked up she saw Dan, driving a silver van that had 'Armstrong's Landscape Gardening' printed on the side. He was kerb-crawling her, grinning.

'Want a lift, darlin'?'

'What are you doing here?'

'I was on my way to a job in Finchley and thought I might catch you on your way to work. Are you going to get in?'

Jemma did as she was told. She had to clamber up onto the seat, which was grimy. Dan was wearing grubby grey cargo trousers and an old sweatshirt, and his hair was hidden under a baseball cap. An empty sandwich carton sat on the dashboard and crisp packets littered the black plastic footwell. As he grinned shyly at her, she felt conscious of her smart black dress and neat heels. There was a client meeting today about a new upmarket restaurant in Abu Dhabi, and she had to be at her most conservative. It was the first time she'd seen Dan in work mode, and it felt as if they were strangers.

Dan put the van into gear and they roared away, and she wasn't sure whether it was for comedic effect or whether he really did drive it like that. He switched on the wipers and the few drops of rain dragged caked dirt across the windscreen in painful curved strata, making the grit shriek against the glass.

'Ouch, sorry,' he said. 'I've run out of windscreen wash.'

Jemma sat quietly for the two minutes it took to get caught in the traffic that led up to the lights by the Tube. She knew it would be quicker to walk from here, but she didn't want to appear ungrateful. She could feel the pull of attraction towards him across the van, and it confused her a little. She still couldn't believe Dan was her boyfriend, somehow – he was unlike anyone else she'd ever been out with.

When they finally reached the station, she leaned over and briefly kissed him goodbye. Just as she was climbing down from the van, she saw her lawyer neighbour, who gave her a decidedly odd look — and Jemma felt so ashamed of her embarrassment at being seen with her gardener boyfriend that she decided things with Dan had gone far enough now. She needed to finish it.

7

Now

Poor Dad. He sounds heartbroken. Six days ago he'd married off his only daughter, at last, and now he gets me crying and ranting down the phone from my bungalow in the Maldives, as incoherent as a child waking up from a nightmare, and at first he can't even understand me.

'Jemma, love,' he says. 'Jemma, please, calm down, sweetheart. What are you saying?'

'*I said I can't find him*,' I shriek. 'He's gone!'

'OK, OK. Have you had a row?'

'Yes. No. He disappeared, in the night. His mask and flippers are gone. Dad, he's *missing*.' I kick viciously at the hand-carved wooden bed-frame with my silver flip-flop, stubbing my toe, trying to let out some of the panic.

'Oh my word,' says my dad. I imagine him sitting at the desk in his book-lined study, sagging suddenly. He gets it at last.

'What am I going to do?' I ask, more quietly now.

'Has anyone told his parents?'

Even the question, less than a week after our wedding, is diabolical. 'No. I don't think so,' I say. 'I haven't, and the hotel wouldn't know how to contact them.'

'Have the police been told?'

'I don't know. They've sent out a rescue boat though. Oh, Dad, I think he might have *drowned*.' I start heaving, and I can't talk any more. The words have got stuck, and they are so alien it's as though I am trying to put the wrong objects through a child's shape sorter. We were meant to be on our *honeymoon*. There is no space in that sentence for words to do with death.

Dad lets me pause for a few moments, and his unfailing patience at the end of the line boosts me, helps me compose myself. I sit down on the bed, and its softness is at odds with the situation. My floaty orange beach dress with appliqué flowers at the neckline is at odds with it, too. I rip one of the flowers off, which takes quite an effort, but it doesn't make me feel any better.

'Look, Jemma, it's all right, love,' Dad says at last, his breath rasping faintly with stress. 'Do you want me to ring Peter and Veronica?'

'I don't *know*. It's too awful. What if he turns up and I've worried them for nothing?'

'Well, then there's no harm done. I think they need to know.'

'Oh, Dad, I'm so sorry.'

'It's not your fault, love,' he says, and although he keeps telling me over and over, I know that he's wrong, and that it is my fault, but I can't tell anyone that, apart from maybe Chrissy, who almost certainly already knows. The regret seeps out of me as if from a weeping, infected wound. *What on earth have I done?*

When at last I put down the phone, I lie on the bed and bury my head in the pillows and sob, for my husband, for the mistakes we have made. I cry my eyes out, for what might have been, for what might yet be. I allow myself perhaps ten minutes of this indulgence, and then I get up, wipe away my tears, tiptoe onto the terrace and walk out through the trees to the beach. The water is sparkling, but it's so vast, and I see nothing, nothing at all out there, although I know that underneath the cool, blank surface the sea is swarming with hot life. As I patrol the shoreline I will my husband into view, try to magic him back. I make all sorts of promises to him, to myself, even to God, just in case. I almost wish I'd taken up Dad's offer to come out here, but I've told him to hold off for now, wait and see. I don't want to make him travel all this way for nothing.

And so here I am – in the bizarre, surreal, numbing position of being on my honeymoon, yet minus my husband. All I have as support are the friendly, ever-obliging resort staff. There's Chrissy and Kenny too, of course, but they're on their own honeymoon – and, perhaps more pertinently and for all sorts of reasons, our fledgling friendship now feels awkward for all of us.

At last I leave the beach and return to the terrace. I sit down, my hands folded neatly in my lap, my feet still covered in sand. I feel my bottom lip vibrate and I bite it, hard. An image of a body comes into my head, with the sea as an aquamarine backdrop, and I push my fists into my eyes, press so hard my engagement ring stabs my left eyelid, try to will the picture away. I feel sick with horror. I have looked forward to this trip for so many years – and now it seems that it has turned to disaster. I don't know how things have come to this, what we could have done differently. Was any of it possible to predict? I just don't know. All I know right now is that if it does turn out that the worst has happened, ultimately it will be because of me – and I will never ever forgive myself.

8

Seven years earlier

It was early December and Jemma still hadn't got around to finishing with Dan. They'd already had a weekend in Bath booked at the time of the kerb-crawling incident, so she could hardly have done it then. And then he'd got tickets to see her favourite band at Brixton Academy, so that had taken them through to November. And of course the sex was great, so what was the point of giving that up for no good reason? The relationship was easy, fulfilling, yet casual for both of them. For a busy twenty-seven-year-old career girl it was fine.

Today Jemma and Dan were on their way to his parents' for lunch, ostensibly for Dan's birthday; plus Jemma had run out of excuses as to why she couldn't ever meet them. Although Dan had delivered a couple of mild warnings on the way, Jemma hadn't taken too much notice, as it didn't really matter what the parents were like. It was just a nice day out in the country, she told herself. It didn't need to mean anything more.

Dan's parents' house was an architectural oddity, set on the steepest of hills, and as Jemma entered, the air had a chill to it that wasn't just from the heating being set too low. The living room was upstairs, and it looked out on to a garden that fell away from the house, like a crater, and the furniture was old-fashioned and of good quality, even though the house itself was modern. Jemma and Dan had been ushered straight upstairs to have some coffee (whether they wanted it or not) and now, even though they'd only been there for five minutes, his mother was going on and on about her newly fitted kitchen, and how it was so amazing, and how Dan's old girlfriend had helped her choose the tiles, and what an amazing girl she'd been. And then she put down the coffee pot and let out a heaving sigh at the memory. Next, she started telling Jemma about her other son, Jamie – how he had such an amazing career, and how he was bound to do well in the City, but of course, he took after his father. And how Dan had packed it all in to start his own business, and wasn't that amazing? Amazing, amazing, amazing. Everything was amazing. Except Jemma, it seemed, judging by the notable absence of interest in her own attributes, her career as an interior designer meriting little more than a sniff.

'So how did you two meet, Jemma?' Peter asked, over lunch.

'In a pub,' Dan said, as Jemma was struggling with a mouthful of stroganoff. 'The weather was so bad, Jemma came in looking like a drowned rat, and so I bought her a drink. And that was that. Wasn't it, Jem?'

Jemma nodded, still unable to speak. She'd happened

upon a large piece of gristle and wasn't sure how to manage it. She tried discreetly to disgorge the meat into her linen napkin and then smiled as nonchalantly as she could manage.

'Oh,' said Dan's mother. Her nose wrinkled as Jemma put down the napkin. 'That's an odd way to meet.'

'Well, I think I was very lucky,' said Dan.

Jemma saw Veronica's eyes harden above her cerise polo neck. She seemed to be one of those people who appeared to be nice, but then would say something ambivalent that could easily be taken as cutting. Passive aggressive, Jemma thought it was called, and she wondered how someone as lovely as Dan could have been spawned from such a fake of a mother. It was a mystery. But Dan's father seemed decent enough, so maybe that was the answer.

As the meal wore on Jemma found herself feeling increasingly nervous and tetchy, and when, during dessert, Dan's mother mentioned Lydia, Dan's ex, for the umpteenth time, Jemma was tempted to lift her fork and stab the older woman in the arm, like in *Betty Blue*, but of course she didn't. Dan apologized afterwards, on the way home, and although Jemma told him it was fine, she couldn't help wondering why Dan had never mentioned his ex-girlfriend. As they made painfully slow progress towards London in the Sunday afternoon traffic, the question continued to thrum inside her, and hook itself on to her nervous system.

'So . . . when was it that you split up with Lydia?' she asked, finally capitulating, just as Dan was parking the van outside her flat.

'What?' Dan was looking over his shoulder as he expertly reversed into the space. A muscle in his neck spasmed, and Jemma had to restrain herself from prodding it.

'I just wondered when you and Lydia broke up.' She clamped her teeth together, to stop herself saying anything further.

'Why? What does it matter?' Dan swung the nose in too fast, nudging the car in front, and then yanked on the handbrake.

'Well, why didn't you tell me about her?'

'There's nothing to tell.' His voice was peculiarly emotionless. 'I presume you've had other boyfriends before me?'

'Yeah, but none my family would go on and on ad nauseam to you about.'

'Well, maybe they would do if you ever gave me a chance to meet them!' Dan switched off the ignition and glared across the cab at her, and his brow was furrowed in a way that she'd never seen before. Jemma stared back at him. It was so unlike Dan to rise to anything. Were they about to have their first row? It was almost exciting.

Jemma pressed her lips together and looked out of the window. She unclenched her fists and smoothed down her denim skirt, willing herself to not say anything further, to leave it there. It was his birthday tomorrow. And besides, she'd already made herself look jealous, which was bad enough; she certainly didn't want to bring her family into it. Dan broke the tension by getting out of the van and, as he stood on the pavement waiting for her, he looked tall, broad-shouldered, impatient – and the thought of him being angry with her seemed intolerable somehow.

'Sorry,' Jemma said as she opened the door. She walked round to his side of the van and put her hand through his arm.

'For what?'

'For being an idiot.'

'It's fine,' he said, although he didn't sound con-vincing.

Jemma forced a smile as she unlocked the door to the flat, knowing better than to say anything more now. Yet still, from that point on Jemma wondered who the mysterious Lydia was, and just how Dan felt about her.

9

Now

It is mid-afternoon and although the rescue boat has been out for hours, there's still no sign of my husband. A toxic scream has formed in the base of my throat, and I want to let rip with it. I long to have a full-on toddler meltdown, but I mustn't, not here at the main bar and restaurant. All the other guests have become aware of the situation, and it has caused a fractious ripple of excitement through the resort. People don't know quite what to do, now that they've taken a cursory walk around the island, calling his name; but the irony is that at least some atmosphere seems to have been created at last. Before all this, the restaurant may well have served truly fantastic food, but it had the personality of a morgue. I wince at my own analogy.

Three glamorous young Chinese couples are sitting together, having just come back from a trip through the bush looking for my husband. Normally, the Chinese tourists here operate as isolated units, sitting opposite each other, playing on their iPhones, or else the men are taking elaborately posed shots of their partners on the beach, with flowers in their hair. The three girls at the table are cute, dressed in their standard uniform of designer mini-skirts with tiny cinched-in waists and sky-high heels, which is possibly not the most appropriate attire for trampling through the jungle on a manhunt. They're all chatting now, engaged in a spirited jabbering discussion which not only makes a change from their usual silent communing with technology, but also creates a suitable soundtrack to the overall mood. An over-affectionate American couple have taken their tongues out of each other's ears for once and are at this moment talking earnestly to the manager, trying not to look excited. Even the older rich couples, the ones who usually seem bored with life itself, as if they've had one Michelin-starred meal too many, look interested in something for a change. The fact that I am, by default, the star attraction is a peculiar feeling in this ghastly in-between time. *What should I be doing? How should I be acting?* How are you meant to behave when your husband has vanished like a magician's bunny on your honeymoon?

I went out on one of the dhonis with Pascal and another of the dive staff earlier, but it seemed so futile, and I could tell we all felt the same, although of course no-one said it. I almost get the feeling from the Australian resort manager that he thinks there's not much point to any of it, and that if my husband has drowned it's his own stupid fault, and what can anyone do about it now? After all, they'd told us enough times that the reef could be dangerous, especially at night, and we'd all been warned never to go out alone, and certainly not when drunk, so in some ways I can see where the manager's coming from.

Pascal's attitude unnerves me, too. He is so unfriendly, and yet when we first arrived he was charm personified. It's almost as though he's blaming me somehow, and yet it's more than that, too. *He knows something.* I'm sure he does, and I long to ask him, but I daren't. The upshot is that everything feels so weird, as if the world is on pause and none of this is real, like it's merely some kind of freaky B-movie where I'm unsure of my lines and have no idea how to play the role anyway. The polarity of my position is killing me. Inside I am distraught that it has come to this, whilst outwardly I cling onto hope, as what else can I do? Yet as the minutes drag by on this ghastly, interminable day and still there's no news, the prognosis feels ever more bleak. The sun continues its obdurate descent through the unblemished sky, and I resent it, that it's carrying on as normal, as if nothing has even happened. It makes me crazy that in a couple of hours it will be too dark for anyone to even keep looking.

Chrissy and Kenny have joined me at the beachfront bar area now, as Chrissy seems to have decided that, in the absence of anyone else, it's her job to look after me. I'm still not sure of her motives, although I want to believe they're benevolent. I find it hard to talk to her, and it's not just due to these extraordinary circumstances. It's also because I can't seem to stop the interminable, jumbled spooling through my mind of our conversation on the beach last night, once the men had bailed on us. *What had I said?* I struggle to remember, even though it was definitely before everything went completely, zombifyingly blank. Surely Chrissy realizes I didn't mean any of it though, that I was just upset, and drunk, and that it's a coincidence. I clutch at straws, try to convince myself that the man I've just married isn't dead, that instead perhaps has intentionally left the island. But if that were the case, *how* has he left? And why hasn't he taken any of his things? I've checked, of course, and his passport, money, flip-flops, everything – apart from his mask and snorkel and flippers – are still in the bungalow.

No. It seems to me that the only plausible possibility is that he really has drowned. I think this thought calmly at first, but then I start to feel the hysteria rising inside of me again. I almost want to laugh, and then I really don't. I try to think straight, work out what will happen next. I wonder whether Dad has told Veronica and Peter yet, and even the thought of them knowing fills me with despair. Surely the police will need to be involved too. If so, where will they come from? From Malé? Or might they even send police out from England – didn't that happen sometimes, in these kinds of circumstances? But, either way, where on earth would they look for him?

I'm aware that I'm getting ahead of myself. I start to feel racked with panic again, and it bubbles inside of me, like sugar melting, and as I look at my skin, faint hives are forming. I attempt to flood my mind with optimistic eventualities. I try to imagine him just turning up, alive and well, with some kind of simple explanation. That's what often happens in these kinds of cases, I think. There's nothing more I can do now, except stick it out, try to keep my cool.

Chrissy beckons one of the waiters, then asks me and Kenny what we're having, and even though I shake my head she orders me a Daiquiri, and when it arrives I take a long, chilled, painkilling draught, and I feel eyes on me, watching, as though they're thinking, 'There she is, her husband missing and she's drinking *cocktails*.' I ignore everyone, and I sit back in my chair, wordless and drawn, and I wait.

10

Seven years earlier

Life went on. Christmas approached, crept up in its insidious tinselly way. Jemma's father and step-mother, Kay, hosted Christmas Day, and Kay's parents, who were as sweet and charming as she was, came too, as did the neighbours – and the day was so sedate and good-natured, so utterly different to Jemma's childhood Christmases, that it unnerved Jemma, and she found herself almost missing the drama. Dan rang in the evening to say hello, but when she heard his mother's shrill voice in the background, calling him insistently to come and play charades, Jemma said she didn't want to hold him up, and could barely get off the phone fast enough.

New Year's Eve was as underwhelming as usual. Jemma took Dan to a mediocre party that Sasha had invited them to, where Dan stuck to Jemma's side and she found it hard to enjoy herself. Her sleep that night was patrolled by nightmares, and on New Year's Day she woke up at her boyfriend's place with a feeling of unnamed dread, of murky apathy, of being there, in the wrong place, on the wrong date. She made a mental note to finish with him, again. Six months was quite long enough for a casual relationship with someone off the Internet, especially now there was a new year to get through, twelve more months of navigating the pitfalls of daily existence. It wasn't fair on either of them – yet how could she possibly articulate how she felt? It wasn't only that Dan didn't fit her usual mould of what a boyfriend should look like. It was also as if Jemma had had enough of being treated well – and as she lay in bed, feeling wrong-footed and ashamed of her feelings, she wondered whether she should just do it now, get it over with.

'Jemma?'

'Yes?' She turned over in bed and looked at him. His eyes were bright, and hopeful. His hair was unkempt, and she wanted to touch it, smooth it. Did he not feel the despair that she felt?

'I said, do you want to go to Suffolk, to the beach?'

'What? When?'

'Now? We can find a place to stay overnight. It'll be fun.'

Jemma's heart jumped at the idea, and then she drew her thoughts in again.

'I thought you were broke?'

Dan looked away for a second. 'No, I'm fine. It's New Year's Day – we should celebrate. We can have fish and chips on the beach.'

Jemma laughed. 'You're crazy.'

'Oh, go on, Jem. There's nothing like an icy blast of sea air to get the new year off to a good start.'

'Has it occurred to you that I might have something else on?' she said, arching her eyebrow, trying to keep her tone light.

'No,' said Dan. He turned and placed his hands on her face and looked deep into her eyes, and she felt her resolve slipping. As he kissed her, she was surprised at how natural her body's response to him was, almost as if their relationship were inevitable, that they fitted together. But sex wasn't everything, she tried to tell herself as his attentions roamed downwards. Solvency and status, and amenable relatives, counted too.

'Well, are you up for it?' he said, afterwards.

Jemma sat up in bed, pulled the duvet up to her chin. Perhaps spending New Year's Eve together had been commitment enough. 'I'm not sure. I . . . I need to tidy up the flat, get some washing done before I go back to work. Maybe I'd better just go home.'

He looked at her then, and it was as if he could see right through her. 'Jemma, you don't always have to run, you know.'

'What d'you mean?' Jemma stared at her fingernails.

'You know exactly what I mean. What are you so afraid of?'

Jemma looked up at last. What could she say? She ran her right middle finger across her eyebrow, massaged the bone beneath it. It was one of those moments that could go either way.

'Nothing. I'm not afraid of anything, Dan,' she said softly. 'Suffolk sounds great. I'd love to go.'

11

Now

The first night since my husband's disappearance descends, dark and fast, and after a dismal meal in the restaurant, where I'd circled the buffet as if it were a dangerous wild animal, trying to ignore the curious looks from everybody, I decide I can't take any more. The tension, the unrelenting worry, is finally too much. It doesn't help that the seven-star resort has become like a circus, and I am its star act, to prod and whip, see what movements I make, monitor how I respond. I just hadn't known what to do, though – whether to go back to my room and order room service, or else stick around the restaurant and try to eat dinner, attempt to show everybody how desperate I'm feeling. It's so hard to judge the situation, but I'm pretty sure my presence is no longer helping anything. I dab at my eyes self-consciously, and suddenly long for my mother. The futility of the thought torpedoes me.

Chrissy and Kenny are still sitting with me, which is nice of them, I suppose, but the atmosphere is tense. Maybe it would have been anyway, after last night, but right now it feels impossible. What is there to say?

I don't like Kenny's hooded eyes any more, and he frightens me somehow, as if there is rage lurking beneath his pink sunburnt skin, although before last night I'd adored him. He keeps scowling at me, as if he's blaming me for everything, and I wonder briefly what he saw, what he knows. When Chrissy heads off on yet another sortie to get him more food, I take my chance to escape. I stand up, mutter a clumsy, tearful goodnight, and bolt from the table before Chrissy has a chance to offer to come back to the bungalow with me, which I wouldn't put past her.

I feel too scared to cycle home alone through the dark woods after dinner, as though the fear that my husband's vanishing has raised in me is swelling in the moonlit ocean, swooping through the bat-swarming jungle. Instead Moosa, my once-friendly butler, drives me to our bungalow in the cream-canopied golf buggy. He seems almost resentful when I ask him to wait until I am safely inside, which is a bit off, I think, under the circumstances, and I stress about why. It's almost as if he thinks this is my fault, and I dread what he might have heard on the grapevine. I give a brief wave of thanks and then I shut the door and turn the lock – and it's only as I lean back against it that I realize I'm hyperventilating.

The bungalow is not secluded or luxurious to me now; it is remote and lonely, full of terrors. I sink to my haunches and try to breathe. I can feel eyes on me, although surely I must be imagining it? But what if there really is a maniac on the loose, watching, waiting until I'm alone, planning to come back to get me too? I try to tell myself I'm being crazy, yet still I stand up and go over to the huge plate glass doors and pull the curtains across, shutting out this lost corner of the world where the sea plummets into the deep and I am marooned. I want someone to hold me in their arms and tell me that it will all be OK, but I am alone. I get into the beautiful super-king-sized bed, which has been turned down as usual, although it doesn't have the petals laid out in heart shapes on the pillows tonight, and I wonder whose decision that was, not to do it. I pick up the phone next to my bed and call Reception, to check again if there's any news. Leena answers, and her voice soothes me, especially as she sounds more composed than this morning, but she's embarrassed that she has nothing to say. I'd known, of course – otherwise they'd have called me – yet the confirmation of the absence is like another sick kick in the stomach.

I hate this island now. Exactly this time last night I was dining in an over-water gourmet restaurant, drinking too much champagne. Now I am lying by myself, barricaded in my honeymoon bungalow, and I feel as scared and alone as I ever have. *Where is he?* The island feels so different after dark tonight, and it is cloudy, rendering the blackness so rich and velvety that when I get up and peer out from behind the curtains I can see tiny strata of stars behind my eyes. It's almost as if I'm making up a vista, in the absence of one. Trying to make up a husband, in the absence of one. There is someone out there, I am sure of it, and I call his name, but no-one replies. Fear and sorrow battle in my throat. A shriek gets swallowed. But who would my screams be for anyway? For him? Or for me?

I am becoming ever more paranoid. I check the locks on the sliding patio doors, yet again, and I bolt the door to the luxurious bathroom, outside in the trees on the opposite side of the bungalow to the beach, and I push a chair up against it, in case someone scales the high white walls, comes and gets me. Even the geckos pinned to the plaster like pictures frighten me now. I lie awake for hours, not even attempting to sleep. My mind is tricking itself into knots and loops, and I can't unthread where it starts, or is destined to end. I can't even remember what is truth or fiction, the fine details of last night, no matter how hard I try. It is almost as if I am traumatized, and maybe I am. But had I really said, and in the *restaurant*, that I hated him? That I wished I'd never married him? I can hear his voice now, can feel his hands on me, but what did he do? What did he say? And, more to the point, who'd heard? As I writhe on the bed, my fist in my mouth to suppress my screams, I so desperately want to go home it becomes a physical pain of longing. I imagine the sea stretching out across the myriad islands like a watery, unnavigable prison. And then I imagine how far a dead body could travel across it, before it disintegrated . . .

I sit bolt upright, hold my breath until my ears are

popping, attempt to drag my thoughts elsewhere. Briefly, I try to imagine him hiding out on one of the many desert islands here in this ocean, with a big bushy beard and an insurance policy. I even picture him turning up jaunty in Rio, a flower garland around his neck and dancing girls in the background. The fact that that scenario feels like the best possible outcome is telling. Yet, really, nothing matters now, apart from knowing the truth. As far as everything else is concerned in this sorry debacle, I don't care any more. What will be will be. Let the repercussions roll.

I lie still, hug a pillow, pretend I have a husband. When I finally slip into sleep, I dream that he's watching me, out beyond the window, and he is screeching with laughter as his skin grows hair and he howls at the moon, and then he is disembowelled, turned inside out like a glove, and I wake up and decide I am going insane. At last, I am going insane, like his mother always said I would. Perhaps I should see the resort doctor tomorrow and ask for something.

Hours stall and dither, but eventually pass. Even as the light starts pestering the curtains I've still barely slept, and so I turn on the television, and its pictures and sounds are such a relief, I don't know why I didn't think of it before. I no longer feel so scared, so alone. The made-for-TV movie is company, and I am grateful to the American actors and actresses, who look so tanned and coiffed and stereotypical: the suave silver businessman, the feisty old lady, the beautiful heroine,

58

the archetypal baddie. I am none of those things, and yet I share something with all of them. They become my only friends, here on my island of smashed dreams. Finally, the inevitable end creeps up, and they leave me, too. I make the screen swallow itself and drift into mercifully blank sleep, at last. Later, when I wake, I look to see him there, beside me, but he's not.

12

Six-and-a-half years earlier

It was Saturday morning and the midsummer rain was chucking itself ostentatiously at the windows, as though purposely reinforcing the fact that there was never any guarantee with the British weather – and that, plus the fact that Jemma was jet-lagged, was the best excuse ever for her and Dan to stay in bed. In the six months since their spontaneous New Year's trip to Suffolk, where they'd marched along a stony, windswept beach, before finding a gorgeous pub to stay the night in (which had cost more than they'd wanted to spend but had been totally worth it), they'd finally settled into a steady, easy relationship which was a complete contrast to the tempestuous ones she'd had before. And although she was still convinced that it would never be serious with Dan, she finally began to realize that at least he appreciated her, unlike most of her other boyfriends, and she was happy.

Jemma's professional fortunes had taken a turn this year, too, which may or may not have been a coincidence. In March she'd been put on a great project at work – the total renovation of a palace in Saudi Arabia, no less – and consequently she felt more valued and was therefore less likely to flip out at her boss, which had never done her any favours. In fact, she'd just come back from her very first overseas trip, to said palace, and her excitement at travelling business class, and staying in a posh hotel, and getting a blacked-out-windowed Mercedes to and from the palace compound had sent her self-esteem rocketing. If she played her cards right, she thought now, she might even be up for a promotion quite soon. She stretched luxuriously, like an over-indulged kitten.

The doorbell rang.

'Who's that?' she asked.

Dan shrugged and made no effort to go, which surprised her. He was usually so gallant. Instead, Jemma got up herself, wrapped her stripy dressing gown around her diminutive frame and padded down the carpeted stairs to the front door. 'Who is it?' she called, and even though the response was unintelligible, she opened up anyway, her security routines quite lacking, as Dan had told her often enough over the last several months.

An unknown man was standing in the porch, scowling, the rain dripping off him. He was holding the most enormous bunch of flowers, which bemused Jemma yet further. He shoved the bouquet into her arms, and promptly turned around and stomped off, yet still she didn't fully understand. She took the flowers into the kitchen – they were a wondrous mix of pale-yellow roses, freesias and daisies that smelled of the summer. There was a card with them, and when she opened it, and it said, 'Happy anniversary, let's hope today's date is better than the first, love D x', she gasped so loudly Dan surely must have heard it from the bedroom.

And now Jemma was back in bed, sobbing into Dan's arms, unable to explain how she felt. How could she possibly articulate it? *I had no idea it was a year. I'm gutted that it is. It was never even meant to go beyond the first date – it was Sasha who engineered the whole thing. You might be a lovely guy but this has gone on for far too long. You're just not the one for me. You're not my type.* It was all too dreadful. Dan held her as she cried, which only made her feel worse. How much had those flowers cost him? A fortune, she was sure. He didn't have the kind of money to spend on someone like her.

'Jemma,' Dan said.

'Yes?'

'I know.'

'You know what?'

'I know you're upset that it's been a year.'

'Oh God, is it that obvious? I'm so sorry.'

'It's OK.' Dan kissed the top of her head and then he gently unravelled himself from her, got out of the bed and walked naked across the room. She stared at the smooth breadth of his back, at the faint T-shirt tan marks on the arms that a moment ago had been holding her.

'What are you doing?'

'I'm going.'

'Where?'

'Home.'

'Oh,' Jemma said. 'Why?'

'Jem, it's OK.' He dressed quickly. Jemma cowered under the duvet, and she felt words forming in her chest, yet still she couldn't say them. All she could do was watch him, her eyes wide and startled, her amber hair post-coitally awry. Was it over? And if so, who was dumping who here?

Dan came over to the bed and kissed her lightly on the top of her head. She pictured the flowers, fresh, delicate, dumped in the kitchen sink.

'I'll give you a call,' he said. And then he was gone.

13

Now

Day Two zooms in, as if it's on steroids. Dad calls me, even though it must be gone one in the morning in England, and that's so typical of him – that he waited until I might be awake, and his considerateness during a time of such crisis makes my heart break. He needn't have bothered, though: I've barely slept. Anyway, he's done it, he tells me. He's rung my in-laws – yesterday evening, England time. Twenty-one or so hours after their son was last seen Peter and Veronica were informed. Was that too late? Should we perhaps have done it earlier? I try to convince myself that there might yet be an entirely innocent explanation; and besides, Peter is unwell, and his heart might not have taken it. I hadn't wanted to worry them unnecessarily.

As Dad and I talk, I long to just blurt out everything to him, but of course I mustn't. I mustn't tell *anyone* what was going on in the dun depths of my shiny new marriage – and then I remember that I might have told Chrissy. *What the hell did I say to her on the beach?* I feel trapped by the hotel phone's cord and wish I was on my mobile so I could move around, run at the walls, get my stress out. Instead, I force myself to stand still, contain my hysteria, keep my feet planted on the smooth, cool tiles: try to let the tension drain downwards, like an earth. As I hear Dad's steady, smooth tones, so clearly he might as well be in the next room, I thank God for his calmness, his ability to make the decisions that need to be made. He was the one who'd insisted my in-laws were told, and he was right, of course he was. He hadn't actually said it as such, but he'd made me realize that we needed to know. We needed to know if they knew where their son was. That he might yet have disappeared deliberately.

Dad is again suggesting he comes out here, but still I don't know what to say. I want him to come, but also I don't. I'm pretty sure he's never been further afield than Italy. We've never had the kind of relationship where we hang out together. And what would he *do*? Poke about in the bushes? Go out on the boats? Lie on the beach? Yet I'm truly grateful that he's offered. I might not have a husband any more, nor a mother for that matter, but if I need my dad, he will come, whenever I ask him to, and that makes me feel better. I feel almost happy about it, in a weird sort of way – although happiness is an abstract construct right now, something pale and off in the distance. Perhaps there for the taking, perhaps not.

Despite how it's looking, I'm praying that there could still be a good outcome. One theory is that maybe my husband has managed to get off the island somehow.

65

They have counted the boats and the kayaks, and they're all here, but you never know. Maybe that's why he spent so much time down at the dive centre, hanging out with the marine biologist. And there are plenty of islands nearby, nearly all uninhabited, all potential hiding places. Maybe Pascal helped him, and then paddled the boat back – that would explain why he'd seemed so odd when I went out in one of the search boats with him. It's a possibility, and I pray it's true. I pray anything is true other than that my husband is dead. I don't care how outlandish it is, or how much we've betrayed each other. 'Please don't let him be dead,' I cry down the phone to my dad, and all he can do is shush me gently from afar.

When I finally hang up, I feel even more bereft. I can feel Dad's absence too, now, as if it has a solid form to it, like a father-shaped force-field – and then I metaphorically shake myself off, tell myself to stop being mad. It's a new day. It's time for action. I put in yet another call to Reception, and my voice sounds like that of an imposter. They finally connect me to the manager, and although I try to keep calm, I soon resort to shouting that he needs to *do* something – but all he says is that he'll be in touch as soon as possible with details of the next stage of the search, whatever that may be. Afterwards, I take a long seething shower that I find hard to end, and not just because the bathroom is so heavenly. When I go to get dressed, I still don't know how I should look. What should I wear? Should I brush my hair, or leave it wild and dishevelled? I search my wardrobe, but I only have beach clothes in bright, vivid colours. I have no widow's black. My thought processes appal me.

Finally, I settle on a simple blue sundress. I comb my hair neatly. I dab some powder on my face, and it makes me look paler. And then I screw up all of my courage and head out on foot to the breakfast buffet – I left my bike there last night and I can't face calling Moosa to pick me up. When I arrive, the staff are so wordlessly sympathetic they make me want to weep. Bobbi is double quick at bringing me my tea, and the buffet servers are more assiduous than ever in trying to offer me food, but all I can face is a croissant. The American woman who normally forms one half of the ear-licking couple is there on her own for a change, perhaps out of solidarity with me. She sits down opposite, without even asking, and tells me her name is Laurie, and then she tries to engage me in pseudo-sympathetic conversation, and I wonder if she's being kind, or just being nosy. I end up making my excuses and legging it, having taken barely a bite out of my breakfast. I retrieve my sand bike and take it for yet another pointless ride around the island, searching for any sign of my husband, although I worry that it might simply look like I'm on a bike ride, enjoying myself. Even going out now, to eat at the restaurant, to join in the search parties, is beginning to feel beyond me. I can't bear what people might be saying.

I give up and head to Reception, where I demand to see the manager. I want to ask him face-to-face what is going on. Leena shakes her head sympathetically and tells me that he's not available right now, but that he'll come to see me soon, to update me. I'm too wired to make a fuss, and so I nod wordlessly and cycle back to my bungalow. I feel exhausted, and it's still only ten o'clock in the morning. I check my phone for messages, but there are none, scan the Internet for any news, but there's nothing (thank goodness), and then I slump helplessly onto the bed.

After maybe half an hour the doorbell rings. It's the manager, as promised. He says he's just contacted the Maldives National Defence Force, and they're on their way, with speedboats, and seaplanes, and thermal imaging equipment, whatever that is. I don't know what to say. He asks me if I want anything else, and I shake my head wordlessly, and he leaves. The scale of the planned operation is utterly numbing. Panic has been replaced with torpidity. Disbelief. I go out onto the terrace and stare out through the bush to the smooth, winking water, but I don't search for someone snorkelling any more. Now I look for pale mottled skin, bloated and buoyant. Now I search out there only for death.

Chrissy comes by the bungalow around lunchtime, ostensibly to see how I am, and it revives me a little. She reminds me in a way of Sasha, and I am grateful to her, although I still can't quite work out her motivation. But perhaps I didn't incriminate myself the other night, after all, and maybe she genuinely cares. I don't dare broach it. I politely offer her a drink from the minibar, and she politely asks for a gin and tonic, and I have one too, and we take them outside and sit down at the table.

'So, how are you doing?' she asks, after an awkward silence. Even she looks a bit rough for a change. Her cut-off denim shorts and vest top are as revealing as ever, but her hair is piled on her head in a messy top-knot and her eyes are tired.

'Oh. You know . . .' I don't know what to say. There are verbal landmines wherever I look.

'Is there any news?'

'No. None.' *Should* I ask her about what happened the other night, now that Kenny's not around to hear? Or will I implicate myself? I tell her that the Maldivian army's coming, and she seems as shocked as I was, and then we sit in silence – and it's as if we're both holding counsel, waiting to see what the other one leads with.

'Don't you think you should ask someone to come out and support you?' she says, at last.

'Who?'

'I dunno. Your mum and dad?'

'My mum's dead.' I'm aware how harsh that sounded, and feel bad for her.

'Oh . . . Sorry.' She fishes in her bag and I hear the popping of pill packets, and then she puts her palm to her mouth, and swigs down whatever she's taking with gin. I almost ask for some tablets too, but not after last time. Maybe that's where all the trouble started. I just wish I could remember.

'That's all right.' I say it softly, trying to make up for my bluntness.

Chrissy sounds hesitant now. 'Have you . . . Have you got a dad?'

'Yes, he's offered to come.'

'Oh, *fab*.' Her relief is touching.

'But I've said no.'

'Oh.' Chrissy drains her drink and stands up. She looks close to tears, and I feel sorry for her. She seems almost tormented now, and I think about Kenny, and his bad leg, and his possible mean streak, and I wonder.

'Look, just call me,' she says. 'If you need anything.'

'Yes, I will,' I reply, although we both know I won't. She briefly hugs me, but I can tell she can't wait to get away, like yesterday at Reception, and who can blame her? I wonder again if I'm becoming unhinged, and for a moment I long to call someone – Sasha, perhaps – to confess what I've done, but I know that I mustn't. That would be a very stupid move indeed.

Once Chrissy's gone I realize I'm ravenous. I've barely eaten anything since that last fateful dinner, but there's no way I'm going to dine out tonight. The shameful dull thrill of being the centre of attention has completely left me now, and I can no longer entertain being seen around the island, cannot stand the suspicion on the faces of the other guests, the faux sympathy. Neither can I stomach the choices that the behemoth of a buffet offers up, and I'm glad to give it a miss. Yet, despite my hunger, even calling room service seems trite somehow. Instead, I'm about to raid the minibar for a chocolate bar and a bag of cashew nuts when, almost miraculously, my favourite chef arrives with a plate of food, a delicious local curry that tempts me even in this state, despite myself, and I would better show my gratitude to him if I weren't so embarrassed. He's so sweet and smiley, it brings a lump to my throat, a sting to my eyes – especially as the housekeeping staff, who still attend to the bungalow assiduously, tend to stare at me now. I worry what rumours might be circulating amongst the staff.

Time becomes fluid, like the ocean. After I've eaten, more hours drift by, hours of rigid boredom and fear and helpless gazing out to the unrestrained sea, and somewhere amidst this torpor army boats start appearing and seaplanes begin to sully the sky. Just as the sun is saying its showy goodbye to this most agonizing of days, more delicate culinary offerings are delivered to me like unexpected gifts, and I'm truly grateful. And then the phone rings in the bungalow, and it's my mother-in-law. She's on her way, she tells me, and terror grips me, but I tell myself I have to be strong, and I say that I'll see her tomorrow.

14

Six-and-a-half years earlier

This time, Jemma almost wished that Sasha would help her out and do her dirty work for her. It was Monday evening, and she still hadn't heard from Dan, although before the events of Saturday they'd taken to speaking most days. More than sixty hours had passed since he'd left her flat on the one-year anniversary of their first abortive date, and Jemma had had time to run through a whole gamut of emotions since then. She wondered whether she *would* hear from him again, although he'd definitely said he would call, and he was usually utterly reliable. She found the thought of him not calling unpalatable, and she wasn't exactly sure why. Part of it was pride, certainly, and part was indignation – but perhaps it was more than that.

Jemma stepped out of her work skirt and put on some old tracksuit bottoms and a pair of Dan's (dirty) thick work socks that she'd foraged through the laundry basket for. She cooked herself a carbonara for dinner, but it wasn't as good as the one he'd made for her two weeks ago, even though she'd taught him how to do it. She sunk into her sofa and put on the TV, but watching *Curb Your Enthusiasm* wasn't as funny without him. *Grand Designs* made her think of him, of his love of the earth and its resonance with architecture, his guileless enthusiasm for life's simple pleasures, the effect he'd had on her own equilibrium. She switched off the TV, picked up her iPad, and browsed online idly and pointlessly. She went on to Facebook, but she wasn't in the mood for other people's clever children, or their latest exotic holidays, or pictures of what they'd had for dinner. Even Sasha, who could usually be relied upon to make her laugh, had taken a serious turn this evening and had shared an anti-global-warming post. The fact that the Maldives were in danger of disappearing in the next few years didn't cheer up Jemma either, and she swore that she would visit before it was too late. And when her next thought was that maybe she could go there on honeymoon with Dan, she knew that she was definitely in trouble, and perhaps ready to grow up at last.

'Hello?'

'Dan, it's me.'

'Hi, Jemma.' His voice was neutral, hard to unpick. She huddled into her pyjamas, curled her toes.

'I thought you said you would call.'

'I was going to call tonight.'

'Oh.' Six words to make her heart leap.

'I'm glad you called first.' Five more.

'Dan, I'm sorry.'

'It's OK. Sasha told me.'

'*What?*'

'I rang Sasha, and she told me to give you some space.'

Jemma couldn't keep up. 'What are you talking about? How did you even have Sasha's number?'

Dan sounded nonchalant. 'We swapped numbers ages ago, when we went there for dinner – just in case, she said, but fortunately I didn't get the wrong idea.' Dan laughed, but Jemma said nothing. 'She obviously knows you too well. Look, I don't want to pry into anything, but Sasha said that you could sometimes be a bit, er, erratic – her words, not mine, Jem.'

'Oh.' Jemma couldn't trust herself to say anything else. Why was Sasha always interfering in her life? She wasn't her mother, for God's sake.

'So she suggested I give you some space for a bit.'

Jemma stared up at her bedroom ceiling, which Dan had helped her paint. He'd taken her to the timber merchant's in his van, too, and put up the shelves in the corner alcove for her. He'd done a good job, she thought, as she looked at them now. He was always nice to her. Why had she pushed him away? What was she frightened of?

'Well, I've never had anyone sob that they were still going out with me,' Dan continued. 'I must admit that was a first. But, you know, unpredictable's good.'

'Dan,' Jemma said. 'Can I come over?'

74

'When?'

'Now. Right now.'

Dan hesitated. She thought his voice caught a little as he said, 'Sure,' and then he hung up.

A few hours later, Dan and Jemma were at his place. They'd had a takeaway and were cuddled up on the sofa watching a movie she'd perversely insisted on. It made Jemma freak out a little, and he squeezed her tighter and asked her if she was OK, but she didn't feel OK. She didn't like horror movies, and she didn't like crying in front of Dan. Yet it felt so safe with him, and he was so nice, and the moment bore the faint poignancy of the ordinary, of normalcy. As if this was what other couples did. She was relishing the mundanity of it.

Jemma looked at him then, and in that moment she knew. She knew, at last, that it didn't matter what he did for a job, or how much money he had, or what the neighbours thought. She knew that here was someone who was good for her, who was looking out for her, who saw the truth behind her painted eyes, and yet still might love her. He calmed her down, made her feel more herself somehow. She smiled, and he smiled, and their faces got closer, until they each became the other's whole vista, and then they fell into each other, as though the world had stopped and they were the only living beings left, and that the cadence of the earth's whispers was theirs, was coming from them.

'I love you,' she said, and she didn't even mean it in that declarative way, and he didn't need to say it back – he had shown her with his heart, and his body, and at last she knew. She knew how it felt to be loved.

15

Now

As the seaplane approaches, I hear the buzz of its engine before I see it, and when it comes into view, it is blue and yellow and minuscule. I watch it bellyflop onto the water, and up close it looks as if it has been cobbled together using spare parts from speedboats, as if it shouldn't even be flying. When the pilot jumps out he has bare feet. It is actually more frightening to watch than it was to be a part of. It seems my seaplane anxiety is far worse now than it was coming here, when the trip itself had been little more than a thrilling ride – but my fears have mushroomed in the last few days, and they are growing still, and exponentially. It doesn't help that there's an army speedboat skimming back and forth along the horizon, and that the wind is up, and it feels as if a dark black storm is on its way.

I am standing on the arrivals and departures pontoon, and it is like waiting for royalty, or death. I'm with Chrissy, who is looking outrageously voluptuous in a tiny turquoise dress, and the manager, and a good few of the staff, the lustrous Leena included, and the mood is sombre yet fizzing with excitement. It's an obscene combination. For anybody unconnected with us personally, I suppose at this stage it could be seen as a gripping adventure, an extra frisson to add to one's holiday. A real-life missing person docu-soap, perhaps. Most people have been appropriately sympathetic to my face, but really, what can anyone say? I still don't know how to arrange my features, and the fact that they seem to have involuntarily defaulted to impassivity makes the scrutiny I am under far worse. No-one has come out and said it yet, but it feels like I'm under suspicion. *I'm not sad enough.* I stand as tall as I can, and my daisy sundress flutters in the choppy breeze. My hair is haywire. My eyes are hollowed-out beneath my dark glasses.

The dhoni is chugging out to the landing platform, which is a little way away from the island, but the sea is rougher than usual and it looks as if the boat is struggling. The suitcases are already being thrown from the plane across the turbulent water onto the platform, and they are expertly caught by one of the butlers, ready to be passed onto the dhoni, to be ferried with the passengers across to the island itself. I know who is on the plane, and yet I still can't quite believe it, until finally my eyes cannot deceive me, and it is undeniably true. At last, there she is, my malevolent mother-in-law, who certainly won't be calling anything *amazing* at this precise moment. She is wearing a long stripy T-shirt over three-quarter-length white jeans and brand new espadrilles, and she looks immaculately age-appropriate, as if she's shooting a Saga commercial. Even her hair remains rock-solid despite the ever-increasing wind. The man that follows her onto the boat makes my heart lurch, and I want to run to him, but I can't – there is water in the way for a start – and, of course, it would be far from appropriate. I take a single raspy breath and try to steady myself.

The person that follows is Dan.

PART TWO
Brothers

16

Six-and-a-quarter years earlier

Jamie pulled up in his black BMW and surveyed the cars that were rammed into the driveway and spread down the street, parked at awkward angles, as if dropped there like litter. He wondered who would be here for his father's seventieth birthday party. He'd decided to come on his own today, as girlfriends often got the wrong idea if they were invited to these kinds of events. There was always a very fine line to tread, and besides, he was pretty sure he and Sarah wouldn't be seeing each other for much longer – their relationship had just about run its course. He took note of the brand-new Peugeot van with the neatly printed 'Armstrong's Landscape Gardening' on its side, and smiled to himself. His brother really was going for it in his new career, and good for him. Perhaps Dan hadn't been able to handle the pressure of being the oldest son, the not-quite-as-high-flying-as-his-younger-brother banker, and so that's why he'd packed it all in and chosen to become a gardener. Jamie secretly found it a relief though, that he and his brother didn't have to compete with each other these days. He knew it was pathetic, but old habits died hard. He blamed their mother.

When Veronica opened the door, she looked even thinner and more pinched than usual. Her hair was blow-dried from its natural bird's nest into a smooth immoveable bob, and she wore a black dress with an Audrey Hepburn collar that aged her.

'Darling!' she said. 'Come in.' She gave him a fierce hug which belied her withering frame. 'It's so lovely to see you! How was the traffic?'

'Oh, you know,' said Jamie. 'Crap, as usual.' As he followed his mother up the half-stairs to the living room, he looked beyond her towards his older brother, on the far side of the room, and immediately noticed the girl he was with. So this must be Jemma. Even the protective way Dan was standing with her peeved Jamie a little, although he knew that it shouldn't.

'Come and meet Jemma at last,' said his mother. She leaned in to him and lowered her voice. 'She's nice enough, I suppose, but a little, what shall we say, odd . . .'

'Mum, you think anyone who goes out with one of your precious sons is odd,' said Jamie, rolling his eyes.

'Shush, darling. I don't want her to hear us. But anyway, I have to say I preferred Lydia.'

'Well, I hope you haven't told Jemma that,' said Jamie.

'Of course not,' said his mother. 'What do you think I'm like?'

Jamie looked at his mother and chose not to respond. Instead he followed her across the room and, after expertly negotiating a couple of dull neighbours, approached his brother and shook his hand vigorously. 'Hello, Dan. How you doing, old man?'

'I'm all right, thanks. You?'

'Yeah, I'm good. So, are you going to introduce me?'

Dan frowned, and then seemed to remember his manners. 'Oh. Sorry. This is Jemma. Jamie, Jemma. Jemma, Jamie.'

'Hi,' Jamie said, extending his hand. Jemma smiled, and she had one of those faces that looked like its proportions shouldn't work, and yet that was what made it extraordinary. She had the most startling green eyes, and flaming elfin-cut hair. Her chin pointed outwards with a touch of defiance, and she had a fierce, spiky energy about her. Jamie wondered what her issue was.

'So, where's your girlfriend?' asked Dan.

'Oh, she couldn't make it,' Jamie said airily. 'By the way, like your new wheels, mate, very smart.'

'Thanks,' said Dan. 'Thought it was time for an upgrade. D'you want a drink?'

'Don't worry, I'll get them. What are you having?'

'No, I'm all right,' said Dan. 'I'm driving.'

'Jemma?' Jamie persisted.

'I'll have a top-up of red, please,' she said. Her eyes were clear and unblinking, impossible to read.

'Course,' said Jamie. He dashed off to fetch the drinks, ignoring everyone, even his father, beyond saying a cheerily dismissive hello. He was keen to get back to talk to Jemma, and not solely to annoy Dan. There was something about her that interested him.

When Jamie returned, Jemma held out her glass to him, and as he topped it up he noticed that her hands trembled slightly.

'I hear you've recently come back from living in Hong Kong?' she said now.

'Yes, that's right,' Jamie said. 'The ex-pat life is great, but I have to say it gets a bit dull after a while.'

'Dan says you're in banking.'

'Well, you know, an apple never falls far from the tree. Except in Dan's case, where he grows them instead.' As Jamie laughed at his own joke, he still wasn't sure what was going on inside Jemma's head, but he could tell that she wasn't impressed. The thought appalled him. He tried again.

'So, what do you do, Jemma?'

'I'm an interior designer.'

'Really? Cool.' He didn't have a clue what that meant, beyond picking carpets and curtains, but he didn't like to show his ignorance.

'Jamie, darling,' said his mother. She swanned across and ignored Jemma completely. 'There you are! Is Dan still hogging you? Come and say happy birthday to your father, he's in the conservatory. And then I must get you to talk to Arthur, he's *so* interested in your job.' Veronica took Jamie's arm, and the way she man-oeuvred herself meant that somehow she turned her back on Jemma, excluding her from the group. As Jamie was ushered away by his mother he couldn't help but clock the furious look on Dan's face, and he assumed, quite rightly, that Dan was serious about this one.

17

Now

Peter's health hasn't been good for years, not since his first mini-stroke a few months after Dan and I split up. I assume Veronica must have decided that her husband couldn't cope with the stress of coming to the Maldives, so she's brought her eldest son in his place. The situation is beyond farcical. I am meant to be on honeymoon with my husband, who's missing. And now my ex-boyfriend, who happens to be his brother, is here, to help try to find him. The shock I experience is so intense that at first I don't know how to react. I have no idea what Dan must be thinking either, especially given our very last conversation, the day after Jamie's and my wedding. The only thing that seems to be instantly clear is that my mother-in-law hates me, now more than ever. I hadn't thought things could get any worse.

Why couldn't Veronica have brought someone else in Peter's place, I think furiously. But then again, who else was there to accompany the matriarch? Dan won't even look at me, but even from this distance the hostility radiates off him almost as much as it does off his mother. I'm glad I have my sunglasses on, so they can't see me crying.

Also disembarking from the tiny seaplane are two police officers, from Malé, and that's when the seriousness of my situation hits me. I don't know the laws here. We just chose this place as a honeymoon resort, so I never even thought about it before, but the Maldives is a Muslim country, and I have no idea what might happen to me. What if the police suspect I'm involved somehow? What if Chrissy says something? Briefly, I visualize crowded, febrile prisons, stoning, that kind of thing, and I press pause in my brain, tell myself I'm being hysterical. The policemen are dressed in smart pale-blue shirts with blue ties, and there are pale-blue bands around their navy peaked caps. They look as well-manicured and perfect as the island itself, but perhaps there is a dark heart at the centre of them, too.

As I continue to stand there, I find it impossible to look out to sea any longer, in case I really do see a body pop up, the dark drip of his hair, the salmon flash of his shorts, the gross pallor of his putrefying skin. Please, no. Not in front of his mother. I need to get a grip. I long to sit down, but I dutifully stand to attention, and when the dhoni finally docks, I am there, and I am waiting.

'Hello, Veronica,' I say, as calmly as I can manage. What do I say next? How are you? How was your journey? You look well. Nothing will do.

'I'm so sorry,' I say, and she looks at me as if she has shards of glass in her eyes and daggers up her nostrils. She is a witch, and she terrifies me, now more than ever.

'Hello, Jemma,' says Dan softly. I offer my hand and he shakes it politely. It's as if we've never met.

There is nothing more to say. There are no hugs between us, no obvious shared concern or grief. It looks odd, and I know the policemen have clocked it too. My card is marked. If my husband doesn't come back, and they start to dig deeper, start to think Jamie's disappearance might be something other than an accidental drowning, then maybe I really will be a suspect.

I find myself thinking back to our wedding last week: the church, the flowers, the pretty dresses. I picture it all. Jamie's waistcoat. Him looking at me, so happy. *Or had he simply been pretending?* And will I ever know? I so desperately want to have that time all over again, so I can stop it right there. I want the world to turn backwards, to how it was before. I want the tides to reverse and wash my husband back in, from wherever he is, so we can say that we're sorry, and we can both be set free.

18

Six-and-a-quarter years earlier

'Hope that wasn't too painful,' Dan said to Jemma, as they were driving home from his father's party through the early evening gloom. The high street was rain-soaked and shiny, following a spectacular thunderstorm, and light was reflecting from the orange street lamps in thick golden pillars. An elderly man was lurching along the pavement, wearing old-man clothes and disconcertingly white trainers, almost certainly drunk.

'No, it was great,' Jemma said, slightly disingenuously. 'I love your dad, and your brother seems nice, too.'

'Are you making your point via the power of omission?'

'What d'you mean?' Jemma looked confused for a second, and then she got it. 'Oh, no! Of course not.'

'But you don't like her much, do you?'

'Well . . . I still think it might be easier if my name was Lydia.' She felt Dan react, almost imperceptibly, and then he recovered himself.

'Sorry, but I'm afraid that that's what my mum's like at times. Don't worry about her. She doesn't mean any harm.'

Jemma didn't believe him. She was perceptive, and she was convinced her boyfriend's mother meant a whole load of harm. Her harm came in the form of verbal arrows and euphemistic slings, in pounding parenthesized catapults, in catty remarks disguised as compliments. Her words and actions swooped and darted, and caught Jemma right in the very centre of herself.

'Anyway,' Dan continued, changing the subject. 'Jamie has invited us over for dinner with him and his girlfriend. You up for it?'

'Uh-huh,' said Jemma again.

'What's up, Jem?'

'Oh, nothing, Dan. I ... I'm just not used to big families, that's all.' She fiddled with her left earring, pulled it a little too hard, so she could feel the flesh stretch.

'When was it that your parents actually split up, Jemma?' Dan asked now. She flinched. She wanted to tell him to mind his own business, but it was an innocent enough question. She owed it to him to talk about it sooner or later.

'When I was fourteen,' she said. She gave a brittle little laugh. 'That difficult age.'

'And why did they? What happened?'

Jemma paused. What could she say?

'They just didn't get on,' she said at last. 'And then one day my dad finally had enough and moved out.' Would that do?

'I'm sorry,' said Dan. He took one hand off the steering wheel and put it on her knee, squeezed it gently.

'It's fine,' Jemma said. 'I still saw him.' She turned her face to the window. As she stared out at the night-time rushing by, thinking dark, poisonous thoughts, she wanted to scream suddenly.

'And how did your mum die?' Even though he spoke softly, the words lashed at her, like a cat-o'-nine-tails. It was the first time he'd asked her.

'What is this? A police interrogation?'

'Sorry,' he said. There was an awkward pause.

'That's OK,' she managed, after a moment. 'Sorry I was rude.'

'It's fine,' he said, although she thought he sounded a little peeved. He was quiet as he drove carefully along the country roads whilst Jemma sat on her fists, the anger ripe in them. Even by the time they entered the motorway and picked up speed, her mood still hadn't quite settled, and the atmosphere between them was uneasy. In the end, Dan wordlessly put on Jeff Buckley, loud and heartfelt, and neither of them spoke for the rest of the journey back to London.

19

Now

The weather is echoing my rage and despair, and it is perversely making me feel a bit better. In the three hours since the seaplane's arrival, I've endured an excruciatingly tactical lunch with Dan and Veronica, followed by a nice friendly chat with the two Maldivian police officers. All the while, the clouds have been descending and the ever-rising wind has been adding to the roar in my ears.

When I finally exit the sanatorium, which has been set up as a makeshift interview room, it's as though the sky is ready to let rip. Big fat hot spots of angry rain start leaking, then pouring, out of the grey – and now the deluge is so great it is as if a gigantic vat of water is being dumped on the island. I get soaked from just a ten-yard dash to the buggy, which has its plastic sides pulled down for once, and is driven by a different butler, which I'm glad about. Moosa doesn't even try to hide his disdain towards me now.

When I get back to the bungalow, I'm shivering. I lock the doors and peel off my sopping clothes, which I know will never get dry in this humidity, and then pull on my pyjamas and get into bed, where I stay for the afternoon, listening to the insistent beating of the rain on the roof. *Where is my husband in this downpour?* I wonder if the army boats are still out looking for him, or whether they've had to come in. The phone rings once but I ignore it, in case it's Veronica or Dan, or the police, or Chrissy. It seems I can no longer face talking to anyone. If it's important, they'll come knocking. Finally, just as I am losing all faith in the universe, the dun sky cracks apart and the sun comes back with a vengeance, and when I open my curtains to see hot steam rise above the sheeny green jungle, my little chef friend Chati arrives on the terrace, like a magical mirage, with my dinner.

There has been a development, apparently. It is first thing the next morning, the fourth day since my husband vanished, and the chubbier policeman has knocked on the door to my bungalow so early he was perhaps hoping to wake me, but he has failed. I still have not slept. He asks me to come with him, and he waits outside as I put on a dress and my silver Havaianas flip-flops. I run my fingers through my hair and wipe under my eyes with a gritty licked finger, but I don't dare take the time to clean my teeth. We get in the waiting buggy together, and when we pass one coming in the opposite direction, I keep my eyes firmly on my lightly tanned knees, study my blossoming freckles, just in case it's Dan and Veronica. When we arrive at the sanatorium, the other policeman is already there, looking pin-sharp as ever, and before I've even sat down he's waving a mask at me, attached to which is a snorkel with yellow tape near the top of it – and I am ninety nine point nine per cent sure it is Jamie's.

'Where did you find that?' I ask.

'It washed up on the beach on the west side of the island, during the storm.'

I am so stupefied I don't know if this is a good or a bad thing. Does it mean they think Jamie's alive, or dead? They are studying me, searching my face for clues, and so I let it crumple, and I start to cry. They ask me again about the last evening Jamie and I spent together, and I repeat that I was quite drunk, that I can't really remember too much of the latter part of it. They look disapproving. I wear too little clothing. I drink too much alcohol. I am a disgrace in their eyes, that's for sure – but am I a murderer? Or is it the sea that's the murderer, that has taken Jamie off to the deep, to one day be returned, putrid and dripping in seaweed? When will the answer reveal itself?

'I feel sick,' I say, suddenly, and I do. 'Can I go now?'

The policemen look at each other. They don't know what to say. There is nothing more to do. They have searched the island and the surrounding seas and found nothing. There is no body, just a mask and snorkel. Jamie might not be found for ages, even if he is dead, and it seems no-one knows.

They let me leave, and I decline Moosa's sullen offer of a lift in the buggy and instead walk back to my bungalow. I can't stand the ill feeling radiating off my butler right now. My head remains bowed as my eyes scan the ants and the lizards on the path ahead of me, and the fog in my head gets thicker and ever more blinding. When I reach the terrace, I settle down onto the daybed slowly, carefully, as if my bones might break. I wrap my arms around my knees and pull my sunhat low over my head, in case someone's watching me. Nothing happens. All is silent: there's just the faint flare of the air and the gurgle-swirl of the sea. Any action is under the surface, where I know it is livid and teeming. But is Jamie under there? Where on earth is Jamie?

Seconds tick noiselessly by, and their passing feels menacing. It occurs to me that we're always at the very end of time. It's always now. And for now there's just more waiting. But for how much longer? What is the protocol in this infernal scenario? How long do we carry on watching and hoping, before we have to declare defeat, admit that *now* is finally over. How long do we wait, before we give up on Jamie at last, and go home?

20

Six years earlier

Jamie's flat was on the ground floor of a Regency house in an up-and-coming part of North London, and it had apparently been decorated with the help of Jamie's erstwhile girlfriend Sarah (who had recently tearfully removed her spare toothbrush from the holder she had so carefully chosen). The cornicing in the living room had been painted over so many times its pattern was slack, like melting jelly, but as the ceiling was high, it wouldn't be noticed by the casual visitor, although of course Jemma clocked it. The walls were a muted grey. The floor was hardwood, wide-planked, covered by a plush thick-piled rug. The sofas rocked a fifties vibe. It was nicer than Dan's flat. She quashed the thought.

Jemma couldn't help but be impressed by Jamie. Although he lacked the raw appeal of his older brother, he was confident, charming, well-dressed. He had an amusing line in self-deprecating anecdotes. He was a good cook. He even folded his washing properly, as she'd discovered when she'd taken a peek into his bedroom. He reminded Jemma a little of one of her previous boyfriends, a thought she immediately tried to quell.

'What would you like to drink, Jemma?' Jamie asked now.

'Oh, a glass of red, thanks.'

'Dan?'

'Just a pale ale, thanks.'

'Ever the sophisticate,' said Jamie, and he laughed.

Jemma glanced at Jamie. Was he taking the piss out of his own brother? And in front of his girlfriend? That's not on, she thought – and she wondered whether Jamie took after his mother. She hoped not, for Jamie's sake. He didn't look much like her, at least. His features were smooth and defined, and his eyes were a pale grey colour that was both arresting in its uniqueness and vaguely unsettling. Dan's face was ostensibly more open, and yet his eyes were darker, veiled even. He was broader too, so he looked less good than Jamie in clothes, but almost certainly way better without them. Jemma blushed at the thought, and then giggled.

'What's so funny?' said Dan, as Jamie disappeared off to fetch the drinks.

'Nothing,' she said.

'Are you OK?'

'I'm fine. You?'

'Yeah,' said Dan, but he seemed troubled somehow. She took his hand and held it until Jamie came back, with two pale ales, as it happened. Jemma decided he must have been joking earlier. It was sometimes hard to tell.

Jamie had cooked a Thai fish curry, and Jemma had to admit it was perfect. It seemed odd in a way that there weren't four of them, but Jamie had said that life goes on, and that he hadn't seen the point of cancelling. Over dinner Jemma tried to imagine what it would have been like to have had siblings, and she sensed that there was an underlying edge between Dan and Jamie that perhaps all brothers had. Sometimes she was glad she was an only child, although of course it had made it even harder at home once her dad had left. Jemma pulled back from her thoughts, as if they were too painful, yet still they screeched across the inside of her skull.

'Hey, Dan,' Jamie said after they'd finished dessert, which was a lemon tart from Waitrose. ('Steady on,' Jamie had said when Jemma had asked if it was home-made. 'It's a school night.') 'While you're here, would you mind taking a look at my boiler? It's making a right racket, and I don't have a clue.' He winked at Jemma, and it made her blush. There was something about Jamie that got under her skin, and when Dan disappeared off to the kitchen as requested, she felt unnerved by the way her boyfriend's brother was looking at her, as if he was laughing at her.

'So, how did you and Dan meet, Jemma?' Jamie said, as he topped up her glass.

'Oh . . . in a pub.'

'Really? What, he picked you up?'

'Er, I guess you could say that.' Jemma didn't know what to say. *She* was fine about it, but she wasn't sure whether Dan would want his little brother to know they'd met on a dating website. Dan and Jamie seemed so competitive somehow.

'Well, well, well. Lucky old Dan,' said Jamie, and at first she thought he was being sarcastic, and then he smiled at her, and asked her what football team she supported, and eventually she gave him the benefit of the doubt, and decided he was just being nice.

21

Now

It's late afternoon on the fourth day and there's still no news. I emerge from my bungalow and walk all of twenty yards along the path through the trees onto the beach. I perch on one of the pair of sun beds that are perfectly positioned for my husband and me. It feels too bright out here, too open. I feel too singular. Too alone. Like I'm the only person on a school trip with no-one to sit next to on the coach. It seems I am regressing. I want to go home so badly the thought tears at me.

I lie down and open the book that I was engrossed in, before, but it's beyond me now. I stare at the pages and struggle not to wail. I don't know what else to do, except feel the panic, try to accept it. I've changed into a beach cover-up (white, for purity, or perhaps surrender), my biggest, floppiest sunhat, de rigueur dark glasses. The umbrella is as low as it will go. I am a parody of somebody who wants to be left alone, yet really, truly doesn't.

I yearn to go in the sea now that I'm so close to it, but how on earth would it look? Does a distraught wife whose husband might have drowned go *swimming*? Yet how does anything I do look? And who really cares? *The police do*, I try to remind myself – and obviously so do those couples who occasionally stroll by along the sand, as if by accident. We all know they're rubbernecking, so let them. What difference does it make?

The sun refuses to surrender. It's still so hot. My legs are getting burnt, so I retreat to the bungalow, where I feel safest. It is a hollow inky kind of safety, though, and I can't shake the feeling that someone is watching me, perhaps from the trees. I almost wonder if it's my husband, playing some dastardly trick on me, to get his revenge. An image of our flower-strewn wedding day flashes through my mind, and the memory is laced with such hopelessness that I clamp my eyes shut, yet the tears squeeze through anyway. Sweat pools in the spot above my Cupid's arrow, and when I wipe at it my skin feels slimy, as if I am putrefying, rotting away.

Jamie has now been missing for around ninety excruciating hours, and as every second passes it feels like the island is getting ever smaller. The image I have of my husband is slowly getting smaller too, as if my memory of him is disappearing over the horizon. I keep turning the crisis around and around in my head, which is fuzzy now, but not in that pleasant, cocktail-induced way you might expect of a honeymooner. The fuzziness expands, melds with the never-ending nausea that my husband's disappearance seems to have triggered, until my skull bangs with the relentlessness of a death knell.

The phone rings. It is Chrissy, telling me the police want to interview her and Kenny again, and I'm not quite sure why she's telling me. I don't know what to say. I'm pretty sure she hasn't said much about that last night so far, but what if she's put under pressure? If pushed far enough, will she tell them what else I might have said that last night on the beach? Is she trying to warn me? I stare at my palms, my delicate wrists, the fat blue veins leading away from my lifelines. I press my right wrist, hard, against the solid wooden edge of the bedside table, and it makes me feel better. I'm almost certain Chrissy knows I hadn't meant any of it anyway. I'd been upset for sure, perhaps even a little demented – but how could I possibly have done anything to Jamie between then and the next morning at breakfast?

What Kenny might think is a different story, of course. But surely he wouldn't think someone like me is capable of getting rid of a twelve-stone man – my own husband – on an island like this. There's nowhere to hide. *Unless, of course, I'd drowned him.* Hysteria rises in my throat like champagne. The dread spirals – especially once it occurs to me that the story could even become interesting back in the UK. Newspapers love honeymoon disasters. To my knowledge no media outlet has picked up on it yet, but I presume they might if Jamie isn't found soon. I'm sure the other guests must be tweeting about it. Perhaps it's only a matter of time before I become an international pariah. I'm almost tempted to go online and Google myself right this instant, but I can't bear to know. I stand up from the bed and shake my head, trying to get the bad thoughts out. I wonder what Dan thinks of all this, but I daren't ask him. He hasn't come near me since that hideous lunch with Veronica the previous day, which I suppose is hardly surprising. The circumstances aren't conducive to him offering a publicly supportive shoulder, seeing as I used to go out with him. It wouldn't be appropriate.

I'm just so restless. I go into the bathroom, do a couple of circuits of the free-standing bath, head back into the bedroom, walk out onto the terrace – and then somehow my feet take me down to the beach again. I can feel hot, hungry eyes preying on my skin. As I sink onto the sand, a young Muslim couple are walking away from me to the right. He is in shorts and a T-shirt, and she's in a full black burka, and I know from seeing them at breakfast that her face is covered. I wonder how happy they are together. It's impossible to tell. I long to yell after them, ask them.

Once the couple disappears around the corner, I stand up and walk down to the water's edge. I let the waves lick at my feet. The sea feels so warm and enticing and I'm tempted, so tempted, but I mustn't. I stare out across the trillions of gallons of water, searching, ever searching. I crouch down to touch the sea with my hand, and I rest there on my haunches, until eventually my mind sways again and bad memories crowd in. I find myself toppling backwards, and as I land on the sand the thud reverberates up my spine like a hammer blow. I lie still for a moment, a little in shock, and then I give up, just go with it. I stretch my legs out in front of me, into the water. I throw my arms over my head and arch my back, yield to the sun. Its rays feel ferocious, as though they're pinning me to the beach. I stretch.

I hear a click, and then another sound behind me. A camera? I sit up quickly, pull my beach throw over my legs. I can see that Chati has appeared at the bungalow, with a tray, and he's putting it down on the outside table, and maybe that was what the noise was. I get up and walk back towards the bungalow. The aroma of the curry is delicate and spiced, and it is served with coconut rice and diced cucumber, and a mango juice, although, as ever, there is no alcohol, which I feel slightly regretful about. Despite myself I feel hungry.

'Thank you,' I say.

'You're welcome, ma'am.' His dirt-brown eyes glow and his smile is as wide as China. 'Enjoy,' he says, and then he edges politely away.

22

Six years earlier

Jemma and Dan saw in their second new year together at his place, just the two of them, and it was perfect. They stocked up on cheese and chocolates and champagne, and Dan cooked the most sumptuous dinner she'd ever eaten, and Jemma joked that she was glad that she'd got him into cooking, even if it did mean that her clothes were getting far too tight for her. They watched the fireworks on TV, and drank more champagne, and when they finally went to bed it was even more wonderful than ever, now that she was excited about a future with him in it. She wondered what this year would bring the two of them. She would turn twenty-nine, he thirty-one. Her job was still going well. She'd been officially promoted to Designer, complete with a decent pay rise, and she hadn't had a career-limiting meltdown in months. The only slight blemish in the overall outlook was that Dan didn't seem to be very busy in his work – but, Jemma thought, that was hardly surprising over winter. She was sure it would pick up.

On New Year's Day afternoon Jemma and Dan went to his parents' house for a drinks party. When they arrived there were twenty or so people already there – a combination of neighbours, family and old friends – and the mood was of general conviviality. Even Veronica's dislike of Jemma was better disguised these days, and in fact her latest tactic was full-on chummy collusion, although Jemma found that almost as alarming as the erstwhile hostility.

'Ooohh, Jemma, do come and meet Carol,' Veronica was saying now, taking Jemma's elbow in a faux-friendly way and marching her over to a sad-looking older woman who was lurking by the buffet, leaving Dan talking to a voluptuous-looking neighbour, almost certainly by design. Veronica spoke loudly. 'Carol's just got divorced, and she's doing up her new flat. Perhaps you can give her some ideas.' She let go of Jemma's elbow, and then turned and called, 'Peter! Can you put out some more napkins, they've all gone!' She stopped just short of tutting at her husband's implied incompetence, and as she marched off Jemma found it inconceivable, not for the first time, that Veronica got away with such behaviour.

'Er, where's your new flat, Carol?' Jemma asked now, as she watched Carol hack haplessly at the salmon.

'Basingstoke,' said Carol.

'Oh. That's nice.' Carol's eyes looked like they were about to fill. She piled some new potatoes onto her paper plate, and one rolled off. 'And, er, did you have a nice Christmas?' Jemma continued, as she discreetly stooped down to retrieve it before it got trodden into the carpet.

'Well, it was –' Carol stopped and grabbed one of the napkins from the pile Peter had fortuitously just replenished. She started dabbing at her eyes.

'Goodness, I'm so sorry.' Instinctively, Jemma put her hand on Carol's arm, and gently squeezed it. She didn't know what to say.

'Auntie Carol!' said a voice behind them. Jemma turned and it was Jamie. His hair was slightly longer than it had been in the autumn, and he was wearing a beautifully cut jacket. Her heart took a tiny leap, which she tried to tell herself was purely because he'd rescued her.

'How are you doing, my darling?' Jamie gave Carol a bear hug, and as Carol stood in Jamie's arms, he winked at Jemma. 'Carol's not my real auntie,' he explained, as he finally let her go. 'Just my absolute favourite of Mum's friends. She even used to take me to Cubs, didn't you, Auntie Carol?'

Carol's face was flushed, and she was smiling now, rather than crying.

'Thank you,' mouthed Jemma to Jamie. His perceptiveness and kindness had surprised her.

'How's Adrian?' Jamie asked Carol, as she started attacking the plate of cold cuts.

'Oh, he's good, Jamie. They've just had a little girl, Ella. I'm a granny twice over now!'

'Oh, that's great,' said Jamie. 'Congratulations! I think that calls for a celebration.' He shot off and soon came back with champagne and four flutes, and as he opened the bottle, he said, 'Here's to little Ella.' He proceeded to pour, as expertly as a sommelier.

'Not for me, thanks,' said Dan, who'd silently appeared at Jemma's side. Jamie nodded and continued his charm assault on Carol. The older woman's twin-setted shoulders were fully upright now, and her cheeks were turning increasingly pink as Jamie kept topping up her glass. The champagne helped relax Jemma too, and soon she and Carol were giggling at Jamie's bath-time stories, with Carol almost crying with laughter at something to do with a Desperate Dan soap-on-a-rope.

'Desperate Dan,' snorted Carol. 'Just like your boyfriend, Jemma!' She thrust her champagne flute towards Dan, who didn't seem to find it as funny as Jemma did.

'Ha, that's what we used to call you, wasn't it, Dan?' said Jamie, holding court.

'Humph,' said Dan, walking off.

Carol peered over her glasses. 'What'sh *hizh* problem?' she said.

'Oh, he's always been like that,' said Jamie. 'Throws his toys out the pram when things don't go his way.' He winked at Carol and Jemma.

Jemma giggled and took another large sip of her drink. Who'd have thought Carol would be so much fun? She, Jemma, should really stop judging people on first appearances – look at how wrong she'd been about Dan. She smiled fondly, and then looked around. Where *was* Dan? She shrugged compliantly as Jamie topped up her glass, yet again, and then she smiled at him, and he smiled back – and she felt a fizzing inside that had nothing to do with the champagne. He was younger than Dan, and richer, and funnier . . . God, she needed to sober up. Jemma wrenched her gaze away from her boyfriend's brother, picked up a sausage roll from the buffet and stuffed it into her mouth, just as Veronica swanned past and asked her how she was enjoying the party.

23

Now

It's still Day Four, or at least I think it is. I fear that I will always count the days from now on. There was everything that came before – and now this. I finish eating the meal Chati brought me, and then I throw it all up. Time unravels. Seconds and hours become interchangeable. *That's it.* I refuse to wait any longer. I'm done.

Darkness is already half-smothering the island by the time I realize that I just have to stretch my legs, *do* something, before I go mad with inactivity and fear. I decide to go for a run, as it's the least outwardly enjoyable thing I can think of, the one least likely to raise merry-widow suspicion. Surely people will understand that I can't sit around this place and wait forever? Moreover though, a run gives me an excuse to go down to the dive centre, try to catch Pascal before it shuts. I haven't spoken to him since we went out in the dhoni on the first day my husband was missing, and he was uncharacteristically abrupt with me then. I still feel there's something about the resort's marine biologist, and it's not just his dark French good looks, his provocative charm, his come-to-bed eyes. Chrissy (who I can't help but think seems way more interested in him than a newly-wed should be) has told me that the police keep questioning him. Pascal knows something, I'm sure of it. I can't wait any more for the police to tell me what's going on. I need to find out for myself.

I put on one of Jamie's T-shirts, which is so long you can't even see the shorts I have on underneath, but of course I didn't bring any more conservative ones – I didn't think I would need them. I wear my husband's favourite cap pulled low over my eyes. I lace up the red Nikes I'd packed in case the mood had taken us to play tennis, and then I step outside, into the jungle. As the door clicks shut I feel so scared I break immediately into a sprint, suddenly worried about what nocturnal wild beasts there might be here on the island. Are there any? I have no idea. You only ever hear of the fish.

My pace is fast and heart-thumping, and I soon cross the interior through the tree-infested paths. When I arrive at the dive centre I'm breathing heavily, due to a dizzying combination of terror and exertion. The lights are on, and one of the dive guys is just shutting up shop, but he's a local and his English is not so good. When I breathlessly mention Pascal, he gestures for me to sit down and wait in the briefing area, but I'm not sure whether he means that Pascal is coming back, or not. I sit there for what feels like forever, and just as I'm about to give up, Pascal appears from the direction of the beach. He is half-wearing his wetsuit, and his feet are

113

sandy and his dark, damp hair is curling at his neck. It's immediately clear he's not at all happy to see me.

'Pascal,' I say. I cut to the chase. 'Do you know what's happened? Do you know where my husband is?'

Pascal's accent has no effect on me now. 'I have spoken to ze police, Jemma. I cannot tell you anything more.' I look at him, and he looks at me, and we both suspect the other of something. My eyes shift to the map on the wall behind him, of the atolls that make up the Maldives. Of all the water. Of all the potential hiding places. I shouldn't have come.

'Sorry,' I say. 'Of course, I understand.' I turn and I can feel his eyes on the back of my head, and it feels like they are burning through, into my brain. His attitude scares me somehow. Is he responsible for Jamie's disappearance? *Or does he think I am?* I turn and flee, and as I run home the trees are like bullies and naysayers, crowding in on me beneath the moon, whispering that it's my fault, after all – and I stumble and trip, blinded by tears. When I get back there is a tray on the terrace and under the silver dome is a glass of cool watermelon juice, a bowl of fresh fruit salad and a slice of coconut cake. I wipe my eyes, sit down at the table and gratefully devour the lot. And then half an hour later I bring it all up again, my head down the toilet bowl in my oh-so-beautiful bathroom.

24

Six years earlier

Peter and Veronica's New Year's Day party was still going strong, thanks to Peter having bought far more alcohol than his wife had realized, or indeed would have sanctioned. Jamie still had Carol and Jemma in fits of giggles, so much so that Carol had fully rallied from her previously maudlin state and was now waxing lyrical about her ex-husband's sexual deficiencies, and Jemma was laughing, mainly because she'd never met the poor man.

'And anyway,' Carol was saying now, in a loud conspiratorial whisper, 'that old trollop can keep the pencil-endowed little goat, and good luck to her.' She threw back her head and guffawed, and some of her drink slopped down her cardigan and onto the long-suffering carpet.

'Jemma,' whispered Dan, who had appeared back at her side and was sober. 'We need to get going soon.'

'Yesh, fine,' said Jemma. 'How are you getting home, Carol?'

'Oh, I'm shtaying here,' said Carol. 'My shitty little flat can wait until tomorrow.' She cackled again. 'I'm going to paint it Rhino's Breath, though. Jemma's told me to.'

'Elephant's,' said Jemma.

'Huh?'

'The paint. It's called Elephant's Breath.'

'Oh, whatever,' said Carol. She stuck her knobbly finger into the houmous and sucked it.

Veronica had just come through from her amazing kitchen and was prowling the living room, looking thunderous, which made Jemma giggle again. She took another glug of champagne.

'Jemma, we need to go,' said Dan, more firmly this time.

'Oh, really? But we're having fun – aren't we, Carol?'

'It's late,' said Dan.

What was his problem, Jemma thought. And then she dimly realized that it was probably because she'd got completely smashed, and he was driving.

'OK,' she said. She smiled sweetly at him. 'I jusht need to go to the bathroom.'

Carol had the same idea and beat her to the guest cloakroom, loudly proclaiming inferior bladder control, and so Jemma staggered downstairs. As she washed her hands her head was spinning, and she felt happy, and free, and it was a new year, and she loved Dan, and they were going to have a *good* year, and she was *sure* Carol would turn her life around – she might look like Mrs Merton but, once she got going, she had the wit of her too. Jemma grinned at herself in the

116

mirror as she dried her hands, and gave a little wave, but her reflection looked hazy, too far away. She unlocked the door and came out of the bathroom, where she stumbled, and almost fell into Jamie's arms. As he caught her, she felt his breath in her hair. He steadied her and let her go. And now they were staring into each other's eyes, their faces moving together as if in slow motion. And then Dan was there, at the top of the stairs in the upside-down house, watching them.

25

Now

It is news. We are news. Someone must have leaked it. The *Mail Online* has it as top billing, which is possibly the most appalling development of all. I flip my iPad case shut and nearly throw it across the bungalow.

I try to keep calm, think straight. My breath feels like it's coming out of my fingertips and I waggle them, push my wrists against the sides of my head, drum my skull. I circle the room, staring at the floor, feeling more caged than ever. I have to will myself not to scream. Memories broil inside of me.

The story's all quite matter-of-fact for now – groom goes missing on luxury honeymoon – but if Jamie's not found soon, what on earth are they going to drag up? OK, let's get the worst of it over with. Girl gets off with boyfriend's brother while drunk on champagne and laughter. Family rift ensues. Brother One never ever forgives her. Years later Girl marries Brother Two, who then vanishes on their honeymoon. Brother One turns up on said honeymoon, to look for Brother Two.

Oh, fucking, fucking hell. It seems that the disappearance and possible demise of my new husband is set to become a gruesome piece of tabloid entertainment to brighten up people's rain-soaked Januaries, and with a backstory like that, it's an editor's gift. Surely it's only a matter of time.

I flee to the bathroom, and at first I imagine that the bats swooping overhead are drones, with cameras, and then I tell myself not to be mad, but still, I wish now the room had a roof. I keep on my dress, just in case, and sink into the plunge pool, and the cool of the water helps soothe me. But then the oppressiveness grows, and grows, as I realize I can't escape the resort, nor the new headlines that will inevitably come, the slurs on my character, deserved or not. Soft waves start thumping in my ears, jungle calls and febrile sounds are trilling through my nervous system. I start to spin and dive my way around the tiny pool like a slippery captured dolphin. The urge to scream is almost irresistible. *I need to get off this island.*

At last I am calm and I loll on my back, numb and silent, depleted. My eyes are closed but I can feel the surface of the water grow smooth, like skin. I make vague, apathetic attempts to rearrange all the strands of the events that have led to this moment, try listlessly to get my head straight. What *was* it with me and Jamie? And where on earth does Dan fit in? How has this all gone so horribly wrong?

I backtrack slowly through the past seven-and-a-half years, looking for clues as to how we all got to here. I'm still unsure why Jamie took such a shine to me, and I've never dared·ask him. I've never wanted to know. Perhaps it really was as simple as him wanting something his brother already had, as if they were toddlers still and I were merely a shiny, tantalizing toy. Veronica's perverse approach to motherhood certainly hadn't helped the sibling rivalry, but whatever the cause, it seems that Jamie had wanted me enough to intentionally steal me off his own brother. So was I just a pawn in their childish little game? At the time I'd believed that the betrayal was all my doing. How hadn't I realized we were all culpable?

And yet, no matter how it's happened, here I am, all these years later, alone in a pool on a tiny island in the middle of the Indian Ocean, and my head is splintering and my skin is crinkling and I am married to Jamie and I don't know where he is, or what has happened, or whose fault it is, and maybe it's mine – and all I want is for him to walk up the beach towards me, and be safe. I long for him to be safe. I would take any punishment that was coming to me, if only he could be safe.

26

Six years earlier

'Well, this is nice,' said Sasha.

'Sorry,' said Jemma.

'It's OK. I'll forgive you for the comedy value.'

'It's not funny, Sasha.'

'Yeah, but if you can't laugh, what else can you do? I can just imagine his mother's face.'

Jemma blushed and hunched into her jacket. It was the second week of January, and they'd been to the cinema to watch a mediocre film that Sasha had slept through, and now they were on the South Bank, in a restaurant made out of a bank of converted shipping containers, eating Mexican tapas. Sasha had insisted on ordering Mojitos, but they seemed to be mainly filled with ice, so even three of them hadn't made any inroads into Jemma's heartache.

'Don't worry, Jem. Dan adores you. You only had a drunken snog, albeit with his brother, but it's not *that* bad. He'll come round.'

'He won't. He won't even take my calls.'

'Well, go and see him then.'

'I did. He refused to open the door.' Jemma sniffed,

and then wiped her nose on her sleeve. 'Sasha, what can I *do*?'

'Oh, Jemma,' Sasha said, reaching over and putting her hand briefly on Jemma's arm. 'I'm sorry, hon. I didn't realize you were even that serious about Dan.'

'Well, I was. And now it's too late.' Jemma picked up her napkin and blew her nose noisily. As she stared out at the blackness of the river, she wondered yet again how Dan must be feeling. And then she took a bite out of a blue cheese taco and tried to smile. It wasn't fair on Sasha to be such an unrelenting misery. She needed to get a grip.

'Look, I'm sorry for droning on,' Jemma said now. She tried to brighten her tone. 'How's work?'

'Busy. Underpaid. My boss is a bitch.' Sasha batted her eyelashes, and grinned. 'Apart from that I love it. How's yours?'

'Well, I had a meltdown this afternoon, so that didn't help. Dan used to calm me down, but now . . .'

'Oh God, I wondered how long it would take to steer the conversation back onto the Brothers Armstrong.' Jemma pulled a face at her. 'Oh, Jem,' Sasha continued, 'why don't you just go out with Jamie and get it over with?'

'Can you imagine?' Jemma said. 'It would almost be worth it, just to see Veronica's face.' And then her smile faded again, and she looked towards the door, in case Dan was coming in, which was highly unlikely. She took a futile draw through her ice-crunched straw. 'D'you think I should ring him?'

'Who?'

'Dan, of course! Who d'you think I mean?'

'Well, I never know with you. For all I know, he might have another younger brother you could cop off with next, like in *Legends of the Fall*.'

'Oh, fuck off, Sasha.'

'Always at your service.' Sasha smiled, and her eyebrows shot up under her dark heavy fringe as her cheeks dimpled. Her voice softened. 'It's OK, Jem. Just give it time. He'll come round, I'm sure he will. And now I come to think of it, he does look a bit like Brad Pitt.'

'Yeah, right.'

'You never know. You've just got to sit tight.'

And so Jemma did. But, for a change, despite her behind-the-scenes machinations, Sasha was wrong.

January and February came and went. March exploded into London with a ton-full of snow, and roads were blocked and buses weren't running. People rang around to check what their colleagues were doing, and then, once they were sure there was safety in numbers, didn't even bother trying to make it in to work. Jemma caught a terrible cold and felt like she was dying, and yet still Dan wouldn't talk to her. She'd run out of ideas about what to do. She'd written, saying that she was sorry. She'd even asked him to move in with her, as a symbol of her commitment, but he ignored her.

It just wasn't meant to be, Sasha told her, over and over, if Dan wasn't prepared to forgive her. 'He wasn't the one for you,' she'd say, and perhaps, thought Jemma, her friend was right.

Finally, Jemma gave up. Now, instead of hankering after the past, she flung herself towards the future with the vitality of a moth at a lightbulb, knowing she'd get burnt, not caring if she did. She went to work. She came home. She went to work. She came home. In the evenings, she ran through the wastelands of her ruined dreams with the fervour of a mother about to be reunited with her lost child. She couldn't share how she felt, so she threw back her head, and shook her pixie hair, and she pounded the streets as if there were a murderer behind her, unable to pace herself. She tried to flee from her feelings until her lungs gave up, but she never escaped, and they followed her like a stream of black smoke, as if her engine were misfiring and she was belching out bad thoughts for everyone to see. *She only had herself to blame.* Night after night she thudded the pavements, past tall red-brick houses split up into flats, along quiet, drab streets lined with unremarkable cars that nestled into each other. Her breath grew ragged as she ran, and ran, and the buzzing of the phone in her ear was persistent and insistent, but it was always Sasha or one of her other friends, checking up on her, never Dan – and so she ignored it.

By May, Jemma's mental state hadn't improved. She caught the flu and took a week off work. She barely washed. She ate out of cans. Kay tried to call, as did her father, but Jemma texted them and told them she was fine. She took to sleeping with a picture of Dan on the pillow next to her. Even she was worried about herself. Her boyfriend's refusal to take her back had left Jemma knocked over by grief, as though it had crept up behind her, tapped her on the shoulder, and then punched her in the face.

More bleak days passed. Jemma forced herself back to work, drew up interiors plans for hotels she would never visit, sat anxiously at her desk through lunch, drifted in and out of meetings, almost as though she weren't there. She took to obsessing about Dan and how she'd betrayed him. Yet he'd always forgiven her in the past, when she'd gone mad about him sending her flowers, or complained about being forced to have lunch with his parents. He'd *loved* her. Hadn't he?

Six months after Jemma and Dan had broken up, just as she was finally starting to feel slightly better, Jamie rang her. She took the call, hoping for news of Dan, and she got it. Dan was moving to Gloucestershire, Jamie told her, to start a new business there, and he was back with his old girlfriend, Lydia. The girl he'd refused to ever talk about. The one that Veronica had claimed to have adored. *How dared he?* And so when Jamie went on to ask Jemma if she fancied meeting him for coffee, she was so utterly enraged and heartbroken and drained, all at the same time, that she found herself saying yes, why not?

27

Now

The British police are involved now. It seems they are the media's puppets, and if the tabloids see fit to investigate Jamie's disappearance, then so must the Met. Two officers are on their way, the Maldivian police inform me on my doorstep, a little bit sulkily. *Lucky them,* my cynical self whispers – someone is getting a free trip to paradise.

As the policemen watch me I can tell I'm still not acting right, but what is the correct response in this hellish scenario? Perhaps I'm meant to be grateful? It doesn't help that I seem to have reached this catatonic state of fear that is occasionally punctuated by a private hysteria. My thoughts are becoming deranged and unreliable, and so I do my best to don an impassive yet suitably grief-stricken mask while retreating ever further into myself. But there's not enough room inside my own skin for all the conflicting sensations, and I know I need to try harder.

After the Maldivian police take their leave I lie down on the bed, exhausted by the charade. As I find myself going over and over that last evening, snippets of memory reappear, and blind me, like the sun in a mirror. If only I could *talk* to someone. Even the prospect of being painted a brother-swapping harlot is nothing compared to the vacuum Jamie's disappearance has created. Yet I daren't call Sasha or Dad to articulate my feelings, in case the police have tapped the phone – paranoid perhaps, but I mustn't risk implicating myself. And of course I can't go near Dan, find out what he makes of it. It wouldn't look right.

When the British detectives arrive on the island at last it doesn't seem appropriate to go to meet them, like I did when Veronica and Dan were magicked out of the endless blue sky, in a buzzy little seaplane as bright and bold as a butterfly. Of course I'd only gone that time because I'd thought it was Veronica and Peter. I'd never have done so if I'd even suspected it was Dan arriving – when I'd spotted him the animalistic desire to fling myself into his arms and sob my heart out had been off the scale, and so now I'm doing my best to avoid him. It's too confusing. It makes me angry.

In truth, I barely leave the bungalow at all any more. Running through the trees was too panic-inducing. Swimming in the sea is out of the question. Being on the beach, I feel spied on. There's no way on earth I can go to the restaurant and endure the excoriating stares, especially now that, on top of everything else, I'm headline news. And even though I'm still too passive to order in room service, it doesn't matter, as dear Chati keeps bringing me food. He's only performing the role that my butler should be doing, but on the rare occasions Moosa does come around now, all he does is stare at me with ill-concealed suspicion, and I want to tell him to just get lost and mind his own business. I think it's fair to say our servant-master relationship has broken down, and I'm glad. It never felt right to me anyway. Who needs a *butler* on holiday, for God's sake?

So what to do? I go into the bathroom and bolt the door, double-check that there's no-one dead in the bottom of the pool – and then I lie on my back on the hard tiled floor and stare at the sky. It's impossible to know what to think any more, how to feel. I am stuck in a vortex of in-betweenness, of not knowing what will happen. Who knew a disappearance was such agony? I've read similar stories before, of course, and tried to imagine what it must be like, but believe me, it's worse. It feels as if I'm in a pressure cooker which is well on its way to exploding. My hopes are being cooked. *And yet.* I told my husband to fuck right off, and now he has. I got what I asked for.

It's a relief when the phone finally rings. As I get up off the bathroom floor and drift through the bungalow, I no longer feel real. My heart chimes to its own erratic pattern. I approach the phone and it looks like it is shaking, and I suddenly wish it would just *shut up.* Before I even pick up, I know who it will be, and what she will say, and unfortunately I am right. When I get off the phone I go straight into the toilet and throw up, yet again – and although I want to blame it entirely on the stress of agreeing to see my mother-in-law, I can no longer deny that things might yet be worse than I even imagined.

I'm beginning to think that I might be pregnant.

28

Eighteen months earlier

Jemma had never known what her best friend had against Jamie. OK, Sasha didn't like bankers. Or gym-obsessives. Or girlfriend-stealers. But, as Jemma had told her a million times, it hadn't been Jamie's fault – *she'd* thrown herself at *him,* and seeing as Dan had never ever forgiven her, she'd had to move on some time. Yeah, but it didn't have to be with the brother, Sasha had said once – that was really closing the door. Jemma had had such an uncharacteristic go at her best friend, Sasha had never dared broach it again.

And now, all these years later, Jemma had almost succeeded in forgetting that she'd once been in love with her boyfriend's brother. The whole debacle had caused such a rift that Jemma hardly ever saw any of Jamie's family, and Dan and Jamie barely saw each other either. Jemma still felt terrible about being the cause of it, about having switched from one brother to the next – but the reality had been nowhere near as callous as it sounded. For a start, Dan had been back with his ex-girlfriend by then anyway. And Jamie had waited months before calling Jemma, and when they had started going out, he'd been so nice to her. He'd booked tickets to films he'd known she would love, whisked her off to dinner in small, intimate restaurants that felt like going to a corner of Paris, taken her to cool markets she hadn't even known existed – and his approach had been seductive, and ultimately effective.

My God, Jemma thought now as she sat opposite her long-term boyfriend, that all seemed like a million lifetimes ago. They were in a hip cafe in East London, and it was the weekend and they were sharing the *Sunday Times*. Jamie had *Sport*, as usual, and she had the *Magazine*, as usual. They'd got up late and walked there along the canal, at her suggestion, but the water had been still and grease-pocked, leaden, as if life within it was not possible, and Jamie had barely spoken. She watched him now, studying the Premier League table. These days, and especially since they'd moved in together, he appeared far more smitten with Chelsea and working out than spending time with her. It was as if, as soon as he'd been convinced of her love, he'd started to take her for granted. She'd been his prize catch, his fraternal victory, but now she could stay flailing around in the net as far as he was concerned. Neither let go nor eaten. He could be such a tosser at times.

Jemma tried to knock back her resentment, which was rising relentlessly in her chest like proving dough. Maybe it wasn't either of their faults that she'd decided it was time they got on with things. Perhaps it was just her age, early thirties, the four years they'd been together, the fact that all of their friends seemed to be getting engaged of late. Maybe it was simply because her biological clock was ticking, ever louder. But whatever the reason, the issue of marriage was forever there now, in the back of his head and hers, like a dirty little secret that they shared. It would be funny if it weren't so painful.

'What are you having, Jem?' Jamie asked.

'Errrrr . . .' Jemma pretended to agonize. 'Eggs Benedict, I think. For a change.'

'You are so predictable.' He laughed.

'You?' she said.

'Four-egg omelette. I need some protein for my weight-training later.'

Jemma tried not to scowl. Why couldn't he do something with *her* for the day, like he used to on a Sunday, instead of going off to his fancy gym for hours? He was so self-obsessed these days.

'Why don't we go for a bike ride?' she said. 'That's exercise.'

Jamie looked appalled, and then tried to correct himself. 'Yeah, if you like,' he said.

'No, it's all right, don't bother.'

'Oh, come on, Jem, don't be like that.' He crinkled his nose, made his eyes pseudo-sad. It was hard to stay cross with him when he looked at her like that. He paused, took a casual tone. 'Anyway, I thought we could go to Amalfi.'

'What? When?'

'For your birthday.'

Jemma stared at Jamie, disbelieving. The Amalfi Coast was the most romantic place in the world. He knew she'd always wanted to go there. She struggled to suppress the thought, but it came anyway, and although at first the words were unformed in her head, the bridal shapes hollow and ghostly, they were there, and it seemed he'd caught her unawares with his gesture. Yet that was all it was, surely: a gesture. June was a great time to go, he was saying now, as he stirred sugar into his coffee, and besides, there was a La Liga match in Napoli that they could catch, so it would kill two birds with one stone. Yes, he really had just said that. And then he grinned, to show he was joking.

Jemma started to laugh. He took her hand. The sky was bleeding ice, and cold, sad, melting chips were sliding down the steamy windows. The world held its breath.

'I love you, Jemma Brady,' Jamie said. 'Really I do. You laugh at my terrible jokes, curtail my drinking, keep my flat at the leading edge of interior design, and pull me up when I act like a fool.' His eyes bored into hers. Jemma's heart had been filling up, like a lock – until he'd said 'my' flat. Now she wanted to punch him.

'What about your boss?' she said, extra moodily. 'She'll probably make you cancel it, like the last time we were meant to be going away.'

'That was a bone fide crisis, Jem. Honestly, Camille's not that bad.'

'Hmph,' said Jemma. She never knew what bothered her more: the unremitting nature of Jamie's job itself, or the fact that his boss was French and impeccably glamorous.

'Oh, come on, sweetheart. We'll have a fabulous time, I promise.'

Jemma said nothing more, and Jamie was uncharacteristically quiet too as they ate. Afterwards, Jamie paid the bill, and as they walked home the cannonball sky split apart to reveal jags of bright, bitter blue, and Jamie suggested that, as the weather had picked up, it might be good to go cycling after all. And so they did, and it was fun, and Jemma did her best to dispel any misgivings that she'd hitched her wagon to a work-obsessed eternal commitment-phobe whose family hated her. After all, she reminded herself later as they sat in front of *Final Score*, not only had Jamie come on a mud-spattered bike ride with her, he was taking her to Italy for her birthday, and he'd sworn he wouldn't let work ruin it. Of course he loved her.

29

Now

The ring on the doorbell is a harbinger. *She's here.* My feelings about my mother-in-law are tortured in their ambivalence – in some ways I dread answering the door, in others I yearn to see her, attempt to protest my innocence. She has never liked me, of course, which doesn't help anything. Yet she has lost her son, and this must be just as tormenting for her. She might even be nice for once.

As I slide back the lock, I find it ironic that I keep the place like a fortress, but then while away the hours on the terrace anyway, where anyone could leap out at me. I think about asking the resort for a bodyguard, as I'm so frightened now, nearly all the time, but I can't work out just what it is I'm so afraid of. The possibilities are limitless – but there again, I always have had a vivid imagination.

When I finally open the door to Veronica's bitter-twist face, I want to turn away, as if we're both magnetic Norths. We repel each other somehow. We always have done – how could I have imagined it might be different now?

'Hello, Veronica,' I say. I stand back to let her pass. She's pristine in white shorts and a navy silk T-shirt, brand-new silver flat sandals. Her smoothly bobbed hair surely should be curdling in the humidity, but the strong lacquer smell gives away her secret, and it makes me feel nauseous. I'm wearing the white beach cover-up again, and I know I look too innocent, too frivolous in her eyes, but I have nothing else better with me. I realized the error of even putting a clip in my hair the first time I was interviewed by the police. My floaty dress had been all wrong, too. Mine is an odd role to try to fulfil. Am I the bereaved bride, or the abandoned bride? Or even the murderous bride? *How do I look, Veronica? You tell me.* Of course, I wouldn't dare say it to her. I don't think anyone has ever petrified me quite as much as she does. I don't offer her a seat.

'I've just come from lunch,' she says now.

'Oh,' I say. I don't know what it is with her that leaves my mouth empty of words. Although she seems frailer somehow, she appears more menacing than bereft, and it is odd. It even makes me wonder whether she really does know where her darling Jamie is. *Surely not.* Maybe it's simply that it's so weird to see her here, in the Maldives. Never in my most imaginative of pre-wedding nightmares did my mother-in-law appear on my honeymoon.

'I just saw that Chrissy woman.'

I stay silent, waiting for her to continue.

'She had the most enormous plateful of food.' Ah, Veronica, a snob to the last. People aren't meant to fill up their plates in a place like this, no matter how bountifully varied or delicious the offerings. Being greedy because it is free is the ultimate sign of ill-breeding in Veronica's book, and is duly noted, even while her precious son is missing.

'She was probably getting food for her husband,' I say. 'He's hurt his leg.'

'Well, she seemed to be enjoying the attention,' Veronica continues, and I still don't know why she thinks I would care. A mini-video plays in my head, of Chrissy strutting her magnificent stuff as people swarm around the equally abundant culinary displays, the atmosphere super-charged, thick with mystery. The fact that I've gone to ground must be making Chrissy and Kenny even more of a talking point. I have no idea what rumours Veronica may have heard about that last evening the four of us spent together. I dread to think.

'Oh,' I say again. Where is this going? 'Look, Veronica, I'm so sorry about what's happened.'

'Hmm,' she replies, turning her merciless gaze on me, and I'm sure she knows something. *Did Jamie tell her?* Did he ring her from here, before he went missing? My eyebrow twitches, and I know it makes me look arch, sardonic. I press my back teeth together, to control it.

'Where is my son?' she says now, and although the question is soft and rhetorically posited, I feel a swift pulling in of my stomach, as if I am most definitely being accused of something.

'I don't know,' I say, and then I start to cry softly, but Veronica's not biting. She just continues to stare at me with that equivocal look on her face. But for God's sake, does she *really* think I would go to all the trouble of marrying Jamie and then dragging him halfway around the world just to kill him? I've had enough.

'I'm so sorry, I need a lie-down. My stomach's a bit delicate.' My voice sounds strong and steady, the opposite of how I feel. I wipe my eyes as I walk to the door and open it. 'Goodbye, Veronica,' I say, as she passes through. And then, in a last-ditch change of tack, I raise the cadence of my tone a notch and add, 'He may be your son but he's my *husband*.' I'm not at all sure of my delivery. Did it convey the despair of a brand-new bride – or not? She turns and gives me a look of such disgust it shrivels my heart, and all I can do is watch impotently as she walks away, her hair immobile, her legs taut and brittle, her silk shirt the only soft thing about her as it swishes gently through the poisoned paradisal air.

30

Eighteen months earlier

Jemma and Jamie were already airside, and miraculously still talking, airports being one of their many pressure points. She'd made sure she was ready to leave the flat bang on time for a change, and they'd got the cab to the airport at the hour of his choosing, rather than hers, and now that they were through security he seemed a bit less tense, although the real ordeal for him, of course, was still to come. But their new strategy was that they each took their own documents and then only met up for boarding, so she could wander around the shops looking at sunglasses and bikinis (even though Jamie said she had suitcases-full), while he could go straight to the gate and stew. Jamie would rather wait for an hour doing nothing than endure the stress of running for the flight, which he said Jemma did *every single time* – before proceeding to pick a fight with him in front of everyone. He'd made it plain he would just pretend he wasn't with her if she was late today, and sometimes Jemma was sure he wished that he wasn't. The thought made her anxious.

Jemma still didn't know what Jamie wanted from her

in the long term, and it bothered her a little more as each month passed. She even wondered now whether the idea of living together had just seemed a pragmatic next step for him, a convenient way of reducing their respective living costs, instead of an expression of his love. After all, Jemma had felt comfortable in Jamie's flat, and had been staying there so often it had seemed to make sense that she help him pay the mortgage, although neither of them had ever put it quite like that. Had she really been that gullible? But if not, why wouldn't he commit to her, after all they'd been through? Had she endured the embarrassment and shame of the long slow rehabilitation into the Armstrong family, as Jamie's girl-friend rather than Dan's, for nothing?

Jamie, of course, had a completely different point of view to Jemma, and that was part of the problem. Why couldn't they just enjoy being together, he used to say, when Jemma had still sometimes broached the subject. What was the rush? They'd been so happy, he'd claimed, before marriage had become an unwelcome agenda item, and then a fractious unspoken part of Any Other Business.

As Jemma tried on a pair of oversized, outrageously priced sunglasses, another thought struck her, and it was the worst one yet. *Maybe he was having an affair.* Perhaps *that's* why he went to the gym all the time, why he refused to get married.

Jemma yanked off the glasses, which looked silly anyway, and fled the shop. As she marched towards the gate, she told herself not to be daft, that Jamie might be many things, but he wasn't a cheat. The balls of her feet were aching in her high boots, so when she reached the never-ending travellator she stopped walking, regretting now that she hadn't worn her Converse. She was still feeling riled when the Tannoy blared at her: 'Ladies and gentlemen, flight BA 2612 to Naples is now ready for boarding through Gate 57.' *Shit. Not again.*

Jemma started to run. When she reached the gate her feet were killing her and Jamie was almost at the front of the queue. Through the window behind the desk the swollen belly of the plane was visible, as was the tunnel which led into it, disgorging the passengers like a birth in reverse.

'Hi, Jamie.' He turned around, and Jemma knew he was relieved to see her. His brow was sweating.

'Where have you been? You can't just push in.'

'I'm *with* you, Jamie. For God's sake.'

Jemma shuffled along with him, and she thought that he hated her now, wished she would just go away. The couple in front of them seemed so relaxed, and Jemma didn't know why she and Jamie couldn't be like that. What was wrong with them? Was it just his fear of flying that made everything else feel so fraught? Or was it because she always managed to make the situation worse? Jemma swallowed, and her throat was tight, as though she had toast stuck in it. He'd never propose to her if she kept on acting like a nutter. She tried to slip her hand into his, but he shook her off.

'What's the matter?' she said.

'Nothing.'

'Why are you being so moody? What have I done?'

Jemma knew she should be quiet, but she couldn't help herself. The woman in front had turned to look, casually, inconspicuously. Jemma felt years' worth of anguish welling up inside of her. She mustn't let it escalate.

'Nothing, Jem, you've done nothing.' He was trying to appease her, fortunately. She got a tiny glimpse into his world, and felt sorry for him suddenly. She tried to compose herself and the tension eased a fraction – until, at the very final check, Jemma found herself rummaging in her bag for her passport, when everyone else had theirs ready. Jamie seemed so embarrassed by her holding up the queue that he walked quickly ahead, almost running to the plane – and as Jemma felt the distance increase between her and her boyfriend, she was filled with a sick feeling of disquiet, mixed with a kind of relief.

31

Now

Oh God. What is happening to me? It feels as if my breath is about to stop, and it's an alarming development. There's a stillness in my head, as though the world is on pause – and then, just when I feel headily half-dead and vaguely glad of it, it jumpstarts again. It's harrowing.

I call Dad. It seems Veronica has freaked me out, and I don't know whether her hostility towards me was because she suspects me of being involved in her son's disappearance somehow, or because Jamie had told her something before he vanished. Either way, I can't cope any longer. I want my dad.

'Please come,' I beg him, and it reminds me of when I was a lost teenager, not knowing how to deal with my mother. I'm pretty sure it makes us both feel guilty.

'Of course I will, love,' he says. I can hear Kay in the background, whispering something, and I wonder if she's trying to stop him.

'Kay's got the flights right here,' he continues. 'I'll book them now and call you straight back. Hold tight, love.'

'Dad,' I say. 'I'm scared.'

'Of course you are, love. Poor Jamie. Poor you.'

'No,' I say. 'I really am scared. I don't feel safe.'

'What do you mean?' he says.

I hesitate, and then say it anyway. 'What if there's a murderer on the loose?'

'Jemma, love.' I can hear it in Dad's voice, that I always have been a drama queen. But I feel as if the island is closing in on me. The jungly branches are ready to tighten around my throat. When I shut my eyes images of gleaming dead flesh flit through my memory, like bats. Jamie seems so far away now, and yet still he's near. He's here. I can feel it. Solitary confinement is sending me mad. I need help.

'Dad, please hurry up,' I whisper, and it seems I can't talk any more. My eyes are flooding. I just about manage to say 'Goodbye', and then I put down the phone.

32

Eighteen months earlier

Amalfi was busier than Jemma had imagined. The hotel overlooked the square, where tourists mingled with locals who zipped about on mopeds, or gathered on the steps of the duomo, to chat, or drink coffee, or just generally hang out, looking marvellously Italian. Jemma was still buzzing, and not just because of the view from the balcony. On the trip from Napoli their cab driver had driven like his life depended on it, butting up to the car in front of them at eighty miles an hour on the motorway, winging his way around sunny blind corners where the sea was too blue to crash into, or the houses on the nearside were too ancient to bull-doze. Jemma had enjoyed it, had never even flinched, as if she couldn't care less if they died, although Jamie had gone quite green – and she knew that this was another thing about her that bemused him. In any given situation she could be calm or hysterical, and he never quite knew which he was going to get – and nei-ther did she. Mostly she tried to be fun and expansive, and her mood would match the light in her eyes and the sunshine in her hair. Yet at other times she behaved like a wild cat, and it appalled him, but once she got going, the more tightly coiled and out of control she became, despite knowing she should stop. And then, at still other times, albeit infrequently, she would become shut down, robotic, scary – and that appalled them both. Maybe *that's* why he didn't want to marry her.

Jamie's phone pinged. 'Who's that?' Jemma said. Jamie frowned as he accessed his messages. 'Oh, just work,' he said.

'What, on a Saturday? When you're on holiday?'

Jamie sighed. 'It's my boss,' he said. 'I need to sort this out. It's about a deal that was meant to be tied up last week. I won't be long.' He disappeared back through the French doors into the hotel room, pulling them shut behind him, and soon Jemma could hear him talking quietly on the phone. Couldn't Camille ever give Jamie a break? Didn't she know they were away? Jemma took a deep breath, leaned her arms on the balcony railing, rested her cheek on top of them, and waited, willing herself not to get annoyed.

When Jamie came back he seemed subdued somehow.

'Everything OK?' she said.

'Hmm,' he said, noncommittally. He stood next to her at the railing as they both looked down onto the throng.

'Wow, I love this place,' she said, as she gently swayed her body behind her, like a boat on its anchor. 'Thank you for bringing me.'

Jamie turned to look at her, and when their eyes met his were loving, a dulcet dove grey. She could feel the atmosphere soften.

'That's OK,' he said. 'It's cool here, isn't it?'

'I love it.' She grinned, determined to make an effort. 'Got over your various travel sicknesses yet? Ready for some lunch?'

'Yeah, well, you know I hate flying, and then that driver was a fucking maniac. I don't know how I didn't throw up.'

'Jamie, I'm taking the mickey. There's no need to be so defensive.'

'Well, I never know with you.'

Jemma's eyes narrowed, and she gave him an evil look, and even she wasn't sure whether she was joking or not.

'Come on, let's go,' he said. He gave her a quick peck on the cheek. 'Before you throw me off the balcony.'

As they got off the bus and walked up the hill towards the villa, the heat was searing. They reached the peak and saw the bluest of skies melding into the sea, and it was her birthday and Jamie had brought her here, and maybe *this* was the place. It was so perfect. A single tree presided over the church and the flower boxes and the fat, low palms, and she didn't know what type the tree was, but its branches were spindly and bare apart from right at the top, where they formed a lush green canopy over the vista of the sea and the cliffs beyond.

Jemma paused to take in the beauty of nature, note how humankind occasionally succeeded in enhancing it. But, as Sasha would have said, that was Italy for you.

Jamie took Jemma's hand and they meandered through the villa's gardens like new lovers. She really didn't know what had got into him, but she wasn't complaining. Finally, they came to the place that she'd read about, where statues were lined up on plinths like soldiers, guarding the view, and the sea and the sky went all the way to heaven. Jemma held her breath. It was her birthday. He loved her. He took her hand, and then he pulled her close and kissed her . . . and surely this was it; it was happening at last. Jemma concentrated hard, to remember the moment, to tell their grandchildren.

'Shall we get going?' he murmured. 'If we hurry we'll get back in time for the Chelsea Liverpool game.'

Jemma stared at Jamie, her mouth opening like an imbecile's, and then she realized he was joking. She faked a swat at him, and he ducked, but the moment had passed, and perhaps that had been his intention. They ended up having lunch in the restaurant, and her hopes were raised briefly again, by the exorbitant cost, the superlative view, the aptness of the setting. But once Jamie had polished off his main course, and she realized that he really wasn't going to propose after all, in fact seemed oblivious to the fact that she'd expected him to, the anger inside her started burning again, fierce and intense, and her thirst for it grew: to become Mrs Armstrong, which even then she knew was a pointless ambition, and one that was unlikely to end well.

33

Now

The doorbell rings again, and I assume it's the British police here to see me at last, but it's Chrissy. Her mood has changed. She's no longer the fun Chrissy, sexy Chrissy, roll-her-eyes-at-Kenny Chrissy that I'd got to know with my husband. She's not even the concerned, salt-of-the-earth Chrissy she'd been when he first disappeared. Now she's super-anxious, although she tries to hide it, and perhaps she really does think this is all my fault after all. It's a bit much so soon after Veronica's visit, and I almost ask her to leave. But I don't. I need her on my side. Instead, I invite her in and fetch her a beer from my minibar, and a Coke for me – just in case – and we sit down on the wooden terrace.

Chrissy's wearing a tight hot-pink halter dress, and her hair is lustrously blow-dried, but her face is blotchy, as if she's been crying. Normally she's chatty, but today she is not. It's hard to find small-talk – too many conversational roads lead to the apocalypse. She tries to ask me some things about Jamie's job, which bank he worked for (and yes, I do notice the past tense), things like that, but it seems odd, and she's making me feel uneasy. I don't know what she's trying to get at. I ask her if the British police have spoken to her, and she says that they have, although she doesn't elaborate on what was said. I wonder again why they haven't even come near me yet – I've still only ever been interviewed by the pin-smart Maldivian officers – and my stress levels rise a notch higher.

Words taper away and disappear over the horizon, as we sit and look silently out across the smooth sheen sea. The perfect shape of the thatched parasol positioned between Jamie's and my empty beach loungers is a cruel, poignant contrast against the afternoon sky. The sand looks whiter than ever. There are too many greens interwoven into the trees and the sea to decide which shade works best against the deep blue air. Still-unknown birds and animals click and rustle in the undergrowth. The island feels so alive, and it mocks the possible death scene we are presiding over. It is a perfect postcard view, and I imagine scrawling on the back of it, *Hi Jamie, Wish You Were Here*, and it makes me almost giggle. The horror has become quasi-comical. Chrissy glances at me, and there is an air about her now, and I don't know if it's that I can't trust her, or that she can't trust me. I wish she would leave.

'I'm worried,' Chrissy says, at last.

'Oh,' I reply. What does she want me to say?

'I dunno if the Old Bill are even going to let me and Kenny go home.'

'Oh,' I say again. I didn't even know people really

said *Old Bill*. I find that the most surprising part of her statement. My reaction is therefore almost indifference, as if it's nothing to do with me, as if she's talking about another story, one in which I play no part. What am *I* meant to do about what the police say to her and Kenny? The way she's acting makes me think she's convinced I'm to blame, or else she has something to hide herself, but I can't work out which it is. It occurs to me that Kenny might have sent her.

'Why d'you think they might not let you leave?' I say, in the end.

'Well, we were the last people to see Jamie alive.' Her tone is odd, not quite threatening. The vowels are whiny and paranoid. 'And anyway, why would they be sending police out from England now, if they didn't think it was suspicious?'

I feel a fear surface, one that has been trapped somewhere inside me for as long as I can remember, when I see Chrissy's expression. Her eyes are colder than I recall. Hers is the face of a stranger. Yet of course it is. I barely know her, not really. We'd become familiar so quickly, but that's what happens when you're on honeymoon, thousands of miles from home, with a husband who is driving you insane. What were her and Kenny's motivations? I'd thought they were just being friendly, but now I'm not so sure. Kenny especially bothers me. On the few occasions that I've seen him since Jamie vanished, he's seemed almost thuggish to me somehow, although he'd been so genial before – with his sunburn, his Sudoku, his endless good humour. Yet now he scares me. Chrissy told me when we first got chatting that she'd met him in a bar, on a Friday night in West India Quay. Apparently they'd been engaged within a month, married in six, in a registry office, with just two witnesses. She's never even met his parents, she'd proudly squawked, because they live in Spain. I think, not for the first time, how Kenny had been alone, back at their bungalow next door, at the time Jamie disappeared.

Don't be ridiculous, I tell myself. Why would Kenny want to hurt Jamie? And besides, he couldn't have done anything anyway – he'd hardly been able to walk that night. He had no motive.

Or did he? Did Kenny and Jamie know each other somehow, from the City perhaps? Is that why Chrissy was asking? It's a very small world, after all. And if so, Kenny was so strong – compared to Jamie, anyway – it might have been quite easy for Kenny to have drowned him.

I feel my head reeling, and I need a drink but I mustn't have one, and when I open my eyes Chrissy is staring at me, and it's hard to tell what she's thinking. There's something not right in all this, but maybe it's nothing more than the mysterious issue of there being a huge husband-sized hole in this diabolical island. It's just adding to my feelings of dissociation, of the world having stopped. It's an abrupt and total mind-fuck.

'Well, anyway, I'm sorry to spoil your honeymoon,'

I say, and it comes out huffy. But I'd hoped Chrissy at least was on my side. She stands up and fluffs up her hair, adjusts her halter top for full knockout effect, sucks in her stomach. Her mask is back on.

'I'm sorry, Jemma, love,' she says. 'I didn't mean to upset you. Are you hungry? Shall I get you some lunch?'

'No, thanks, I'm fine,' I say, and I am. Chati will be sure to come by soon. It has become a routine, and although I still feel a little awkward about it, I find myself almost looking forward to his twice-daily visits. I don't know whether it's the food, or the breaking up of the monotony. Or perhaps it's simply that he's the only person around here who doesn't seem to be judging me.

'I just can't resist the food here,' Chrissy says now. She's trying hard to be normal. She pats her concaved stomach. 'And so what if I put on a bit of weight?'

I stare at Chrissy's perfect figure and want to hate her, for being so shallow when my husband is missing, quite possibly dead. But then she claps her hand over her mouth, and goes, 'Oh, sorry, love!' We stare at each other. I wonder whether I should smile, even make a quip. Instead I look down at my own stomach, which is softly rounded now, and the thought that there might be a baby in there makes me so sad. This was not how it was meant to be.

'It'll be all right, Jemma,' Chrissy says, after a pause that is so long it appears to eat itself.

'No, it won't!' The desperation in my tone shocks

me. I'm almost crying now. 'You don't know what it's like. I've lost the love of my life!' Even I don't know if I'm acting any more.

Chrissy looks at me, and she doesn't need to say anything. It's there in her eyes at last – that she thinks this could all be quite convenient for me.

My heart pumps, then stops, then pumps again. The blood seems too thick to work itself around my veins. I wonder whether Chrissy has told the police what I told her. She will, eventually, if it saves her own skin. But hopefully she won't, unless she absolutely has to. I try to hold onto the belief that Chrissy and I shared something that made us want to look out for each other, perhaps makes her trust in my innocence. She's a nice girl, and we're friends still; I'm sure we are.

My food delivery rescues the situation, rendering more potentially incriminating words unnecessary. Just as Chrissy is about to leave, Chati appears around the side of the bungalow, and I'm even more relieved to see him than usual. He removes his sandals as he steps onto the terrace. His feet are wide and spread out, as though he has barely ever worn shoes. When he puts down the tray, the curry is rich and enticing, the meat cut into perfect-sized glossy chunks, its aroma dizzyingly spicy. There is a tomato carved into the shape of a flower, and I want to put it in my hair. I want to scatter the pure white rice like confetti. I want to drink the coconut water as if it were champagne. I want to rewind time, spool it back just a week or so, to my wedding day, so I can work out what on earth is going on. My head is spinning with utter confusion as Chati places his palms together and bows, and then quietly takes his leave.

34

Eighteen months earlier

Jemma had known what was coming as soon as Greg and Donna invited them to dinner. Greg and Donna never invited anyone for dinner. Donna was a terrible cook for a start, and their flat was always a mess, and not at all suitable for entertaining. Donna normally suggested a night out at a comedy club somewhere, followed by a curry, and would take great pride in matching the guys pint for pint. She and Greg hosting a dinner party was completely out of character.

Although Jemma was delighted for her friends, convinced they were the best match ever, she didn't dare tell Jamie what she suspected. It would only have caused a fight, especially so soon after their trip to Amalfi. And anyway, maybe she was wrong. Jamie had grumbled regardless, of course, saying that dinner parties were for old people, and that her friends were all so pretentious it would be another night of one-upmanship over who had seen the most obscure show, or read the most impenetrable book. It made Jemma insecure. Why didn't Jamie want to do things with her any more? She just wished he'd be a bit more committed. Yet that was the way things seemed to work these days. People lived together, and then, only once they knew they were compatible, did they decide to get married. There was no need to take the plunge too soon, Jamie had always said. But *four years* was hardly the plunge, was it?

Jemma tried to empty her mind of these thoughts. They weren't appropriate here, and certainly weren't helping her yogic breathing. She stared straight ahead at herself in the studio's floor-to-ceiling mirror, trying to follow the directions of the calm-voiced instructor, who was dreadlocked, pale, bare-chested, oddly sexy. Beads of sweat oozed menacingly towards her eyes, but she managed to ignore them as she kept her left foot pressed into the top of her right thigh, her back straight, her hands in prayer position. She breathed. *Jaya ganesha jaya ganesha jaya ganesha*, she said, over and over, in her head. She tried to bully out unwanted thoughts, stop them entering her mind, but despite her private mantra, they refused to go away – it was as if her brain were in stereo, with two channels going on at once, and she couldn't turn off the negative one. It was doing her head in.

Jemma was fully aware that she was becoming fixated. Why was she letting an unhealthy obsession with an outdated institution ruin her life? And Jamie's too, come to think of it. After all, her own parents had more than proved the fallibilities of marriage – and as she remembered the screaming tantrums, the thudding flung shoes, the smash of crockery, she wondered if she would ever move on from growing up in such an atmosphere. No wonder her father had left her mother. No wonder Jamie didn't want to marry her, the way she'd been behaving lately. Perhaps she, Jemma, was just like her mother, after all. Maybe it was simply in her genes, and nothing, least of all yoga, could fix it.

The room was sluiced in heat. The man to the left of Jemma was wearing nothing except a pair of tiny, close-to-obscene shorts, and he was working himself too hard, failing to listen to his body. He was hairy, and drenched in sweat, and far too near to her – but she had got used to it, this communing with strangers, as they each pulled themselves into shapes and curves that were meant to help their minds as well as their bodies. Jemma had tried to get Jamie to come once but he'd just laughed at her and said it was a freak show, so now it was something she did separately from him, at least three times a week. She and Jamie consumed so much time separately these days, what with their jobs and their hobbies and their separate friends, that the least he could sodding well do was come for dinner at Donna's.

Jemma came out of Rabbit Pose and lay face down on the floor. She breathed. As she folded into one of the final postures, she felt her throat constricting and blood rushing to her head, and the overall sensation left her mind light and floaty and free . . . and at last futile deliberations about boyfriends and marriage and babies started to melt away, like the last of the snow, as

Jemma settled into a rhythm of unfailing trust, and optimism, and eternal harmony with the universe.

'Yay,' shrieked Sasha, a few hours later. 'I *knew* it!' She jumped up from the makeshift table and rushed around to Donna and consumed her in a congratulatory hug.

Greg seemed faintly embarrassed, and Jemma wanted to do something to acknowledge his happiness, so she leaned over and kissed him lightly on the cheek. Jamie sat still, looking like thunder, and the aura he gave off was noticeable.

'Another one bites the dust, eh, Jamie?' said Martin, Sasha's boyfriend. He shovelled a lump of dried-out chicken into his mouth and ruminated amiably, like a cow.

'Ha,' said Jamie, mirthlessly. He picked up a bottle of red wine from the centre of the table and filled his glass to the brim. 'Congratulations,' he said, in a way that made it clear he didn't mean it. There was an awkward pause.

'Thanks,' said Greg, at last, wiping his cheek where Jemma had kissed him. Donna was smiling so hard that Jemma swore her face would split, and it was lovely to see – Donna was normally far too cool for such shows of emotion.

'D'you know where or when yet?' Sasha asked.

Jemma didn't dare say anything after Jamie's reaction, so she just did her best to look neutral as she waited for Donna to answer.

'Hmm, we're thinking of running away and doing it on a beach somewhere, aren't we, Greg? Saves all the family arguments.'

'Oooh, how lovely,' said Sasha. 'I'd love to do that.' It was Martin's turn to look alarmed now, and it made Jemma cross that they all had to pussyfoot around their boyfriends like this, as though the men thought they were trophies to win, and the women mere desperate harpies who were obsessed with the contest.

'Not with you, Martin,' said Sasha, not missing a beat. 'When I find someone I love enough.' Everyone laughed, and the pressure lifted, just a little.

Jamie got up and went to the bathroom, and while he was gone Sasha asked Jemma in a low voice whether everything was all right. Greg was struggling with the cork on the champagne he'd had ready in the fridge, and Donna was collecting up an assortment of glasses to serve it in. One of them was cloudy from the dishwasher and another looked like an ice cream sundae dish, or a vase, but as it was Donna and Greg, no-one minded.

'Of course, why?'

'Just you and Jamie don't seem . . .'

'Don't seem what?'

'Oh, nothing. Sorry, we'll talk about it another time.'

'OK.'

Jemma knew what Sasha was going to say, and she also knew Sasha only had her best interests at heart, but frankly, her best friend hadn't a clue how her and Jamie's relationship was. Sasha didn't see their private moments, when they did the crossword in bed, or when they went out for breakfast, or belly-laughed at *Peep Show* together. She didn't see Jamie sorting out her washing for her, tidying away her knickers, folding up her socks, so she'd always find what she needed when she was in a panic in the mornings. She didn't see him planning her route when she had to drive somewhere unfamiliar, as he knew she got so stressed by her inability to map-read. Neither did Sasha realize quite how into football Jemma was now, nor how exciting the end of the season could get. Sasha had never trusted Jamie, but Sasha was wrong – and anyway, Jemma thought, people couldn't help who they fell for. So as she sat there drinking champagne with Greg-and-Donna and Sasha-and-Martin and Kate-and-Angus, her brain became alcohol-softened, and she grew certain that her time would come, as it would for everybody. She and Jamie had been through so much already, and they loved each other. Everything would work out; she was sure of it.

When Jamie came back to the table, he still seemed angry. His face said it all, as if he thought the whole thing was a conspiracy, and once they got home he would surely tell Jemma that her friends were all so competitive that they wouldn't be content with trying to prove how highbrow they were any more. Now the contest, according to Jamie, would be wedding venues and baby names. Jemma had heard it all before.

'More chicken, Jamie?' said Donna.

'Oh. No, thanks.' Jamie upturned the bottle in front of him, but just a dribble of red slid out of it. 'Have you got any more wine?'

Jemma gave him a look, but he ignored her. The evening was already in danger of disintegrating into tearful drama when they got home as it was, although hopefully they'd be drunk enough to simply pass out and avoid any unpleasantness – or would she try to pick a fight, even if he was unconscious? Nothing would surprise her, and if Jemma were honest, that was part of the problem. Why *would* he want to marry someone like her? She might have her good qualities, and the guilt-laden soap-operatic nature of their getting together had definitely heightened the romance, but perhaps he thought she was just too neurotic to be a keeper. Maybe he needed someone more stable as a wife, someone his mother didn't hate. *Jemma and Jamie. Jamie and Jemma.* Did it sound right, or not? Jemma put down her knife and fork and picked at a patch of dry skin behind her ear.

Sasha was staring at Jamie, who was still acting like a dick, and Jemma saw him blanch. Sasha took no prisoners, and it was good for him to know that her friends were looking out for her. But what could Sasha do? What could she, Jemma, do? She couldn't *make* him want to marry her.

'Jamie, should we get going soon?' she stage-whispered after the dessert had been served and the

163

conversation had turned to engagement party venues. 'We've got an early start tomorrow.'

Jamie looked startled, as though he'd been let out of jail, just when he'd been least expecting it.

'Uh, OK,' he said.

'Sorry everyone,' Jemma announced, as she stood up and her chair toppled over behind her. 'We've got to go home.' Jemma was aware her words and her mouth were very slightly out of synch.

'Oh, OK, Jem. Lovely to see you.'

Jemma's eyes danced around the room, taking in the saggy sofa and the art house movie poster prints, and the 'Congratulations' cards already propped up on the over-filled mantelpiece amongst the candles and the photos, the happy homely chaos. It all felt out of reach to her suddenly.

'Thanks for having us,' Jamie said, as he took hold of Jemma's elbow, a little too firmly in Jemma's opinion. She teetered next to him, her heels unmanageable. He smiled apologetically. 'I think I need to get her home.'

'Yessh, I'm very, very tired,' Jemma said. She beamed at her friends. 'Shee you all shoon.'

Everyone was laughing at her, in that affectionate way old friends do, and Jamie went along with it. But once they were in the cab, Jamie wasn't laughing at her any more; he was telling her she was a bloody disgrace. And when they got home Jemma didn't remember much, or at least not until the next morning, when

Jamie came into their room to get his work clothes and he was obviously not talking to her – and he had a deep red scratch beneath his eye, like you might get from a cat, if they'd had one.

35

Now

The spectre of Jamie swims about in my head, gurgles through my internal network. The more time that passes, the more the fear grows, like hunger. In desperation I turn to yoga, to see if that will help. I daren't do it on the terrace, in case someone spots me, so instead I retreat into the confines of the bungalow. I start to download a yoga app, but then think better of it, in case the police go through my phone. It might look frivolous. I don't have my yoga gear, so I put on a fuchsia-pink swimming costume, the only one-piece I brought with me. I keep the doors open, turn off the air conditioning, let in the hot jungle air to help make me bendy.

I find it hard to concentrate at first, but I burrow my thoughts into my stomach cavity and focus on my breathing. *In out in out jaya ganesha jaya ganesha jaya ganesha.* I start with side bends, back bends, forward bends. I move into Downward Dog. I do the Cat. I instantly fall over when I attempt the Tree. I'm not sure what I'm meant to be doing, can't remember the sequence, but it doesn't matter. I feel a release I haven't felt before now. My mind is planing over the surf of the anguish, instead of being mired in its swirling waters. I lie on the floor, put my fists under my thighs and arch my back. I breathe. I lift one leg high in the air. I shut my eyes, and breathe. I lift the other leg. I use my arms and my elbows to arch my back and prop up my pelvis. I breathe. When I open my eyes again I am looking up past my body at two people standing in the doorway, and the sun is behind them, and at first I think it's Jamie and Dan, and I just can't believe it.

'Mrs Armstrong?' says the taller of the men. 'I'm Detective Constable Neil Simpson of the Metropolitan Police. I'd like to talk to you about your husband's disappearance.'

I stare up into the policemen's faces and never have I felt so naked. I move my elbows, drop my bottom to the floor, clumsily sit up, hunch my shoulders. I virtually curl up into a little ball, hiding the bold pink-covered pubis which a minute ago I'd been thrusting at them. For a second I wish I could just vanish too, like Jamie.

'Of course,' I say.

'You might want to get dressed,' Detective Constable Simpson says. I'm not sure of his tone. Is it disapproval, or is he mocking me? 'We'll be waiting out the front.' The two men turn on their heel and leave the terrace. I stare at the space where they were, as if transfixed by their absence . . . and then I remember myself. I spring to my feet, run in to the bedroom, yank open the wardrobe, and proceed to put on as many clothes as I think I can get away with, layer upon layer, without looking mad. I lick my palms and smooth down my hair. And with that, I leave the relative safety of my bungalow and head out to where the policemen are waiting for me, to face the metaphorical music at last.

36

A year or so earlier

'Jamie, I've got something to say,' Jemma began. It was a few weeks after the dinner at Donna and Greg's, and things were a little better again, and perhaps the hot yoga was finally starting to work, as she hadn't lost her temper once since that diabolical night. She and Jamie had been getting on well, he'd uncomplainingly missed a key Chelsea game and a night at the pub to come to a work event with her, and she'd been gracious in the extreme regarding his weekend gym visits. Everything was fine-ish. But Jemma had made up her mind. 'Ish' just wasn't enough.

'*Jamie.* It's important.'

Her boyfriend looked up at her at last. The note in her voice cut through his concentration on the football, which Chelsea were cruising anyway. The blinds were closed. The side lamps were lit. They each had a glass of red wine, viscous and blood-temperature. The room exuded a warm familial glow, although it was just the two of them. She could tell he was irritated at the interruption.

'Yes?' he said.

'I can't do this any more.'

'What do you mean?'

Jemma picked up her wine glass and took a sip. 'I can't carry on, not knowing where it's going.'

There. She'd said it. It felt like playing Russian Roulette, with just two chambers.

'Jemma, sweetheart,' Jamie said. 'What on earth are you going on about now?'

Jemma spoke calmly, and she was glad that Sasha had made her rehearse it so many times. She refused to let him make her feel that she was the one with the problem. She stood up, and positioned herself between him and the TV.

'Jamie, we live together. We have been together for four-and-a-half years. I love you. And if you don't want to marry me that's fine, but I can't wait around any longer for you to make up your mind.'

Jamie said nothing, just stared at the floor. All his bravado was gone, and she'd never seen him like this. Maybe he wasn't used to her being so controlled.

At last he spoke. 'Jemma, I'm just . . . I'm just not ready.'

Jemma put down her wine glass very, very carefully. She thought of the hours he spent at the gym, the hours he spent at work. 'Is there someone else?' she said.

Did he look away for a fraction too long? She wasn't sure.

'No,' he said. He didn't seem indignant to be asked, though, and weren't people usually ultra-defensive when they were guilty? Her dad certainly had been. 'Jemma, it's not that, I promise,' he continued. 'It's just that you're too . . .'

'I'm too what?' She tried to keep the menace out of her voice.

Jamie changed tack. 'Look, Jem, I . . . I just need to think about things. Will you give me some time?'

'How long?' she said.

'I don't know. A couple of days?'

'OK.'

'Jemma?'

'Yes?'

He stood up, moved towards her. She took a step back. 'I'm so sorry.'

'About what?'

He shrugged his shoulders helplessly. 'That it's come to this.'

'Jamie, I don't care. I don't need to hear it. I just need to know what you want.' Jemma didn't know where she'd got this strength of purpose from, but she was determined not to buckle now.

Jamie looked a little bewildered, as though he was expecting more drama. Maybe he'd have preferred her to have just stormed out, rather than leaving the ball in his court.

'I, er, I'll sleep in the spare room if you like,' he said. 'For the time being.'

'Yes, that would be good. Thanks.'

Jemma went and sat back down on the low leather

sofa, which had never been comfortable anyway, and thought how, if they did split up, she wouldn't miss it. She even considered taking a carving knife to it, as if it were skin, to let out the tension, but she wouldn't, of course. She wondered where she would live if her gamble failed to pay off. She couldn't go to her dad's as he and Kay wouldn't want her, although they'd never put it as starkly as that. It would all be about there not being room, and how Totteridge was too far from her job, and that it would be a terrible commute for her. There was always Sasha, who had a spare room and a whole heap of empathy, as ever, but Jemma didn't want to burden her friend, or risk unbalancing Sasha's relationship with Martin. So, 'Spare Room' it would be, then.

Jemma's mind was so vacant now it was as if it had been flushed of feelings. She had taken back control at last. Ironically, her destiny was finally in her own hands, one way or the other, and she was glad. It felt good in a way. She went to the bathroom, took off her make-up, brushed her teeth until the spittle ran red, removed the delicate necklace he'd bought her last Christmas (and as she'd opened its box, had been convinced was a ring) and put it carefully, wordlessly, next to the tap. Jamie was obviously agitated by her actions, and he didn't know what to say, what to do. Neither of them knew how to handle it, but when Jemma crept from their bedroom in the early hours, ostensibly to get a glass of water, or perhaps to launch herself at him, she found that he had gone. He was not in the spare room after all, nor watching TV on the leather couch. He'd just left a note saying he was sorry, and that he'd be in touch soon.

37

Now

The British police have taken over the sanatorium, and at last they're about to officially interview me. In the buggy on the way over we chat as politely as if we were on the way to Manager's Cocktails. None of us refers to my recent yoga practice. I still wonder why it's taken them so long to speak to me, but I try not to over-analyze it. Trepidation laps at me like the ever-advancing waves of an incoming tide.

Detective Constable Simpson and his colleague are youngish, and excited, although they try to hide it. Once we are all seated and they have gone through the formal stuff, they announce that they have some news. I stare mutely at them, terrified at what they're about to tell me. I feel so alone suddenly, and someone might as well have garrotted me, chopped me up, the ache in my gut is so intense, and I long to know what's causing it. I sit on my hands, to be sure they don't betray me.

'Do you know Pascal Anais, the marine biologist here?'

'Oh, yes, of course. Jamie and I went on a snorkelling trip with him.'

'Do you know his sister, Camille Anais?'

The name is familiar, but my mind is fuddled. 'No.'

'Are you sure? She worked with your husband in Deutsche Bank.'

Of course! Camille, Jamie's boss, until just a few months ago. The one who used to be a slavedriver, emailing him day and night, even that time we went to Amalfi. The one who went to the same gym as him, even though Jamie had insisted that loads of people from work went there. The one I became so jealous of. I picture her now. Slim. Groomed. Gorgeous. What did Camille have to do with all this? Pascal, sexy louche Pascal, is her *brother*?

'It seems Camille was the last person Jamie tried to contact before his disappearance. We have traced the calls made from the phone in your bungalow.'

'Oh.' I don't know what to say, or what to think.

'We have interviewed Mr Anais, and he claims not to have seen Jamie since the afternoon of the day he disappeared.' They pause, as though I'm meant to interject here, say something helpful.

'Uh-huh,' I manage. The silence goes on and on. There's just the gentle rustle of the palms, reminding us of the discordance of the conversation, here on my honeymoon. 'What a coincidence.'

'Now, that's just it, Mrs Armstrong.' I grimace at the name, and it makes me think of Veronica. 'It seems that it isn't a coincidence.' They pause again. Detective Constable Simpson has a wide, round face, and he looks so baby-innocent, it belies what he's saying, the accusations he appears to be making. It doesn't help that he's wearing shorts.

'I, I don't understand,' I say. I'm struggling to keep up, but the fact is I don't much care what they're trying to imply. I just care about what they think has happened to my husband.

'Mrs Armstrong, I'm sorry to have to ask you this, but do you know why your husband would be contacting Ms Anais on his honeymoon?' I can feel them watching me closely, forensically, for my reaction.

'No,' I say, at last. The word feels very small, as if it has been dropped out of a plane, into the ocean. I want to tell them that it's OK, that that's the least of my worries, but a survival instinct kicks in from somewhere, and I force myself to be quiet.

'We think there may be a link to your husband's disappearance,' says DC Simpson now.

'What do you mean?'

'Well, Mr Anais has access to the resort's boats. It is possible that he helped Jamie get off the island.'

I am so astonished I just gape at them, my mouth a round hole that the words have fallen into. Is he suggesting that Jamie really has disappeared *on purpose*? That Pascal helped him? I start to cry, with relief that maybe they think he isn't dead after all, and they take it to mean I'm distraught about what he may or may not have been doing with Camille, which I suppose is no bad thing.

'That's ludicrous,' I say at last. 'Why would my

husband want to do that? It's just so far-fetched.' I cough, and the bile I drag up is bitter and stringy, like seaweed. 'Surely it's more likely that he's . . .' I struggle to even say it. '. . . That he's drowned?' No-one says anything, so I plough on. 'When would you expect him to be found?' They just stare at me, and it's clear I've made an error. 'Er, if that *is* what has happened, of course?'

'Well, that's just it, Mrs Armstrong,' says DC Simpson. 'We've been talking to the Maldivian police about this. If your husband has drowned, the body could wash up on any one of the hundreds of islands here. It could be years, if ever, before anyone finds it.'

It seems DC Simpson doesn't have the same sensibilities as me, and I wince at the word *body*, at the thought of my husband, so full of life, devoid of it, lying abandoned somewhere with only the sun to cook him, the maggots to eat him. How will we ever know? *Will* we ever know? It seems that drowned people are hard to find in this most dispersed and sparsely populated of countries.

I have managed to just about compose my thoughts now, and I have to know. 'Are you honestly saying that you think Jamie might still be alive?' I say. 'That he might have absconded? *On purpose?*'

'Yes, it does sound rather unlikely, I must admit, but we are looking into it as one possibility.' DC Simpson pauses again. It seems the other one doesn't speak, and I wonder why they needed to send two of them.

'Mrs Armstrong, at the risk of sounding intrusive, how was your honeymoon?'

'What do you mean?'

'Well, were you enjoying it?'

They know. I struggle to compose myself. The silent one looks alert suddenly, and I can sense the shift in him. Of course it has occurred to them. I could have done it. If only I could recall what I'd blurted out to Chrissy during our drunken, rampageous evening, on the very same night that my husband vanished. I still can't remember exactly. I still can't work out what Chrissy's capable of.

'Mrs Armstrong? I *said*, how was your honeymoon?'

'Um, well, it was fine.'

'Fine. That's a very strange word to use.' The other one has spoken at last, and I am reminded of a fisherman with a spear. The baby-faced one casts the bait, and the silent one stays still, his weapon primed. And then he pounces.

I'm not sure what to say. I say nothing. I begin thinking whether I should be asking for a solicitor. The world has gone mad, taking my sanity with it.

'Mrs Armstrong? I was asking about your honeymoon?'

'It . . . it was good. I mean, it's so beautiful here. How could it not be?'

'We have reports from some of the other guests that you and Mr Armstrong didn't seem very happy together. That's rather strange, on a honeymoon, don't you think?' There he goes again, the thin, quiet one, in the loud floral shirt.

178

I need to think fast.

'Well, it's true that I've been feeling a bit unwell. Apart from that it was fine.'

'Apparently you had an argument on the night your husband vanished. Is that right?'

Shit. Yet how could I have hoped to get away with it? I wonder who told them. I try to keep my tone neutral. 'Well, we did have a bit of a row, it's true, but what couple doesn't?'

They don't bother answering that. Instead they just stare at me, unblinking. I'm floundering. I decide to plunge onwards, in the absence of any other choice. And anyway, no-one knows what was really going on in our relationship. (Except Chrissy, who I'm ninety-nine per cent sure I told. Except Dad, who guessed, I think. Except Dan, who has now arrived on the island. This is a mess.)

'It's just that I've been feeling very odd, and sick, and —' I stop. I can't face voicing my suspicion after all, under these most dreadful of circumstances. I might not be pregnant anyway, and besides, it's none of their business. ' . . . And I, I've had rather an upset stomach . . . I think it might be something I've eaten.'

I look down at my knees, push them together. The two policemen look impassive, and I wish I could remember the thin one's name. Still I wonder whether I'll get away with this. What has Chrissy said to them? Has she kept quiet, or not?

'I see,' says DC Simpson.

'And so *of course* I'm upset if he's deliberately done this, if he's disappeared on purpose. We've just got *married*. It seems too improbable, too unbelievable – too much to take in.' I raise my voice a couple of decibels, and I am not putting it on. 'And at the end of the day, my husband is *missing!*'

'It's all right, Mrs Armstrong,' says DC Simpson. Have I done and said enough?

'Can I go now?' I say, as I wipe my nose with the back of my hand.

DC Simpson seems unsure whether to let me. There's another awkward pause, but then I start to stand up anyway.

'There's one more thing,' cuts in the thin one. 'You're aware, of course, that we found his mask and snorkel?'

'Yes.'

'Well, we've also found his dive torch.'

'Oh?'

'In a drawer in your bungalow.'

I say nothing.

'How many dive torches did you have, Mrs Armstrong?'

'Two.'

'Yes, that's what we found. Now, why would your husband go night-snorkelling without a torch?'

I'm quiet for a trifle too long. 'I don't know.'

'Unless someone meant us to find the mask,' he says. He looks pleased with himself, as if this is a game and he's just put me into check, with checkmate imminent.

Again, I have no idea how to respond. I choose to say nothing, and my eyes grow wider as the silence expands, letting in the dulcet jungle noises through the open window. Everything feels light and bright, bleaching out to blankness.

'Is that it for now?' I say at last. 'Can I go?'

'Yes,' says the quiet one. 'Although we'll need to talk to you again.'

'Of course,' I say. 'I know you're only doing your job, but, honestly, it's all such a shock. I can't bear to think what might have happened.'

I stand up, and my pretty sundress is incongruous amidst this inference of dark deeds, done by me, or Jamie, or perhaps someone else altogether, or maybe by the great mysterious forces of the sea. Who knows? I am longing for a drink, and I wish I could call Chrissy, ask her to come over. But I can hardly drink cocktails any more, and certainly not with her. It seems everyone might suspect me now, and it is devastating.

Again, I try not to think it, but the person I want to speak to most at the moment is Dan, if only to make sure I get my story straight. I daren't risk it, of course. We are both locked in a private Venn diagram of purgatory, and it's hard to tell where there's an overlap.

I move towards the door. 'Thanks,' I say, although no-one knows what for. My legs weaken as the nausea returns, and I stumble a little, yet I manage to steady myself before leaving the room. Outside, the leaf-filtered sunlight fails to permeate my psyche. Everything feels devoid of colour, like an over-exposed photograph. I refuse the smiley porter's offer of a lift and start making my way back towards my bungalow. As I traipse along the path through the paleness of the trees, I see someone coming from the other direction, and from his distinctive gait I can tell it's my husband, come back at last, and my knees go soft in a way that I had no idea knees could do.

And then I realize that it's not Jamie at all, but his slightly taller, slightly stockier, slightly moodier brother. We can't avoid each other, like we couldn't at our first meeting, in a London pub on a rain-swept night, seven years and a world away. I don't know what I should say. I don't want to compromise either of us. Between us is a yawning gap of silence, of the unspoken.

'Dan,' I say, at last. I speak formally, sombrely. 'I'm so sorry about Jamie.'

He looks at me now, and his eyes are impossible to read. 'It's OK,' he says. 'It must be awful for you.' It's like we're reading from a terrible film script.

I lower my voice to a whisper. It might be my only chance to see what he's thinking, without his dreadful mother sniffing around. 'The police think he might have absconded. That one of the guys at the dive centre helped him.'

'I know,' Dan says. He has a peculiar expression on his face, and his eyes are searing into mine. It's hard to look at him.

'I almost wish he *had*,' I continue, twisting my left

flip-flop into the sand, studying the indent I'm making. 'I'd rather that, than the thought of him lying dead and alone somewhere . . .' My voice tails off. And then I look up at Dan, and start again. 'But, unless he has done it deliberately, which seems too incredible, what other outcome is there now?'

I can tell that Dan's thinking about the snorkel, and what a strong swimmer I am, and how Jamie wasn't particularly confident in the sea. I'm sure he's thinking his ex-lover, his new sister-in-law, might be a murderer, and it seems I am forever tainted in his eyes. I try not to blame him.

And then I remember that this might all be Dan's fault anyway, and suddenly I *hate* him for it, almost want to run at him. How *dare* he be standing there, when Jamie is not, with that weird, ambivalent curl to his lip? I can't trust myself to do or say anything further, and so I force my anger inwards and march straight past him, without looking back, even when I hear him call my name, and the only saving grace is that he doesn't follow me. But now we are both lost souls on this island of secrets, and in the silence of my room the sense of foreboding grows and grows, until it is fizzing and fermenting, and horrendous.

38

A year or so earlier

A week had passed since Jemma had given her ultimatum, but she hadn't heard from Jamie. She was determined not to ring him – she had laid down her gauntlet, and now it was up to him. Jemma still felt spookily calm, in control at last, even though she knew that the longer his silence went on, the less probable their staying together was. She was busy at work, having been put on a new residential development in Morocco, and she was enjoying it. And at least with Jamie temporarily gone from his own flat she was able to imagine what living without him would be like, and it felt OK. There had been something about waiting for him to propose that had infused virtually every situation with angst lately, had dialled up every single one of her overwrought tendencies, all of his defensive ones. Sasha had been right. It couldn't have gone on forever. She might have ended up killing him.

Jemma finished checking the project's mood boards, which were a satisfying blend of neutrals with a single pop of deepest magenta, and sat back in her chair. All she needed to do now was the fee proposal, and she'd be ready for the meeting in Marrakesh the following day. She was proud that not only did she get to go to the overseas project meetings now, she was also running them on this job. She'd come a long way since the early days of being a stroppy little trainee, before she'd met Dan, had benefitted from his calming influence.

Dan. Jemma had tried not to think about him these past few years, but she wondered now what he was up to. She'd heard from Jamie that he and Lydia were getting married. Was that partly why she, Jemma, had given Jamie an ultimatum? No, she was being ludicrous. Dan had nothing to do with it.

Her mobile rang. It was Jamie. Her heart felt like it would stop, and she could barely breathe.

'Hello,' she said, as she got up from her desk and walked the long, sleek length of the office towards the exit. Her heels clicked busily on the herringbone oak floor.

'Hi, it's me. Can we meet?'

'Sure. When?'

'Now? I'm round the corner.'

Jemma felt wrong-footed. She had to get this work done, and if he told her it was over she would definitely have to go straight home and cry her eyes out. But if he was going to dump her, surely he wouldn't have been so mean as to doorstep her at work to do it?

'OK,' she said at last.

'I'm in the tapas bar,' he said. 'Hurry up.'

*

Jamie was sitting at a table in the corner, looking tired and anxious. His eyes had dark circles around them, and she felt for him suddenly, that she'd forced him into this. She sat down across from him. There was a natural-coloured linen tablecloth placed diagonally on the distressed wooden table, and the menu was printed on a sheet of brown paper, with prices that were just single numbers. A tortilla was '6', which she thought was extortionate. She didn't usually come here.

The waiter bustled up, and he had a large ice bucket and a bottle of champagne, and that's when she knew.

'Jemma,' Jamie said. 'You drive me nuts, but you make life interesting. The thought of you not being in mine is unbearable.' And then he reached into his pocket and brought out a ring, and it was the most beautifully set diamond she'd ever seen.

'We've waited too long, Jem. Please, will you marry me?'

She looked into his silver-smoke eyes and felt her heart expanding. She smiled shyly. 'Yes,' she said.

39

Now

Who is the person I married? Who is he? Where is he? And who, incidentally, am I? What ghastly part have I played in this unimaginable conundrum?

I have so many questions, and I want Jamie to come back, to answer them. I want to ask him exactly why he married me. I want him to look me in the eye and tell me whether he was sleeping with his boss. I want to find out if he'd truly loved me, or if my gamble had failed, and I'd simply forced him into this, after all. I want to know his side of the story at last. Jamie is a mystery to me now, and it's as if he is far out of reach, and yet near still. I miss him. The longing becomes febrile. I keep throwing up, and yet I need to eat. Maybe it's nothing more than the stress, and I pray that's true – this isn't how I'd imagined becoming a mother. Even Chati heard me retching earlier, when he brought me my supper. He looked so concerned, and I wanted to give him a hug, tell him that I was fine. I feel almost responsible for him, somehow. I hate to leave any food on my plate and so sometimes, when I just can't manage it, I flush it down the toilet so as not to offend him. I don't know what I would have done without him.

Dad will be here in the morning, and although it will be good to see him, have someone else on my side, I find I'm going out of my mind tonight. I don't care any more if there is someone out there, waiting for me. I need to get out. I leave the bungalow via the terrace and run barefoot through the wandering-handed trees onto the dark midnight beach. My head races as I fling myself to the sand, which is colder than I expect it to be. The sky over the ocean is endless, unfettered by green jungly growth, and its star-pocked hugeness is a relief. As I stare upwards, I let my mind track its familiar journey into my romantic hinterland . . . but tonight it surprises me, slows in a different place. The landscape here is unfamiliar, like getting off at the wrong train stop. Instead of placing myself at the centre of the action, for a change I'm not even present. Tonight I find myself thinking solely about Jamie and Dan, and how they were with each other. There is something not right about their relationship, I know it, and it feels as if it is more than just sibling rivalry. Even the fact that Dan is here on the island feels twisted somehow. I can still see his expression from when I bumped into him earlier. What was he thinking? *What has he done?* But how *could* Dan be responsible? He wasn't even here when Jamie went missing. And anyway, even if it turned out that Dan was involved in some way, would it still ultimately be my fault?

I hear a noise, near me. A cough? Or just a rogue wave? The urge to scream fills my lungs. I cower in the darkness.

Nothing.

I wait, too scared to move.

Still nothing – just hot, salty, night-time air.

I feel so sick.

There is a roaring in my head, like there'd been in the seaplane, as I realize there's no-one else out here. The presence is closer. Much closer. I lean over, and vomit into the pristine white sand.

40

Nine months earlier

'Jamie,' Jemma said. 'Can we talk about the flowers?'

'What flowers?'

'The wedding flowers! What other flowers are there?' She picked up her glass of red wine and took a sip. The glass was smeary at the top, and she considered sending it back. Then she recalled having read that restaurants were full of germs, even the top ones, and decided not to be a princess.

'Oh, right . . . none . . . What do you want to talk about?'

'Well, what kind we want, what theme, whether we have the same at the reception as we have in the church.'

'Jem, darling, we're not getting married for months. Surely we don't need to make these decisions now.'

'Well, I'm sorry, but we do. We're working on a pretty tight time-frame compared to most people, you know. And I thought, as I've got your undivided attention right now . . .' Jemma watched Jamie slide his eyes away from the giant screen above her head, back to his pint, which he took a slurp of, and finally back to her.

'Jemma, my sweet,' he said. 'I don't care what flowers

we have.' He saw her face. 'No, no, I don't mean it like that, I just mean I know how good you are at that stuff, so I'm more than happy to let you work it out.'

'That's just a cop-out, Jamie,' Jemma said. 'This is meant to be *our* wedding, remember?'

'Well, you're the one who wanted . . .' His face fell as Jemma stood up. 'I didn't mean it like that,' he said quickly.

'Really?' she said. Her eyebrow lifted. 'I'm going to the bathroom. Maybe you can think about your position while I'm away.'

As Jemma climbed the stairs in the centuries-old pub, she felt the ripple of old traumas radiating upwards through the worn-away stone. What was her stress about floral displays compared to all that might have happened here over the years – births, fights to the death, gut-wrenching affairs, lung-bursting sicknesses. And what were flowers, anyway, compared to their own thorny journey to get to this point? Maybe Jamie was right. She was turning into a Bridezilla. But it was mean of him to imply he didn't want to get married. Why would he be like that? A flicker of fear ignited somewhere beneath Jemma's ribs. As she dried her hands, the noise from the drier was discordant, unpleasant, and it clashed with the voice in her head, the one that said it was her fault for forcing Jamie into this, leading him to the altar against his will – until, like a dog on a lead, he'd finally given up straining to go in the other direction and had succumbed. It was no good. Did he really want to go through with this? She needed to ask him.

The walk back down the haunted stairs escalated Jemma's anxiety, made her feel that something was about to go very, very wrong. Perhaps she should have let Jamie come to the pub on his own, instead of tagging along with him. Going on about wedding flowers when he was trying to watch the football and then stomping off in a huff wasn't cool; it was painful. Were they both going to have to put up with another nine months of this?

Jemma crossed the bar towards Jamie, and as she watched him down half his pint, she saw he had that look he got sometimes, as if she were another species entirely. He knew the rules, did his best to play by them, but still it seemed she confounded him. The institution of marriage confounded him.

'Hey, Jem,' he said, as she reached the table. 'I'm sorry . . .'

'Yeah, it's fine, forget it,' Jemma said. She shuffled into her seat and picked up her drink. 'What's the score?'

'Nil-nil still.'

'Fascinating.'

'Do I detect a bit of cynicism, my darling?'

'No, of course not. But Jamie . . .'

'Ye – es.'

Jemma took a breath. 'Did you mean what you said about getting married?'

'No, of course not. I *want* to marry you, Jem, really I do. I wouldn't be doing it otherwise. It's just, I sometimes get a bit tired of talking about the wedding.'

'Oh . . . Do I do it that much?'

'Well, we've decided on the font for the name tags. We've bought the guest comments book, the one, after much deliberation, with the cream pages rather than the white ones. We've plotted the route between the church and the reception to the nearest millionth of a mile. You've made me pick that terrible waistcoat . . .'

'Oh God, sorry.'

'It's OK. I just don't want to have to come to the pub to talk about it.'

'OK, point taken.' Jemma leaned over and kissed his cheek. He smelled of French aftershave, and it made her love him even more. And he *must* be into it, she thought; he'd even chosen and booked the honeymoon himself, which was beyond a miracle. She finished her red wine, in what she hoped was an impressive single gulp. 'I wanted to watch the *Bake Off* anyway. Shall I see you at home?'

'Are you sure?' said Jamie, but she could hear the relief in his voice. As she looked up she saw his mate Mark coming in, and her hackles rose. Mark was one of those types who suggested one for the road, and then another, and who nearly always managed to cause a fight between them. Jamie must have given Mark a look, as Mark's smile suddenly faded and he sidled off to the other side of the bar. Jamie got up and ushered Jemma out of the far door.

'What's got into you?' she laughed, as he gave her a passionate kiss goodbye, and then she realized he thought she hadn't seen Mark.

'Nothing, Mrs Armstrong. It's just I love you.'

She felt a flush of pleasure. He'd never called her that before. 'I love you too, Jamie. See you later.'

'Yeah, I won't be late,' he said, and then he sauntered across the bar towards his friend.

By the next morning, Jemma's goodwill towards Jamie had vanished.

'Are you going to get up?'

No response.

'It's gone 8 o'clock.'

Still no response. Jemma felt a rush of rage, as if there were hot air blowing in her face, with sand in it, making her skin livid. She lifted the bottom right corner of the duvet, and flicked it. A wave throbbed through the feathers: white, goose down, from Heal's. She was in her new navy dress with tasteful white birds on it, her high wooden clogs. She was showered, made up, dressed for work. She needed to leave. Jamie normally left before her, yet he wasn't even awake. She shook the edge of the duvet again, harder. It rose a good half a foot off him, before settling back like a cloud in summer, as if she'd never done it.

'Ugh,' he said. He grunted, turned onto his side, and pulled the duvet fully over him, covering his pale bare shoulders, his sandy head. He started snoring, a low, rasping strangled noise he made whenever he'd been drinking.

'Jamie,' she said. 'YOU ARE GOING TO BE LATE FOR WORK.'

'I texted Camille.'

'Oh.' That unbalanced her attack, and she felt almost foolish for a second. And then she felt even angrier somehow.

'You said you weren't going to be late.'

He didn't reply.

'Did you hear me?'

Nothing.

'Jamie!'

She tried to pull the covers off his head. He held on tight. They got into a brief tussle, and a glass of water was knocked off the bedside table.

'Now look what you've done,' she shrieked.

'Leave me alone, Jemma. Go to work.'

'You said you'd be back! Why didn't you come back?'

Jamie sighed. He pulled the duvet down far enough to make his eyes visible. His hair was sticking up at broken angles, like trampled-on straw.

'Big deal, Jemma. I bumped into Mark after you left. We just had a couple of pints.'

'It wasn't after I left. Why are you lying?'

Jamie sighed. 'Jemma, you need to chill out, darling. What's got into you?'

Jemma walked carefully around the perimeter of the bed, towards the door. The room stank of beer and bodies. No, not bodies – body, singular. His body, and all its effusions. She held her head proudly. She was willing to take the moral high ground, on this occasion, although unfortunately Jamie didn't seem to have noticed.

Jemma knew she was overreacting. He'd just had a couple of pints with his mate. *But he'd lied to her.* She needed to chill out. *She hated Mark.* She took a deep breath and turned back to her fiancé. 'Well, I guess I'll see you later then.'

Jamie didn't reply. He'd retreated back under the duvet. Just one shapely foot was sticking out at an odd angle, as if it wasn't attached to him. As Jemma passed the end of the bed, she grabbed his foot and yanked it, hard.

'Owww,' he said. 'What is *wrong* with you?'

Jemma was filled with a shame that was hard to put a name to. She rushed from the room and fled down the corridor and out of the flat, just as the divorced man who lived above them was coming back from walking his dog. Jemma muttered hello and stalked off, head down. Usually she would have been friendly, stopped and patted Buddy, made some comment on the weather, and she could tell that her neighbour had clocked her mood, and she hoped he hadn't heard her shrieking. She hurried down the street towards the bus stop, and the world felt like it was out of pace with her. She was alone, completely alone, on her boiling island of rage – but why? Because her boyfriend was late home from the pub. No, not her boyfriend. Her *fiancé*. That terrible word for that terrible thing, the process of being engaged, on a promise, but not yet past the finishing line. Jemma had wanted Jamie to marry her for so long, and they'd been through so much, and they loved each other. What was it that had made her so angry?

As she reached the main road, the cars were whizzing by, and they contained little children in smart uniforms being transported to school, and one day those would be their children, and she would be that mother, and she couldn't go around digging her pink-painted nails into her husband's foot and twisting, just because he was late home from the pub.

During her commute Jemma surreptitiously surveyed the other people, and she wondered. Did anyone else feel fury like she felt? There was the full spread of humankind on the number seventeen bus. The plump teenagers in their shiny polyester blazers, eating crisps for breakfast. The City type, in her smart pure-wool suit with her black leather briefcase. The man in stained, worn-out clothes with misery etched through his features, like dirt. The fat woman with a buggy who huffed when she was told to fold it up, but failed to erupt, like Jemma might have done. The foreigners, who had fled their countries and who lived here now, scratching out a living, when perhaps they'd once been lawyers or doctors. Were they this angry at what had happened to them, which was surely far worse than someone being late home from a night out? Or was she, Jemma, simply still enraged by past traumas, which permeated everything, and would do forever?

As the bus thundered on through the city's brick-lined arteries, Jemma's heart rate began to slow. She took out her phone to text Jamie. She composed it several times, until finally she was satisfied.

I'm sorry Jamie, I don't know what got into me. There's no excuse for my behaviour. Please forgive me. See you later. Jx

Jemma pressed 'Send', and then she felt cold and clammy, and terrified. The bus was crowded now, and a woman sat down next to her. She smelled of Poison, which was the perfume her mother had worn, and Jemma suddenly wanted to bury her head into this stranger's ample breast and sleep, but of course she couldn't. It was odd how it was always when she felt at her most fragile that she most missed her mother, who'd never been much help anyway. As her journey continued, Jemma sat stiffly in the enforced proximity, waiting fruitlessly for her phone to ping with its message of acceptance of her apology, until at last the bus reached the Gray's Inn Road, and she had to get off.

41

Now

It's the morning of the day Dad is due to arrive at last, and I've lost count of whether that means it's five or six days since I last saw Jamie, but it doesn't matter. What matters is that the British police want to talk to me again – although they rang me up this time, perhaps reluctant to risk interrupting another yoga session. At least seeing them gives me something to do, I suppose. It pulls me back from emotional shutdown. The unreality of the situation, its malevolent undertones, the not knowing, is finally becoming too much. My world is continuing to slowly close down, like the onset of death. Even the shrill thrill of the phone a moment ago had been a notable event, and that's how weird and suspended life feels right now. Worst of all, I can't seem to summon up much fear for my husband any more. It all feels too pointless, too late.

I refuse the offer of a buggy, and instead I cycle across the island to the sanatorium. It gives me a legitimate reason to be out, and I'm glad of the activity – it rouses me a little. When we first arrived I loved biking here. It made me feel like a little kid again: just a quick, fun way to get from A to B. Get on. Get there. Get off. No hills, no special gear, no complicated locks to wrestle with; no fear that your bike might not be there when you get back, like in London. The irony almost makes me laugh. I might not have a husband any more, but at least I have a bike. My husband might have been cheating on me, but at least I have a bike. All our lives are in tatters, *but at least I have a bike.*

I need to calm down, hold it together, especially in front of the police. As I approach the sanatorium, I find myself going through the exact details of how Jamie and I got engaged, and of our wedding day, in case they decide to ask me about any of it. I get the feeling they'll be going in for the psychological interview today, and I need to get my thoughts clear, my story straight. The irony is that Jamie's proposal – albeit after I'd put a gun to his head – had been way more romantic than any of the mini-break scenarios I'd dreamed of. When I'd said yes, he'd stood up, come around the table to my side, and held onto me as if he were drowning. He'd said that he'd realized he was happier with me than he'd ever been without me, and that in his book that was the best reason in the world to commit to someone. And I'd thought that was so lovely and heartfelt, I wonder now whether it was before or after he started fucking Camille.

I reach the sanatorium and get off my bike, prop it up on its stand, resist the urge to kick it over. The path to the door is leafy and the sun stipples through it, and as

I walk along it, I try to work out what I should tell the police about my relationship with Jamie. Whatever I do, whatever I say, I need to hold it together, not let them rattle me. I need to hold onto the fact that this is my husband here, and it's not my fault if he was having an affair, and that I've done nothing wrong. All I can do is answer the questions they ask me, and make sure I do so in an appropriately wifely way, although I have no idea what that would be in these most appalling of circumstances. But the one thing I mustn't do is let the police think I'm hiding something, which of course I am.

I knock on the sanatorium door, which is pointless as it's open, but it seems I'm playing for time. I stand back and look up through the trees at the sky, and there are faint white clouds in the soft muted blue, and they are so neat and rhythmic in their thin, straight patterns it's as if somebody has raked them. I breathe. It will be OK. Maybe they even have news of Jamie. It's possible. Whatever I do, I mustn't tie myself up in knots, risk saying the wrong thing. For the next hour or so, I mustn't worry about what has happened to my husband, or how I'd truly felt about him, or what might be happening inside my body. For the next hour or so, I mustn't worry about anything other than watching my back.

42

A week or so before

As Jemma paused at the back of the church, tiny and picturesque and how she'd always imagined, the first person she noticed was Dan, and she wondered if she should be doing this. Every single event, large or small, insignificant or otherwise, had led her here, to this moment, and yet now it felt so wrong. But when was it right? Had it ever been right? And how on earth had she let it get to this point?

As the music struck and she failed to start walking, the murmuring and the shuffling increased, just a notch. The organ filled the void, the joyful notes of Bach's 'Wachet Auf' cutting into the silence, and it gave her a respite. She felt her father nudge her, oh so gently. She was frozen in time, in this minuscule moment when it wasn't too late, when she still had the chance to change her mind. Still she could turn. Still she could flee. *It wasn't too late.* Her eyes were wet behind her veil. She could feel everyone looking at her. Everyone she loved. There for her. No, not for her, for her and Jamie. *Jamie.* Oh God.

'Come on, Jemma, love,' whispered her father. 'It's all right.' He started to propel her forward, and although she let him, her legs felt heavy and useless, and she had the walk of a defeated, broken-in elephant underneath the froth of her skirts. She saw Veronica turn and look, a hazy smear of antipathy clouding her eyes, and Jemma paused again, halfway down the aisle. She fast-forwarded in time to the day ahead – to the saying *I will*, to the *you may kiss the bride* moment, the photos, the speeches, their first dance, falling into bed together, her new lingerie. *The honeymoon.* She couldn't go through with it. Not after last night.

'Dad,' she whispered.

Her father was squirming. What was he meant to do? This wasn't his fault. She needed to sort it herself.

'I'M SO SORRY EVERYONE, I'M MAKING A MISTAKE.'

Silence. Jemma couldn't understand it, the lack of response. And then she realized that she hadn't said anything at all, except in her head, and the words were crowded inside there, trapped. The space was filling up with *I'm making a mistake I'm making a mistake I'm making a mistake I'm making a mistake* and it felt as if her mind might even explode, shatter into a million tiny pieces of horror. Her father subtly nudged her, and as she started walking again she concentrated on her feet, on her dainty little feet, in their dainty little princess shoes, transporting her, lumbering her towards this terrible image of hell. The day she had dreamed of, ever since she was an innocent little girl, going to hell.

Jemma managed to reach the altar without looking at Dan again. His presence was merely a faint electric buzz behind her now. Instead she focussed on Kay, who was sitting in the front row in a simple burgundy dress, her cream fascinator equally elegant and understated – but although her step-mother smiled at Jemma, her hazel eyes were troubled. And now Jamie was turning to her. She hadn't even glanced at him yet, let alone acknowledged him, not since she'd seen him from the entrance to the church. He didn't deserve this.

'Hello, Jem,' he said quietly. He was beaming. 'You look beautiful.' And then she realized that Jamie couldn't see her eyes beneath the veil. *He didn't know.* Her father was hovering, unsure what to do. Eventually, he sat down and refused to engage with his wife, who was whispering anxiously to him. Jemma stared at the vicar, begging him to rescue her. He was a nice man. Surely he had an obligation to do so? Yet they'd had all the meetings. She and Jamie had been so pleasant, so respectable, so well-suited. They'd seemed textbook, had given the vicar nothing to doubt. But now? Did he see? Please let him see.

As Jamie helped Jemma remove her veil, her eyes were shiny still, and he seemed to see that as a radiance of her happiness. He squeezed her hand, but she couldn't squeeze his in return. Her hands were like dead fish, her face was the face of a simpleton doll, and yet Jamie hadn't noticed. Jemma stared at the vicar, and she knew he caught the look, the plea in her eyes. He hesitated. He glanced at Jamie. Jamie smiled back. Whose obligation was it here? They were in God's house. The vicar was the servant of God. This was not God's will.

'Jemma?' said the vicar, softly. 'I said, "I, Jemma Marie Brady . . ." He paused, waiting for her.

What? What had happened? Surely they hadn't got to this part already? Who on earth had pressed 'Play'? She didn't know what to say.

Jemma's eyes were leaking. Jamie looked alarmed, at last. The pregnant pause in the church was infinite, to the end of time and back. And then Sasha, her best friend, her beautiful bridesmaid, handed Jemma a tissue. As she dabbed at her eyes she looked straight ahead, focussed on Jesus, who was hanging emaciated from the cross in front of her. She could no longer see her friends and family behind her. She could only remember the gaudy colours that she'd passed by as she'd cut her lonely swathe through the church: the reds and cerises and the glorious emerald greens of her friends' dresses, the floral patterns of the aunties, the dark backs of the men. She couldn't see the cream of the cosmos and the dahlias and the phlox and all the other flowers that she'd spent hours selecting, to bring to mind a summer meadow. On her way to the altar, the blooms had been but a backdrop, mere scenery. She'd been the main event. She, and Jamie. Now she wanted to whisper an apology and turn around and bolt down the aisle and out of the door. She wanted to disappear in a cloud of fairy smoke, and wake up tomorrow to find it never happened.

43

Now

The police were surprisingly nice to me, and it only took half an hour or so, but that has just made me feel yet more suspicious. They claimed they had nothing more to update me with, but I'm certain there's stuff going on in the background that they're not telling me. I am now so paranoid about what everyone's thinking, I even wonder if the police have found out somehow that I hadn't wanted to go through with the wedding. Maybe Chrissy has told them, and how I wish I'd never confessed to her. But I'd been drunk that night, and distraught, and I'd had to tell someone – and how was I to know that Jamie was about to vanish off the face of the earth? It's like the cruellest of practical jokes.

It's a relief, therefore, to get back to the confines of my self-appointed prison, and I'm grateful that at least it's a luxurious one. My breakfast is just being delivered, and Chati is polite and unobtrusive as he puts down the tray. And although I never feel like eating anything at all until the food arrives, it's so beautifully presented, and the aromas are so sweet and spicy and jungly, I usually can't resist. Today, as well as fresh fruit salad, there are steamed buns, and when I take my first bite, I can taste coconut and ginger and another unidentifiable local spice, and I vaguely wonder what meat it is. It tastes like pork, but then I decide it must be chicken. The food is delicious, whatever it is, and before I know it, I've finished it. Just as I'm wiping my mouth with a starched white napkin, Chrissy drops by to see how I'm doing, update me on the mood in the resort (palpable excitement, she implies, somewhat undiplomatically). I hardly say anything, and she doesn't stay long, and I'm relieved. Despite our attempts to be normal, our exchanges feel increasingly difficult, for both of us.

Jamie has been missing for so many days now that a new routine on the island has been established. It seems that even trauma can be normalized through structure. I still spend most of the day on the terrace, staring out through my own bit of jungle at the sea beyond, still looking for something, still dreading it. In my brief snatches of sleep, I still have nightmares. The army continues to zip about on boats or in seaplanes, checking every nearby deserted island in case Jamie's been shipwrecked there, which is yet another possibility they're investigating. The British detectives carry on interviewing people. Honeymooners try to get on with the business of loving each other, albeit with a camera phone and Twitter handle to hand. And although, to my knowledge, no-one has snapped me on the terrace yet, the fact that someone might just makes me shrink back further into the sanctity of my bungalow. I long for my dad to get here.

I've only seen Dan twice since the day he arrived – that awkward, highly charged time we bumped into each other on one of the inland paths, and briefly the other day with his mother. They are staying in an over-water bungalow on the south-east side of the island, and the police have been the ones liaising with them mostly, so there's been no need for us to have any contact with each other. Neither Dan nor Veronica choose to come near me, which must seem odd to the casual bystander – we're part of the same family, after all – but my mother-in-law's suspicion of me rises off her like low mist in a valley, and I can't face trying to justify myself to her. I'm pretty sure Dan hasn't told her anything, but that doesn't stop her doubts. I can't help feeling devastated for Veronica, though, that her youngest son is missing. It must be the most flailing feeling in the world to lose a child – surely even more so than a husband.

The doorbell rings, and it is jarring, that ding-dong noise, in my wood-and-thatch haven, and I assume it is Chrissy again, or else Housekeeping, or, worse, the police, wanting to speak to me once more. I don't want to talk to anyone, but least of all them.

My feet are soft and silent as they slide across the smooth, hard tiles. I feel solid, and heavier than I should, weighed down by regrets. I pull the door open and try to rearrange my features into a neutral expression.

'Oh. Hello,' I say.

'Can I come in?'

I hesitate, nearly tell him to go away. 'OK,' I concede.

Dan walks through my bungalow, past the oversized bed I shared with his brother, past the beautiful carved furniture, on to the terrace with the gorgeous glimpses of the sea through the trees. He sits down at the table. I worry that there may be nosy holidaymakers outside, with cameras. I don't want us to be seen together. I don't want anyone to hear our conversation. I try to warn Dan off with my eyes. I attempt to silently convey to him that I don't know where Jamie is. That what I want more than anything in the world is for my husband to be found. That I don't want to speak about anything else, especially Dan's role in all this – I still can't decide how much he's to blame. But of course there are too many conflicting emotions to express in just one look, too many contraflows of feeling. Everything is messed up.

'Jemma,' says Dan. His voice is curiously impassive. 'I want you to know something before the police tell you. They've found an account of Jamie's.'

'What do you mean?'

'He had another bank account. It seems he was siphoning money into it.'

'Oh . . .' I'm stunned. 'But why would he do that?'

'I don't know.'

'I know they think he was seeing his boss,' I say, after a long while, as the sands shift sightlessly under the gentle waves a few yards away from us. 'Did you? Before, I mean.'

'No,' says Dan. 'Though I must admit I wasn't that surprised . . .' I'm unnerved by the hatred in his voice. It's so faint, but I spot it. It's there.

'But if he was seeing her, why would he have bothered marrying me?' There's more silence, as the question stumps both of us. Neither of us is willing to discuss the possible reasons. It's so weird being in the same space as Dan, talking to him again face-to-face for the first time in years. Until he arrived on my honeymoon, I'd only seen him a handful of times, and never alone, since the day he walked out of his parents' drinks party. As I wait for him to reply, my mind meanders back through our past with a regret that is delicate in its construction, like a spoonful of bubbles. I thought I'd found in Dan a good, steady man, who loved me, made me feel safe, brought out the best in me. My love for him had been like the coming in of the tide, so gradual as to be barely noticeable. Enter his dashing brother, a veritable tsunami of glamour and charm, buoyed with a bottle or two of champagne and the sociopathic ruthlessness of his mother. The fact that I was drunk when I first kissed Jamie will never excuse it. *But what about how Dan has behaved since?* I'm pretty certain it's worse.

'Why are you telling me this, Dan?' I don't need to try to inject hostility back into my tone. Blame is easier than regret.

It still takes him an age to answer. 'I don't know,' he says. 'I thought you ought to know, before the police tell you . . .' His eyes drift away to the sea, making them seem brighter, browner. It is a spiky, painful kind of silence between us now. He shifts in his chair. I'm not sure what it is that he wants to say. When he turns back to me, he looks broken, and it occurs to me that he might be trying to make amends, but it's too late.

'Oh God,' I say, so quietly I'm almost speaking to myself.

I need to think about something else, other than Dan, our past, so I move back onto safer territory, which, bizarrely, is to talk about the disappearing trick it seems his brother has engineered, willingly or otherwise. My tone turns formal, a bit like a radio announcement. 'I'm so sorry about Jamie. I just pray they find him.' He looks at me hard, and it's clear he doesn't know what to think. He suspects me, I know he does. I shift my gaze away.

'Me too,' he says, eventually. 'Me too.'

Dan gets up and so do I. We walk back through the bungalow towards the front door, where he stops and gives me the briefest of hugs, how someone might say goodbye to their sister-in-law in a situation such as this, and a couple passing by capture the moment – and I presume the photo will end up online soon enough, and my reputation will take another battering. And it's only going to get worse now, I'm sure of it. It is only a matter of time.

44

A week or so earlier

I will I will I will. She had she had she had. The words floated about, blurry and indistinct, and she felt like she might even pass out. It was done. The register was signed. And now Jemma was sitting on the closed seat of the church toilet, which was not the cleanest, and her precious white dress was making contact with the porcelain, and she didn't care. She was crying, great racking sobs that she was managing to keep inside of herself, as she knew people might hear, and she couldn't tell anyone. She couldn't admit how she felt. She had made her decision, and now her job was to get on with it.

There was a knock on the door. Sasha.

'Jemma, sweetheart, are you OK in there?'

Jemma wiped her eyes. She took a breath. Her voice was steady enough through the cubicle door. 'Yeah, I'm fine, Sasha. My . . . my stomach's a bit dodgy, that's all.' She feigned a laugh. 'Not very bride-like, I'm afraid . . . Anyway, I'm just coming.'

She pulled the flush and when she came out she couldn't look at her friend, and she knew in that moment that Sasha knew, but couldn't say anything either. Not now. It was too late. Instead Sasha watched her as she washed her hands at the tiny sink, with a soap that smelled of hospitals. Her new wedding ring felt bulky and uncomfortable on her finger. Sasha briefly squeezed her shoulder, and then they left the sanctuary of the chapel toilets and made their way out to the front of the church, for Jemma to see her husband, have her picture taken with him, as irrefutable proof as the marriage certificate that she really had done this, that her new life had begun. That now, officially, she was Mrs James Armstrong.

In the little church garden, just before the graveyard, there was winter-crunched grass, scattered with snow-drops, and the whites and greens were so sparkling and vibrant that the photographer was almost orgasmic about the light. Maybe it was normal to feel like this when you get married, Jemma tried to tell herself. Perhaps everyone has a wobble at some point, even on the day itself – and in her case it was hardly surprising. And yet, as she stood with a fixed smile on her face, she felt like an imposter at her own wedding, and rarely had she felt as wretched.

'Okey dokey, lovely . . . that's really lovely. Smashing.' Click click. 'Jemma, can you put your hand on Jamie's arm, so we can see the ring?' Click click. 'Beautiful. One more.' Click click. 'Got it.' The photographer's face popped out from behind his camera, as if he were play-ing peek-a-boo with a baby, and he had a handlebar moustache and bouffant hair, and he was so bouncy and enthusiastic it made Jemma want to weep. Jamie seemed to have got over his years-long commitment issues and was playing the part of the happy groom with gusto. As he touched her, it made Jemma's bones jolt, and she wasn't remotely sure what the feeling was.

'Can we have the bride and groom kissing now, please?' the photographer said. Jamie turned towards her obligingly, and his waistcoat was awful, and he'd been right about that. What had happened to her judgment of late? The colour looked gorgeous on Sasha, and her two little flower-girls, but very pale pink sapped the life out of Jamie's skin. And although in these situations Jamie could sometimes seem a little ungracious, Jemma had to give him his due, not today. Today he looked so happy, and his happy, smiling face loomed towards her, and she caught a fresh, clean whiff of his happy-smelling aftershave. A few days ago she would have been ecstatic, and yet in this moment it made her feel – what?

Jemma's feet went from beneath her, and she staggered. Even though Jamie caught her, her princess heels dug into the turf and ripped through to the dirt, and they were ruined. Her shoes were ruined. Her wedding day was ruined. She'd planned every last detail to the nth degree – *apart from the little matter of the identity of the groom*. How had it got to this?

'Careful, Jem,' Jamie said. He laughed. 'There's no need to swoon.' She felt hot breath and the spittle wet of Jamie's mouth as he kissed her on the cheek.

'Perfect!' said the photographer.

Click, click, click. Sick, sick, sick. That was the word that was looping through Jemma's head now, and she was unsure of its meaning in this context. Did she feel physically nauseous? Or was it sick as in depraved, terrible, that it seemed she may have got married purely because it was too late to turn back? But when would have been an appropriate moment to change her mind? A month before? The night before? At the altar itself, in front of Jesus?

The wind whipped through Jemma as the photographer kept prodding and cajoling the smiles out of her, as her mind kept drifting back to eighty or so minutes ago, in that other life. If only she'd listened to her innermost feelings then, and had refused to get out of the car. They wouldn't have been able to force her from a vintage Rolls Royce – a gentle prod from her father wouldn't have been enough to propel her towards her doom. She could have just sent him in, without her, to have a quiet word, try to minimize Jamie's humiliation. Then the driver could have taken her back to the house, and she could have taken off her beautiful dress and kept out of the way until everything had died down. It would have been awful, certainly, but the long-term consequences might have been better for everyone.

But was that even what she wanted, Jemma thought now, as Jamie leaned in for another choreographed kiss. Didn't she *love* him?

Jamie's lips were soft beneath the fuzz of his stubble, but when he tried gently to prise open her lips she was having none of it. As he gazed into her eyes, he looked confused for a second, and Jemma ached for him. It was as if he'd made a decision that had felt agonizing for so long, but now felt so right he was wondering why he hadn't made it years before, and his puzzlement at her resistance was pathetic, in the true meaning of the word. Jemma felt such sympathy for Jamie at that moment, that the graphs of his emotions and hers seemed so uncalibrated, it made her kiss him back suddenly – and the photographer said, 'Ooh smashing, that's what we're after,' and afterwards she felt a teeny bit better.

45

Now

It's mid-morning, and it's breezy, and the waiting is torment. *Finally* I hear the seaplane from my terrace, and knowing Dad's on it makes me feel faint with relief. I wonder how we'll be with each other. It is just so unlikely for him to be here, and he sounded anxious when he called me from Malé to let me know he'd made it that far. The one thing he and my husband always had in common was their fear of flying – and it seems strange, now I think about it, that Jamie endured the journey to this particular resort. There are plenty of other islands in the Maldives that we could have just got a boat to. I am so addled by the trauma that I can't even begin to guess what his true motivation was.

I search in the sky for the plane, and although I can't yet see it, the droning is getting louder, and I find I cannot wait any longer. Although I wasn't planning on going to the pontoon, I just have to see my dad. My trusty sand bike whizzes me there in five minutes, and as I carefully get off it, I feel so many eyes on me. I move along the pontoon as though I am walking to my death. I arrive just in time to watch the plane land, and it skids all over the choppy water, and I wonder how my poor dad is coping. Finally I see him climb out onto the landing pontoon, and although he seems a little wobbly, he looks debonair in beige linen trousers and a white shirt, and his outfit surprises me. It's almost as disorientating to see him here as it was to see Veronica and Dan.

The sun is burning fiercely, and the sea is blinding as I watch the dhoni chugging towards us. And now Dad is getting off the boat to say hello, and as he hugs me I feel so nauseous my head swirls and shimmies and my legs almost give way – and I don't know if it's the heat, or the shock, or the food, or whether I really am pregnant, but I don't care. It feels like the least of my worries. Yet, whatever the cause of my condition, when we get in the buggy to take us to Dad's bungalow I have to make Moosa stop so I can throw up at the side of the path – and my butler seems so pissed off, anyone would think that he's the one who has to clean it up. But I can't help it. I'm sick of this island. I'm sick of waiting for Jamie. I'm sick of being sick. *I'm sick of worrying that I'm pregnant.* It is sending me crazy.

After Moosa has shown us in and taken his laconic leave, Dad just stands there, looking helpless, and I realize he's not young any more, and Kay's not with him, and he must be exhausted. I feel so bad for him. I take two glasses and some water from the fridge and lead him out onto his terrace. We sit down across from each other at the table, and the water tinkles daintily as

I pour. Neither of us speaks. Ambient jungle noises fill the void.

'Jemma, do you want to tell me what's going on?' Dad says at last.

'Nothing. There's nothing going on, Dad. I don't know where he is.'

He stares at me. I haven't seen him since my wedding day, when he gave me away. I don't like the look in his eyes. 'I miss Mum,' I say, and I'm not sure of my motivation. Maybe it's simply that, when you think you might be pregnant and your husband is missing on your supposedly dream honeymoon, that's when you need your mother. Or maybe I'm trying to deflect my father from the truth.

'I know you do, love. It must be hard for you without her.'

I start to weep. 'That was my fault, too.' I have no idea why I've brought this up. It's really not helping.

'Oh, Jemma, of course it wasn't. It was no-one's fault. And I'm sure this isn't your fault either.'

Dad and I look at each other, and neither of us knows whether he's right. I still feel the need to broach it. I can't cope with not knowing any more.

'Dad,' I say. I try not to adopt that little-girl whine. He makes me feel like a teenager again, but maybe all parents do that. 'Why did you leave me with Mum?'

The look that crosses Dad's face is one of guilt and sorrow and shame. I can see every single nuance of his regret.

'I just couldn't take any more, love,' he says at last. 'And when you refused to come with me, I didn't know what else to do.'

I want to tell him I understand, and in a way I do, but it still makes me mad, enraged, that he'd thought it was OK to take the risk of leaving me with her. I remember my mother now, drunk, her eyes dancing with derangement, launching herself at my father. Over the years I'd seen her kick him, punch him, pull his hair, and he never, ever retaliated. He'd just packed his bags one day and walked out for good.

There is quiet, filled with the breeze and the crickets and a single low call – from a bird, I presume. I have to say it. 'Dad . . . I'm worried I've taken after her.'

'Oh, Jemma, love,' says Dad. He looks grey. 'What happened? Tell me about that last night with Jamie. What went wrong?'

'I just can't remember.' I'm crying and he stands up and comes over to sit next to me, and the feeling of sobbing into his arms is almost as alien as this tragic mystery we find ourselves at the heart of. 'I'm so sorry,' I say, but Dad just shushes me and strokes my hair. I feel myself regressing to the last time we were like this, when I was eighteen, with a punky art-student haircut, and Dad's own hair wasn't grey yet. He'd sat me down and told me that of course I should go off to university – but I hadn't wanted to leave Mum. Some-how I'd known it would end badly.

'You need to put your future first,' Dad had insisted.

So had Mum, to be fair. Mum had always wanted what was best for me, even if she was a little misguided at times. She'd assured me over and over that she'd be fine, and that I wasn't responsible for her anyway. She'd been drinking less, definitely, and she looked good – like my sister, the postman used to joke.

'No-one could have predicted it, Jemma,' Dad says now.

Perhaps. But when I'd got the knock on the door of my first-year halls' room, and opened it to find a woman in a skirt-suit, accompanied by my tutor, I'd known it was something. I'd found it hard to follow what they were saying. I hadn't even known back then that people could die from asthma, and the fact that my mum had done so felt discordant, impossible, as if reality had been shunted, barged out of the way . . . and then the earth was turning, and twisting, and turning, and twisting, until my throat was constricting, and I'd had to sit down.

And so that had been it. Dad had come up to Warwick to collect me and I'd gone home to his and Kay's, and they'd been marvellous, but I'd lost the one person who, in her own way, had been there for me through everything. Nothing can change it, of course, and maybe it wasn't directly my fault, yet I still feel so guilty. She needed me, and I wasn't there. But who knows – maybe *that's* why I'm so fucking furious all of the time.

I leave Dad on the terrace and walk out onto the sand and shift my gaze upwards. I can feel more angry tears threatening, but I don't want my dad to have to see them – he's done his best to make his own amends over the years. I watch the loss expand up and outwards, until it's filling up the sky, and I can see Mum's face in the faint wisps of cloud, and then somehow it turns into my husband's, and I know for sure that Mum has gone, but I don't know about Jamie.

Jamie, where on earth are you? The regrets balloon and billow as I pray for him to come back. My heart rate slows. *Jamie, please come back,* I whisper. *I'm so sorry for what I've done. I'm so sorry for everything.*

Oh God. The status quo has ended at last, and the timing is almost comical. Just a few hours after Dad turned up to save his innocent little girl, all hell breaks loose. Here I am, as good as shipwrecked, stranded in paradise, and the world has outed me. Twitter, that master snowballer, has done its work. Its democratic machinations have taken a sand-sized grain of truth and made it a lie as big as the Earth in an instant. Thanks to the photographic prowess of one of my fellow holidaymakers, my fears have come true – the picture of Dan giving me an innocent goodbye hug has gone viral, and it looks a million times worse than I thought it might. Even the tabloids have picked up on the story now, and according to them not only am I a brother-swapping harlot, but perhaps I'm a murderous witch too, with devilish trickery that makes husbands vanish in the night-time. I would laugh if it weren't so tragic. But they have dug into all of our backstories and found gold, and it's as if we truly are on a real-life treasure island now. *X marks the spot, folks.* Even a media ingénue like me knows this story is going to run and run. The chronic anxiety feeds on my innards, as if I am eating myself.

It's early evening on the day Dad arrived, and after a brief sortie with him to Reception, for another fruitless yet increasingly uncomfortable meeting with the manager, I have excused myself for the day, pleading a stomach bug. Dad didn't mind – he's jet-lagged anyway. So here I am, lying in my honeymoon bed, in my honeymoon bungalow, and I don't care how comfortable or opulent it is any more, I despise it now. The curtains are shut and it is completely dark. The low thrum of the air conditioning drowns out the soft wash of the sea. I could be anywhere. Yet again, my mind starts to dredge through past events, tries to make sense of what is going on – of how everyone's lives have been turned upside down so brutally, and seemingly irreversibly. A week or so ago I was a supposedly blissful bride at the threshold of a flower-scented church. Now my husband is missing, and my father and ex-lover and mother-in-law are all here on my honeymoon, and the police almost certainly suspect me of something, and the dregs of my private life are being disinterred by the media. *Guilty*, they might as well splash across their mastheads. Sasha has rung me, close to tears, but her voice sounded so far away, and at least here on my island of nightmares, marooned in the midst of this impossible ocean, there are only a hundred or so people, and I can hide away in my bungalow, protected from the furore. As long, of course, as I stay off the Internet. And then hopefully by the time I get home the fuss will have died down, and someone else will have taken over the weary mantel of world notoriety.

Not if Jamie's not found, a voice whispers through the chill artificial breeze of the bedroom. If he's not found it will be an eternal unsolved puzzle, like Lord Lucan, or that estate agent. I will live out my days under the taint of suspicion. I will forever be looking over my shoulder, just in case.

I lie completely still. My stomach is hollow, and yet it feels full of something indescribable. Wakeful hours pass. The sun rises, inevitably, although I don't see it. Instead, I continue to stare up at the fan as it whirrs and circles, pernicious like rumours. At last I get up, open the curtains a slice, peer out to the endless deep sea, look hopelessly for my husband. Dark clouds are ganging up on the blue again today, and fat drops are pock-marking the ocean. I welcome the rain, am glad of the temporary interruption in utopian service. Thunder clatters above me, and I can hear the thudding jungle-drench on the roof. The violence of it is comforting, but still my mind is flighty, can't concentrate. It's the shock of exposure, perhaps. Or is it the effect of a baby, growing inside of me? I would have been happy with a honeymoon baby once, in fact had deliberately been letting nature take its course the last few weeks, but not like this. Never like this.

I go back to bed, in the absence of any other options. I'm tired. I'm bored. I'm racked with neuroses. My fear is as deep as the ocean. Memories flit at the edges of my mind, and I try to hold them back. I refuse to acknowledge them. I shut my eyes, will away the images. I must be like my mother, unbalanced, imagining things. But still the recollections swarm in, as relentless as the returning tide, and they are just so dreadful that I long to get up, run across my terrace and onto the beach, swim out into the waves, and, like my husband, never ever come back.

It did not happen.

Or did it?

46

A week or so earlier

When Jemma first woke up she wondered where she was, and she felt hot and confused, and momentarily fearful, as if there were a murderer lurking. And then she heard the soft rasps of her new husband's snores, and she remembered. She remembered the church, and the vicar, and the photos, and the reception, and the speeches – the excruciating nature of the speeches – and she recalled trying to smile herself out of it, as though, if she smiled hard enough, the feelings of remorse would go away. Jamie had got drunk, and she'd got near-suicidal, but she'd smiled and she'd smiled and she'd smiled, like the damned villain she was, and now the whole of her jaw ached and her head was pounding from the sustained effort. She would have congratulated herself on her acting skills, if the situation hadn't been so nightmarish.

Jemma managed to creep out of bed without Jamie stirring, and the sheets were so crisp and yet soft, and the thread count must have been sky-high, and she should have been the happiest girl in the world and the fact that she wasn't was an insult to this room, to the very institution of marriage. She tiptoed in her silk nightgown past her wedding dress, which was discarded and inert on the sofa, like a dead person, and she couldn't believe she'd ever worn it. Its bodice was stiff and its skirts were foamy, and it was an interloper, an imposter. She continued on to the bathroom, turned the key in the lock, and then sank down onto the black-and-white tiled floor, her back against the door. She stared at her pale bare legs, the muted pattern of their freckles, and she put her head on her knees and tried to calm the feelings of panic and confusion. She longed to go for a swim or a bike ride, clear her head, but she knew that she couldn't. She couldn't exit this room alone, not without Jamie. She might bump into someone, even at this hour. People would ask her what she was doing, where her husband was.

Jemma shifted her weight, and her bones crunched against the tiles. Did Jamie know how tormented she felt? She was pretty sure he didn't, and the way she'd fallen into bed last night, pretending to be as drunk as he was, she thought she'd got away with it. And anyway, apparently no-one had sex on their wedding night. Sasha had told her, and Sasha knew everything.

There was a knock on the door. 'Jemma,' Jamie said. 'Are you in there?'

'Oh, yes, sorry,' she said. She sprang silently to her feet and tiptoed across the room to flush the toilet. As she needlessly washed her hands at the art deco basin she called out for him to hang on, and when she finally opened the door she was so fraught her heart felt as though it might explode out of her chest, like a Tom-and-Jerry comedy clock on a spring.

Jamie swept past her into the bathroom, naked, looking rough, his broken-straw hair cute and mussy. He came within half an inch of his wife, but their skin didn't quite touch. She sleepwalked across to sit on the edge of the bed, unsure what to do. If she got back under the duvet he might get in too and try to have sex with her. If she perched on the edge he'd know something was wrong. She wanted to absent herself, and be regenerated somewhere else. What could she do? Should she tell him how she was feeling? *No.* Not now.

Jemma stared at her hands, at the shiny, winking ring. Perhaps these feelings would pass. Maybe she just needed to give it time. She felt so confused and exhausted that she got into the bed, after all. She hugged the duvet to her. She waited. She heard the sound of the toilet flushing, and then Jamie brushing his teeth, and she knew that was a bad sign. He only brushed his teeth at this time of the morning if he wanted sex, and she pulled the covers tighter to her, as if she were a little girl again, scared of the dark. She tried not to acknowledge that conjugal relations were what was expected of her. The world felt as if it had become unstable, and everything was in the wrong order, and she cared about all the wrong things. Was it possible to keep a thought so tightly bound inside yourself that you could spend ages, years if needed, pretending it wasn't even there? Could she really have deceived herself so assiduously?

Jamie came out of the bathroom. The sight of him without clothes made her feel odd, as though he were a stranger and she was spying on him, and she averted her eyes. He hopped into the bed, shuffled over, took her in his arms. Jemma buried her head into his shoulder and it felt OK. Her panic subsided a little. Maybe her feelings were entirely normal, after all. Surely she couldn't have been the first ambivalent new bride? Perhaps it's just that no-one ever said it.

'Hmm, you OK?' Jamie said. He ran his hand up her thigh, squeezed her rump, kissed the top of her head.

'I feel a bit sick,' she said.

'Really? Did you drink that much?'

'I don't know,' she said. 'I didn't think so.'

'Poor love.' He tilted Jemma's chin up and she tried to resist but it was too obvious. She looked into his pale-grey eyes, and they lacked something, but she didn't know what.

'Hello, Mrs Armstrong.'

'Hi,' she murmured. Jamie leaned in to kiss her and his breath was minty and beery, and it turned her stomach, although she'd used to love it.

'Jamie,' she said, fighting him off. 'I'm sorry. I . . . I've just got my period.'

His hand was still roving around her upper thighs, but at this he stopped. 'Really?' he said. 'Shit. That's bad timing.'

'Yeah, I know. I'm sorry.' She lay still, willing him to remove his hand completely. She felt so bad for him. She could tell he suspected she was lying, and that she didn't usually mind much, anyway. They were both lost for words. At last Jamie decided to go with it – what choice did he have? – and he moved his arms to encircle her waist, and they lay there together. She rested her head on his chest, and now that the sex issue appeared to have been resolved, at least temporarily, she found it a little easier. And the room *was* lovely: large and luxurious, with grand swags at the windows, which looked out across acres of serene, bucolic parkland scattered with grazing umber deer. When they'd first come here, she'd known immediately it was the place. She'd loved the faded grandeur, the stateliness, the upholstered seats at the windows, where she'd imagined she would sit and look out, swamped by a fluffy white robe, sipping tea, eating biscuits, after hours of hot newly-wed sex, her body clammy and perfumed by her husband. Jemma closed her eyes. She tried to sleep. The desire to push him away was almost animalistic. Jamie's breathing slowed and became heavier, and when he fell back into hungover sleep, the relief was momentarily sharp, like a brief sweep of autumnal sunshine as the clouds split apart. Jemma dared not get up again. It was too early. At last she managed to extricate herself from her sleeping husband's arms, and then she lay there silently, and thought about Dan.

47

Now

My missing husband has been spotted in Colombo. Unfortunately he has also been seen in the bustling streets of Jakarta, deep in the jungle in Venezuela, and, perhaps most improbably, in a service station in Gloucestershire. I suppose it's inevitable that the sightings have started, but it's painful, and I hadn't been prepared for the gut wrench of any proof that it might be true, that he might be out there, walking around, living his life. That he really might have done this on purpose. The comparisons with the Canoe Man are also being made now, and so not only am I a potential murderer, I'm also a possible colluder in the disappearing trick of the century. I have sworn, yet again, that I will stay off the Internet, but in some ways I feel like I should be on top of it, be aware of the latest theories, so I know what the police might accuse me of. It's hard to know what to do.

The British police questioned me for a third time earlier, in the sunny little room in the sanatorium – about Jamie's clothes this time, although we've already gone over and over it. I repeated that the last time I saw him he was wearing salmon shorts, and a white linen shirt, and flip-flops. He wasn't dressed up, even though we were in the à la carte restaurant over the water. He was on a beach holiday, he'd said, not at the sodding Dorchester. I don't know why they had to ask me again. Would he have gone snorkelling in those shorts, they wanted to know. In normal circumstances, no, I'd said – but after our argument, maybe he'd stormed back, grabbed his mask and flippers off the terrace, and plunged into the water. But without his dive torch? *I don't know*, I'd wanted to yell, *you're meant to be the detectives round here*, but of course I hadn't.

Anyway, the upshot appears to be that if Jamie did go snorkelling he must have a) been unable to see anything, and b) done it in the clothes he was wearing that night at dinner, as they haven't been found anywhere either. Or else the mask and snorkel they found on the beach was planted, and he hadn't gone swimming at all – and that theory seems increasingly likely. But who on earth would plant them? And where are his flippers? None of this makes any sense. I've nearly reached breaking point, and I have to be careful in front of the police. Yet the truth is, I'm almost past caring what has happened to my husband, or whether or not I'm pregnant, or how I feel about Dan. All I care about is getting off this infernal island. Now, more than anything else in the whole wide world, I just want to go home.

Dad is struggling with the humidity, and he seems out of place, and older than I remember – and although he tries to hide it, he carries an air of deep sorrow with him. I can't say I blame him. Last time I saw him, he was proudly marrying off his only daughter. Now he's stuck on a desert island with her, having to negotiate untold drama as well as the latest headlines. The *Sun* has excelled itself with the most recent pictures of me, one in which I look as if I'm having a whale of a time lying at the edge of the water, eyes closed, arms flung back in orgasmic release, apparently offering myself to someone. The other shot is one of me and Dan from years ago, arms around each other, at a party, coupled with the headline: 'The bride and the brother – missing groom mystery deepens'. Someone's told them all about my history with Dan, complete with pictures, and I wonder who has betrayed us. I am seriously worried now. The circumstantial evidence against me is mounting. Jamie and I were overtly miserable honeymooners; we'd just had a row; I used to go out with his brother, who incidentally has been caught hugging me on my doorstep; and now there are these latest photographs, where I appear to be luxuriating at the edge of the waves in some kind of insouciant celebration of my husband's disappearance. It's a PR disaster.

A whole week has passed since Jamie went missing, and he and I should have been flying home tomorrow. But instead I'm here on my exquisite terrace with my father, and although I am grateful to him, it still feels so odd. He gets on with his John Grisham, and I try my best to sit still, concentrate on my latest literary endeavour, but I can't focus on a word of it. I give up soon enough and instead practise my yogic breathing for a bit, but that just seems to alarm Dad, so I stop that as well. I can't remember when I last spent any time alone with my father, which is sad, now I come to think about it. Neither of us speaks. We have said everything there is to say. Everything apart from what was really going on in my life.

Finally I capitulate and go back on the Internet. I can't help myself. It terrifies me to discover that Jamie's disappearance is still front-page news, and therefore so am I. I no longer care if anyone thinks he did do it deliberately, or does have a secret bank account, or was sleeping with Camille. At least that means they don't think it's me. It seems Camille's a great actress, though, if he truly has disappeared off to South America with her blessing, as she's been pictured on the street looking distraught, albeit dressed as chicly as ever. I can't work out why I don't hate her.

I lie down on the daybed and close my eyes, feeling weak with apathy and ongoing nausea. It's as if I've reached a place where I'm thinking, *OK, just sock it to me, tell me what's going on.* If Jamie accidentally drowned then that is tragic, but that makes him definitively dead, and although I will always feel terrible about it, at least there's nothing that can be done. But if it turns out that he has absconded, I will be glad. Glad that he's alive, and that I won't need to feel guilty, as he will be the villain of the piece, not me. Yet the most likely outcome is that we'll never know, and the situation is a paralysis, and I don't want to stay here for a single second longer. I am *desperate* to leave. But when will they ever let me? And whose decision even is it? Perhaps I should ask Dad to talk to the British police, who surely need to go home soon too. Haven't they got families, and responsibilities?

Yet here's the rub: I'm too terrified to risk disrupting the catatonic status quo, as I have reached a new stage in this absurd tragedy. Even more than wanting Jamie to come back, or longing to go home, or wanting to know what has happened, or yearning to find out whether or not I am having a baby, I now care about just one thing. More than anything in the world right now, I don't want to get arrested.

48

A week or so earlier

Jamie and Jemma were staying the following night after their wedding at his parents' house, as it was near the airport and Veronica had insisted. On the trip down the motorway the silence in the car was brooding, inescapable. It hummed along with the rubber on tarmac, burred with the strokes of the engine. It needed curtailing.

'Can we put the radio on?' Jemma said.

'Sure,' Jamie replied. Jemma pressed the button and Taylor Swift burst through the speakers, telling them to shake it off, and Jemma wanted to laugh. She wanted to laugh hysterically at the predicament she and Jamie found themselves in.

'I'm sorry about being so quiet,' she said. 'I think I'm just a bit hungover still.'

'That's all right,' he said. It seemed he had greater powers of forgiveness than she'd ever had. He put his hand on her knee, and his fingers felt as if they had electricity running through them. It was only when the motorway took a slight leftward turn, and Jamie put both hands back on the steering wheel, that she felt able to breathe again.

'Are you nervous about flying?' he asked.

She gave a little laugh. 'No, that's you, Jamie, not me. I'm . . . I'm fine. I think I'm just exhausted.'

'Well, you're certainly not yourself. Normally you never shut up.' He was trying to be jokey, but it came out like a reproach, and a rude one at that. How had they become such strangers? How had they got married yesterday?

Jemma rested her head against the passenger window, and her heartbeat rose through her head and thudded into the hard, unforgiving glass, and she thought of prisons, made of crystal, and sledgehammers. She shut her eyes. The adverts were playing now, and Jemma wished they'd shut up, but even though they were terrible, they were better than the silence. Anything was better than this silence. Her breath still couldn't escape her body properly, and it felt like she was being inflated, as if there wasn't enough space in the car for all the air in her lungs, and she couldn't let it out anyway, and that soon her skin would be pressing against hot metal and cold glass, expanding, ever expanding, as she puffed up like Veruca Salt, or was it Augustus Gloop? She yearned to explode her way out of her husband's smooth-pistoned, leather-seated BMW like a flesh-and-bone bomb, and be free.

When they finally arrived at his parents' horrid upside-down house Veronica made such a fuss over Jemma, anyone would think she hadn't seen her daughter-in-law in months, instead of this morning at breakfast. And then she told Jemma that she looked ill and should go and have a lie-down. When Jemma demurred, Veronica proceeded to ignore her, talking to Jamie as if Jemma wasn't even there. It was peculiar, and Jemma even wondered whether Veronica had some kind of personality disorder. She shuddered at what effect such a mother must have had on her children. In Veronica's eyes, her sons were her golden boys. Her boys could do no wrong. Her boys always got what they wanted. Perhaps that was why Jamie had always been so uber-confident – not because his mother had instilled in him a healthy sense of self-esteem, but because she'd given him an unedifying sense of entitlement. Jemma couldn't believe she hadn't seen it before.

Jemma finally made her excuses and went to her room, after all. She was too scared to ring anyone. She was desperate to ring someone. Her phone burnt a hole in her hand. She stared at it and willed it to dial. She almost asked Siri. But who could she call? She thought of her mother's ashes, at home on the mantelpiece. She didn't want to upset her dad. There was only one person she wanted to talk to, but she couldn't do it here. She couldn't ring Dan, ask him to come and rescue her, not here in his parents' house. She'd married his brother. It was too late.

49

Now

It's night, and a bird squawks, and I can't sleep. I get up, go to the toilet, but the absence of blood still is like a harbinger. I scrub, to be certain.

They have finally called off the search. It seems I'll be going home soon, but without Jamie. The unimaginable really is happening. I will be going back to a different life. One without a husband. A new life, of notoriety and suspicion and doubt. I lie still, on my back, and I imagine I can feel a baby kicking, but that's ridiculous; it would be far too early, even if there is one. As soon as I get home, I will take a test, and I'm still not sure what it will say. Maybe my failure to menstruate, my near-constant nausea, is simply due to this horrific situation. But whatever the reason, I can barely face even eating now, no matter how delicious the food that's delivered to me. Chati doesn't seem to mind, though. Sometimes he just waits quietly, as I pick at his offerings, and we don't need to say anything to each other. His assiduousness helps somehow. His kindness is like balm. And besides, feeding someone is the most primal response to grief that there is. Maybe that's why people deliver lasagnes to bereaved people. Or even why babies cry to be fed: their hungry wails make the mother feel too bad not to oblige, and I have to say it's an ingenious survival mechanism. The thought makes me picture a baby growing inside of me again, and I'm pretty certain I need to be strong.

I get up again, visit the bathroom again, lie back down again. I have endured so many hours here in this room, there on that terrace, but now it seems I really can't bear these last several. It feels like I may as well be in an actual cage, with strong, thick bars and a giant, gleaming padlock. I put my hands on my stomach and breathe, and I feel my gut balloon up, and down, up, and down. I'm hopefully leaving, at last. But going home to who? To what? Nothing matters.

Eventually I drift off into a beautiful, luscious sleep, and I am so grateful to the universe, for allowing me this respite, this escape from the nightmare. I can feel water lapping at my ankles, and then my thighs, and now it's over my head, and I am fighting it, I am fighting so hard, but it's so strong, and the waves are like arms. And now I'm fighting Jamie, and we are thrashing about in the sea, and he tells me I'm drunk, and a nightmare, and I fucking hate him, I hate him more than the worst corner of my memories. I wish so desperately that I wasn't here, here with him. I wish he would just fuck off and go away, and I tell him so. I shriek it as loudly as I can, such is my hysteria – and now I can hardly breathe, and I am drowning, I'm drowning, *I am going to drown.* And then, suddenly, it is quiet, and the sea is calm, and I walk out of the water and my dress is sopping and my eyes are stinging and so I screw them up as tight as I can, and when I open them again I am in bed, and I am going home soon, and I am burning a fever that's soaking into the sheets . . . and at last, at long last, I remember.

50

A week or so earlier

The dog was looping through the grass, backwards and forwards, in and out, sniffing, ever sniffing, and just watching him run exhausted Jemma. She'd said she wanted to get some fresh air, and apparently Samson had needed a walk, and so she'd offered to take him, just for twenty minutes or so. Jamie hardly ever went with her, indifferent to both dogs and country walks, so it hadn't seemed too odd that she'd gone alone. Veronica had still given Jemma one of her looks, though, and it had frightened the life out of her, even more so than usual.

Jemma soon reached the other side of the meadow, and instead of continuing along the public footpath towards the village, she skulked along the hedgerow until she found an opening into the field beyond. Only once she was certain that no-one could see her did she take out her mobile. She wasn't one hundred per cent sure who she was going to ring until she did it. She handled the phone as if it were a grenade.

'Hello.' His voice was dull, muffled.

'It's me.'

'I know it's you. What are you ringing me for?'

'Dan . . . I've made a mistake.'

'What do you mean?'

'I shouldn't have married Jamie.'

Silence.

'Well, it's a bit late for that.'

'I don't know what to do.' Jemma could hear her voice crack.

There was more silence. And then there was muffling and scuffling. She hunched into her coat, the phone clamped to her ear.

'Dan?'

'Yes?'

'What should I do?'

'Jemma, I have no idea. Where are you?'

'Walking Samson.'

'Where's Jamie?'

'At the house.'

'Jemma, I'm sorry, but you've made your bed. What you do now is up to you.'

'Please . . . Dan . . .' She was shocked at how hostile he sounded, and she didn't know why she'd rung him. It seemed there was no point bringing up their last conversation.

'Jemma, please. Leave me alone. I'm sorry, but I can't talk any more.'

'But . . .'

'*No*, Jemma. You made your decision. Go on your honeymoon. Enjoy it. Bye.'

Jemma stared at the phone after the call cut out, and then she dropped it into the coarse winter grass and hid her head in her hands. She was so confused. She longed to confide in someone, but it felt too disloyal. *What, more disloyal than calling Dan?* She ignored the thought.

Jemma gave herself a few moments to grieve for the life she might have had, for the mistakes of her past, before forcing herself to confront what she'd done. It seemed she'd got everything wrong, and she needed to fix it, as soon as possible. She bent down and picked up her mobile, looked up the definition of annulment. When she was finished, she cleared her phone's history.

Jemma always felt better once she had a plan. She just needed to get on with it now. She broke into a run, the dog chasing after her, snapping viciously at her heels, like its owner. When she couldn't run any more, she threw herself into the long scratchy grass and lay on her back, panting. She stared up at the sky, at the capricious clouds. Ever changing, ever shifting, like life. Samson came and sniffed at her, bemused now. What should she do? Didn't she *love* Jamie?

Or did she love Dan still?

Jemma put her finger in the air and drew patterns in the sky. She tried to shut out the cacophony of other people's opinions, tried to access how she really felt. She found she didn't know. But the Maldives were booked and paid for. They were meant to be flying in the morning. Jamie needed her to hold his hand at take-off.

What should she do?

At last Jemma's mind started to clear. Maybe this was all simply a blip, and she had to forget about the last couple of days, forget that she'd ever spoken to Dan. She wondered how he could have been so coolly dispassionate on the phone just now. It had felt almost cruel.

Finally Jemma stood up and brushed herself off. She called Samson, ruffled his shaggy, oversized head as she put on his lead, and started walking again, more calmly now. By the time she'd reached the lane, she'd made up her mind. Who knew what might happen between her and Jamie in the future – but she'd married him, and so for now she owed it to him to at least give it a try. Yes, she decided, she would go with Jamie to the Maldives, would do that for him. She would do her best to act like a honeymooner, try to forget about the past all over again – do her utmost to make their brand-new marriage work.

PART THREE
The Honeymoon

51

Jemma

The airport was crowded, and Terminal Four had that hemmed-in atmosphere, where the lines were long and people were bottling up their stress and frustration at the thought of flying through thin air, or of having to take off shoes and belts and bracelets as they were herded through beeping machines that undressed passengers' souls and pried into the secret pockets of their lives. Jemma's sunhat had a length of fine metal wire that ran the perimeter of the brim, keeping its shape – but it had come loose and the end was protruding through the straw, and she reckoned that, if she so chose, she could pretty easily poke a crew member in the eye with it, really cause some damage. The hat was airily waved through, of course, although she had to put her nearly empty lip gloss in a transparent plastic bag so they could take a look at it, in case she was planning on using it to blow up the plane. On the plane itself she could put her can of Coke under her jumper and disappear into the toilet and crush it under her heel to fashion a sharp, lethal edge from the busted red-and-silver metal . . . but still she had to show the security guards her oh-so-dangerous mascara wand. The whole world has gone mad, she thought, it wasn't just her.

Jemma offered to meet Jamie at the gate as usual, just so she could get away from him for a bit, but he said he was happy to come with her. As they wandered about, she had no interest in the airport shops, or in buying a magazine, or grabbing a coffee, and she was sure that Jamie had noticed. Yet no matter how much she'd resolved yesterday to kick-start her heart, re-energize her feelings for her husband, it simply wasn't working. Her tongue felt hoary in her mouth, furred up. Her feet were dragging. Their lives together stretched before them like hell. The travellator dumped them at the gate, and Jemma found a single seat where she sat and stared into space. Jamie disappeared off, and she was glad. This wordless antipathy felt far worse than their normal fights at the airport. Jemma was wrestling with dark, bitter thoughts that were surely alien to a love-flushed new bride, and it made her wonder what she might be capable of.

The waiting was interminable. She played aimlessly on her phone, darting through headlines, raising an eyebrow at celebrity outfits, reading about breakups and murders and bombings. All there, in the palm of her hand, to further poison her mind. At least in the air she'd be free of the world. The latest depressing news wouldn't be able to reach her high in the sky. Instead, she would be stuck up there with her husband beside her, and the thought was so oppressive she could feel the pressure building in her heart, and she really thought she might implode, fall in on herself.

'Jemma,' said Jamie as he sat down beside her, taking the place of the impatient-looking man who had just got up to start queuing to board already, as though that would get him to his destination quicker. He took her hand. 'What's wrong, darling?'

She couldn't look at him. 'I just don't feel well, Jamie, that's all. I'm sorry.'

'Normally I'm the one who can't cope with flying.' He laughed. And then she understood. He hadn't noticed her mood after all. He had an ego the size of his mother's, and he didn't know.

It still wasn't too late for this to be over. She could just walk up to the gate staff and tell them that she'd changed her mind, that she couldn't board after all. But were you even allowed to do that these days? Jemma wasn't sure. It was as if a thick mist had descended, had turned her feelings to fog, her heart to a half-life. She longed to do the right thing, for her, for Jamie, who didn't deserve this. She wasn't sure about anything any more. The announcement for boarding intruded into the mayhem in her brain, and it was only as she stood up that she definitely knew what to do. She moved with Jamie along the snaking queue quite steadily now, her mind calming. After all, they were on their way to paradise. Surely that would fix it.

52

Jemma

'Wow, this is *amazing*,' said Jamie. They had just been shown into their bungalow, which was beyond gorgeous, set back from a beach that was like those you only saw in brochures. They were standing in the magnificent bathroom, the pictures of which hadn't been able to do it justice. Jamie had taken off his shoes and shirt and was in just his jeans. Jemma stared down at the floor, as timid as a child. His toes were attractive, she'd give him that.

Jemma felt ambivalent still. Not even being met off the flight in Malé and being treated like royalty had helped her state of mind. And although travelling over the atolls had been unlike anything she'd ever experienced, almost as if she were looking at another universe entirely, it hadn't shifted the feeling of unspecified dread lodged inside her. In fact, in a way it had added to it, seeing as it was clear that they were travelling to the middle of absolutely nowhere. As they'd flown over all the tiny islands, Jemma had thought they looked like green fried eggs, swimming in a sea of turquoise oil, and that had reminded her of the Dr Seuss books her mum used to read to her, which had made her even more sad. But, on the plus side, at least Jamie's terror had rendered him apparently oblivious to how his new wife was feeling, and she knew it would take nothing short of tranquilizers to get him back on the seaplane to go home again.

The sick tinge to Jamie's face was fading at last. He put his arms loosely around her waist, but that made her feel uncomfortable. He didn't seem to notice the bleak look on her face. He glanced over at their plunge pool. 'Fancy a dip?'

Jemma wasn't quite sure of his motivation, but she couldn't risk it. 'Sure,' she replied, gently detaching herself and moving towards her suitcase. 'Just not that kind of dip, though. I've got my period, remember.'

Jamie looked crestfallen, for just a moment, and although sex was probably not what he'd meant at all, she felt bad for pulling away from him. She was pulling away in a way he wasn't used to, and it seemed the yin and yang of their relationship was confounding him. Where had needy Jemma gone, who flew into a rage the minute she felt rejected? Where was the girl he'd thought he was marrying, who'd adored him, had been desperate to be his wife? Where was the girl he'd last seen three nights ago? Neither of them had a clue.

As Jemma entered the pool, she was sure Jamie knew she was lying, and the atmosphere between them was quiet, stilted somehow. Afterwards he was silent as he dressed, in beige shorts and a linen shirt, and Jemma liked his outfit, liked his stubble. She liked the way his skin furrowed on his forehead when he smiled. Yet it seemed it had been a mistake to come, after all, and she knew she must be careful. They might be married, but she still hadn't slept with him, and as long as that remained the case Jemma knew that all was not lost — and that at least she still had options.

53

Chrissy

Chrissy stood waist-deep in the sea and carefully dunked her face into the water, into a magical world full of flashes of silver and relaxed flaunty colours and undulating waves of tiny fish darting between the bigger ones – and it was like nothing she'd ever seen before. She stood up straight again and looked around. Kenny was just coming up for air, and he looked comical with his mask on, and she wondered if she looked as silly. He waved at her.

'Come out here,' he yelled. 'It's amazing.'

Chrissy shook her head. She didn't like the idea of getting out of her depth, or of getting her hair wet.

'Later,' she called. 'When I get some Dutch courage.' As she sashayed out of the water she knew Kenny was watching her, so she wiggled a bit more than usual, just for effect. She dried herself off with a huge, soft towel and then lay down on her splendidly comfortable sun lounger. A misting green cocktail was on the table next to her, glinting in the sunshine, and she downed it, almost in one go. She stretched luxuriously. Five minutes passed.

'Are you coming back in, love?' Kenny called from the water.

'No, not yet,' she said. She wiggled her toes. 'This is far too nice.'

'It's like a bloody aquarium in here. It's unreal.'

Chrissy smiled and picked up her paperback. She'd imagined nothing better than this. A good book. Sunshine. Drinks on tap. Their own private bit of the white sandy beach. Palm trees. It was heaven. And Kenny might behave like an overgrown toddler at times, but it was endearing, and at least with the kayaks and the boat trips and the snorkelling there would be enough to keep him entertained while she relaxed. And then, at night, they could have dinner in the restaurant over the water, and wander home through the palm groves, and sit outside drinking cocktails on the terrace, before tangling between the cool silk sheets, and the world was really quite wonderful. And *so what* if the other guests looked down on them – they were just snobs. She and Kenny had as much right to be here as anyone. Kenny had done well for himself in the City, and Chrissy was proud of him. And even if she still wasn't sure exactly what he did there, no-one at this resort needed to know that. They had nothing to be ashamed of.

Chrissy watched as Kenny pulled off his mask and waded out of the water, and she admired how hunky he looked as he strode up the beach towards her. He grinned as he shook himself over her, like a naughty puppy.

'Aaagh,' Chrissy yelled. 'Gerroff.'

Kenny ignored her and put his hand on her waist, and when he kissed her, he tasted of the sea. His nose was freckly and his eyes were bright, the pupils reduced to mere pinpricks.

'I bloody love it here,' he said. 'I wish we never had to leave.'

Chrissy laughed. 'We've only just got here,' she said. 'I'm sure you'll get fed up. Give it a few days, and we'll be like them.' A couple were wandering by, and they looked so bored and despondent it was noticeable. The girl was walking on the edge of the water, and her feet were sinking into the soft, saturated sand. Her partner walked further away from the water, just ahead of her, his arms crossed, his expression grim. Chrissy wondered what was wrong. She wouldn't waste time here being miserable, what was the point? Make the most of life, that was her motto. You never knew when happiness was going to be snatched away from you.

Kenny plonked himself onto the sun lounger next to her. He stretched his arms over his head, flexed his toes and let out a sigh of satisfaction.

'This place is wicked,' he said.

'Hmmm,' said Chrissy, back in the grip of her book, the truth of the protagonists' deteriorating marriage unfolding before her, word after word. It wasn't really a honeymoon read, and the irony made her smile.

'They're in the next-door bungalow,' Kenny said, after a little while, having busied himself with applying more sun cream, flicking sand, studying the cocktail menu, adjusting the umbrella angle.

'Who?'

'Mr and Mrs Miseryguts.'

'That's not very nice.'

'Ha, you were the one who said it, you hypocrite.'

'How d'you know, anyway?' she said.

'Maybe because I just saw them go in there. Doh.' He sat up and tickled her under the chin.

'Kenny,' she said. She giggled, but in truth he was annoying her now. Did he ever sit still? Maybe she'd get him to go and order her another drink.

Kenny stood up once more and walked down to the edge of the sea, and he looked pale against the sand. She should have made him go on a sun bed before they came. He needed to be careful – this sun was so strong, and he was getting burnt already. As he started humming an unknown song her skin prickled. Being here felt almost *too* perfect, as though there was something that was bound to spoil it, and she hoped it wasn't going to be her brand-new husband. She suddenly wished he'd just bugger off, so she could lie on the beach, reading her book, with no-one bothering her.

'Chrissy, I'm hungry,' Kenny said, as he came back and sat down. 'Shall we go and get lunch?'

Chrissy demurred, saying she wanted to finish her chapter, and so he picked up a magazine and carried on humming. A few minutes later, he leaned over and took her hand, rotated her wedding ring as he stared into her eyes, and it was a little disconcerting. She knew she needed to be careful. Kenny wasn't a man who liked to be kept waiting, even on holiday. She reminded herself how lucky she was, here on honeymoon in the Maldives, with her successful banker husband – and when he asked her again if she fancied some lunch, she knew better than to refuse him.

'Oh, all right, babe,' she said, with a smile. She stood up, put on the teeniest pair of shorts over her bikini bottoms, and then she let him take her hand and lead her along the beach, past the other bungalows, towards the infinity pool, and the bar, and lunch.

54

Jemma

Jemma gave up on the beach bar's lunch menu and made do with just a cocktail, too stressed to even think about eating. She was glad they'd booked a boat trip for the next morning. It would be a distraction from just lying around, having to pretend to be enjoying herself.

'Psst, there they are again,' said Jamie now. His voice seemed to carry across the calm slick of the pool to further around the bar, where a couple were sitting, leaning into each other, flirting, drinking cocktails.

'Shush! You are so indiscreet.'

'There's enough gold on them to sink a ship.'

'*Shush*, Jamie.' Jamie looked a little hurt at her tone. 'Sorry, I just don't want them to hear us slagging them off.'

'They can't hear, Jemma. What's got into you?' Jamie took an exaggeratedly long swig of his beer as Jemma picked up the menu again and hid behind it.

A Chinese couple entered the bar area and sat down at one of the tables beside the pool. They were young and the woman was pretty, slender as a teenager, dressed like a little girl at a party, with alabaster skin and flowers in her hair. Her partner was earnest-looking, bespectacled, and even in just swim-shorts and a T-shirt, his overall look was pristine, and expensive. They sat opposite each other in the wide wicker chairs, placed their iPhones on the table, and proceeded to stare silently at them, and occasionally prod them. Another couple were in the infinity pool in matching rash tops, snorkelling, presumably practising. A faint flurry of air lazed across the water towards them, and the man spanked at the glinting water with his hand, as if the ripples were threatening him. Two more couples were dining together on the other side of the beach bar, and they seemed happy enough, although one pair were perhaps a little too ostentatiously in love, with a good deal of nose-rubbing – as if it were a competition, Jemma thought. It seemed that that was the problem with these couples-only places – it felt like you almost had to put on a performance, and it just augmented her and Jamie's predicament. She looked over at the barman, who was round and chirpy, his frequent smile a brilliant gash below his flared, turned-up nose. He was wearing the resort's uniform of a brown-and-gold flowered shirt (with a prominent name badge announcing that his name, rather improbably, was Arnie), and he was taking the various cocktail orders as if each were a gift, and a pleasure. Jemma watched now as his dark-brown eyes settled briefly on the blonde girl's spectacular cleavage and then shifted away almost immediately, like a caught-out child's.

'D'you want another drink?' said Jamie.

'No, thanks.' Jemma was trying to absent herself, blank out her feelings, and yet still she felt dreadful. She watched Arnie expertly mix the girl another cocktail – a Sex on the Beach this time – but once he'd served it, he turned away from her again, as if he thought she were bad news somehow.

After lunch Jemma and Jamie returned to the beach, in the absence of anything better to do. As Jemma lay down, she felt weird rather than sad, as if she were floating on the top of a mountain, and it added to her feelings of dissociation. She pretended not to notice when the blingy couple walked past and Jamie's eyes lingered on the girl for just a little too long. They looked so happy together, and it made Jemma furious at herself. What had she been thinking? She and Jamie should never have come on this trip; it was just compounding the cataclysm. Jemma picked up her magazine, tried to focus, but she really didn't care what shape autumn coats were set to be, or how to make her lips fuller. She gave up, tried to shut her eyes for a bit, but the sun was too strong on her face. She turned over, lay on her front, but she needed sun cream on, and she couldn't bear to ask Jamie to do it. Finally, after how long she had no idea, Jemma found that she couldn't lie there for a single second longer, and so she leapt up from her sun lounger, careered down the sand and dived into the warm, lapping water, trying to drown out her ever-growing feelings of shame, and bewilderment, and anger.

55

Chrissy

A few hours later, Chrissy was lying in the bath, and she could hear the faint swoosh of the breeze through the trees and the popping of the bubbles in her ears, and above her the stars were winking at her, as if in approval of something. Kenny had wandered down to the beach to look for bioluminescent plankton, whatever that was, and she'd been happy to let him. As she looked about her, she knew she would never take another bath more perfect in her life. She sighed and closed her eyes, and felt herself sinking into a golden well of inner peace and happiness. She'd had three cocktails at lunchtime, plus two lots of co-codamol that she knew she didn't really need, and the buzz was like a very low motor, oiling her heart, her mind, her very being. It was paradise lost, and then found again, and she tried to remember who had written that poem. She knew it was something to do with Adam and Eve, she remembered that much from school, and although everyone had written her off, she'd been brighter than anyone had given her credit for. And she'd certainly known how to make the most of herself – otherwise she wouldn't be here, would she?

She heard the pad of Kenny's footsteps coming back through the bungalow and her mind quickened. She opened her eyes and smiled at her new husband, her mouth glossy and seductive. Kenny leaned over and kissed her, and she put her hand behind his neck and pulled him towards her, and then fully into the bath, and he laughed as water went everywhere, and next he was pulling her up and out, and dragging her, giggling, into the plunge pool, where there was more room, and she felt swept away on a tide of pills and passion and Pina Coladas, and afterwards they lay down on the bed and did it again, and she liked the feeling of his bulk on her, pinning her down . . . and then they showered and got dressed and went for dinner.

56

Jemma

The sky was ever darkening as Jemma's honeymoon edged further towards the abyss. As if things weren't bad enough, she could hear the people next door having sex now. Here she was, on the second evening of her honeymoon, and her misery had metamorphosed into rage. She wanted to stick pins into her husband and make him disappear. She wanted to kill the neighbours. She wanted to tell Moosa, their obsequious butler, that they could walk the two minutes to the restaurant, thank you very much, that they didn't need him to fetch them a golf buggy. It was as if the switch for her feelings for Jamie had been flicked off forever, and now, no matter how hard she tried, she couldn't turn them on again, and it was infecting how she felt about everything. Their honeymoon had the dismal downbeat of a funeral dirge – and surely something would have to happen soon to break the tension.

Jemma flinched on the day-bed as she heard her neighbour squeal again, and it sounded a little affected to her, put on almost. She and Jamie still hadn't consummated their marriage, although he hadn't pressed the point, thank goodness. Last night Chelsea were playing any-way, and he'd got Moosa to come around specially to find the channel, and it was an important match apparently, so that had killed a couple of hours. Today they'd swum and sunbathed and snorkelled at the beach outside their bungalow, and it had been beautiful, but she'd been barely able to sit still. It was ironic that she'd wanted to come to a place like this *because* there was nothing much to do, except be together, enjoy their union. Yet now they were here, it seemed as if the world had been emptied of people and purpose, leaving nothing more than a faux happiness, a mere apparition of paradise. There was something about this island, and Jemma didn't like it. It wasn't just her own circumstances – it felt more sinister than that somehow, and she couldn't work it out.

'Bloody hell,' said Jamie, who thankfully was lying on the other day-bed, although there was room for them both on hers. 'Will she ever shut up?'

'I know, it's just too awful.' This was perhaps the first completely natural exchange they'd had with each other since they'd been married, and to Jemma it felt like a relief. There was nothing like eavesdropping on some-one else's intercourse to lighten the atmosphere. There was a violent rhythmic slapping of water, and then a final squeal of satisfaction, and it was over. The world grew quiet, and large, the blackening sea expanding into the universe, becoming one with the sky. Jemma felt so bad for Jamie, that their honeymoon wasn't the romantic idyll either of them had expected, but at least he seemed to assume it was just her hormones – being perennially histrionic did have some advantages. Jemma still had no idea how to play it. She couldn't decide what she wanted. What was best for him. What was best for her. It was a train wreck.

'Has she got fake boobs?' Jamie said now.

'I'm sorry?'

'The girl next door?'

'Doh! What do you think?'

'Does that mean yes?'

'Well, have you seen anyone else's breasts defy gravity when they're lying on their back?'

'It's odd, isn't it . . . She's attractive, though.'

'Gorgeous,' Jemma said, and she didn't know what had got into her. She used to get so jealous. But maybe it would do her a favour if he did fancy someone else. Make the honeymoon easier to bear, any annulment proceedings easier to arrange, if the regret were mutual.

Jamie huffed as he took a swig of his beer, and she felt guilty again. How could he possibly understand how she was feeling? And besides, this was his *life* at stake. She needed to try harder.

The silence pressed in on them. There was nothing to say. There was no-one around. Even next-door was post-coitally quiet now. Giant bats flew soundlessly above their heads as the last of the daylight receded.

'I think I might go for a bike ride,' she said finally. She nearly asked him if he wanted to come, and then she didn't. It seemed she couldn't try harder, after all.

'Fine.'

Jemma got up and padded across the terrace to the large wooden bucket, which, as ever, was full of clean water. The housekeeping staff appeared to glide around and through the bungalows when the guests weren't looking – topping up the foot-rinsing tubs, sweeping the sandy paths clear of every last leaf, polishing the already-shiny taps, folding away clothes, arranging petals in heart shapes on the beds, replacing the fluffy robes, restocking the minibar. Faking perfection. Jemma could feel Jamie's eyes boring into her back as she bent over and poured. His mood felt unstable, as though he wasn't quite sure which way it would go, how he would handle her. A shimmer of disquiet skimmed through her as he followed her into the bungalow and watched her put on her running shoes. She didn't like to run here. No-one ran. This was a place for relaxing, not running. But she could cycle, thank goodness, and the tyres of her bike were fat and soft as they squished through the sandy trails between the coconut trees, and at least it was one thing she enjoyed doing here.

'Where are you going?' Jamie asked.

'Just across the island,' she said. 'I need to get some air.'

'It's dark.'

'It's fine, the paths are lit.'

'Are you going to the dive centre?'

'Of course not. It'll be shut anyway. Why?'

'Just wondered.'

Jemma didn't answer.

'What are we doing for dinner?' he said.

'Shall we go to the buffet?'

'Yeah, great.' His tone was hostile, not that she could blame him.

'Well, I don't know, Jamie. What do you want to do?'

Jamie gave Jemma a look of disgust, and she knew she deserved it. She needed to get her head straight. Maybe they should have it out, and then arrange to fly home tomorrow.

'I'm sorry, Jamie,' she said. 'I won't be long.' She walked out through the front door and took her bike, which was leaned up against the bungalow, unlocked of course, because there was no crime here, there were no criminals. There was nothing but peace and beauty and sun-kissed perfection, and she loathed it. As she pedalled through the moon-fringed darkness, the swish of the sand was both silky and grating. Once she passed the apex of the island, all three feet of it, the path continued slightly downhill, and it became easier going. Jemma dared herself to leave the brakes alone now, and as the bike picked up speed, it was exhilarating and frightening – and suddenly too much to bear. She slammed on the brakes, far too hard, and her back wheel skidded sideways through the sand as she crashed off-course through the thickest part of the undergrowth. She only spotted the brown and gold of a resort staff shirt, the stricken face above it, too late. The face twisted with pain as she made contact.

'Owww, sorry. Sorry sorry sorry,' Jemma said, over and over, as if it were a verbal tic.

'Are you all right, ma'am?' the man said. His voice was muffled. Her knee was bleeding, and he was doubled over in obvious agony. Jemma was mortified.

'I'm so sorry, I was just taking a shortcut,' she said, and they both laughed, but she knew it wasn't funny. She recognized him as one of the staff from the buffet, and although usually he was cheerful, his face wore more of a grimace right now. Yet he was as polite as everyone else who worked here, and he helped dust her down and then insisted on wheeling her bike to the dive centre, where a golf buggy miraculously was waiting to whisk Jemma back to her husband, who was stewing alone in their beautiful bungalow, on the other side of this idyllic tainted island.

57

Chrissy

The boat was large and wooden, traditional in style, with a wide, shallow belly and a covered roof. There were only eight people on the trip, although there was space to fit five times that. The sky was unabridged in its blueness, and when they first headed out across the calm cobalt sea towards a reef where the coral breathed and the turtles swam, Chrissy tried to remember a time in her life when things had felt as clear and pure, and she couldn't. The sea breeze was cool and comforting, a welcome antidote to the fierceness of the sun, which was high in the sky and all-powerful already.

Chrissy was lying on top of the flat roof of the boat, with Kenny sitting beside her, taking hundreds of photos, which she was sure would be fantastic but would undoubtedly all look the same. As she'd climbed the steep steps, Chrissy had felt more pairs of eyes on her than just her husband's, and it gave her a guilty thrill of pleasure, that she had this effect on people. The apparently joyless couple were on the trip with them, plus another obviously English pair who were assiduous in their coupledom, and although they'd all nodded at each other, no-one had attempted to strike up any kind of conversation. In the end she'd suggested to Kenny that they go up on the roof, and sod everyone if they were going to be snooty. One of the Chinese couples was also on the trip, dressed in matching Lycra suits which reminded Chrissy of flies, or those people that get flung at a Velcro wall for some unfathomable reason. But, she thought pragmatically, good for them – at least there was no risk of them getting sunburn – and she'd given them her biggest, most friendly smile, which seemed to have frightened the life out of them.

As the boat headed further out, the waves gradually increased in size, and the sea got bluer and darker, like a developing bruise, but still the swell was just about gentle enough not to break. The boat bumped rhythmically beneath them as Chrissy watched the island getting ever smaller, and it became even more stunning to her the further they travelled, unveiling itself as tantalizingly as a stripper. The wooden jetty, the shipwreck beach, the tasteful resort sign that blended in with the land: ultimate luxury in tune with nature rather than discordant with it. The fringes of palm trees. Glimpses of the little bungalows nestling in amongst them, hiding luxurious open-air bathrooms surrounded by bush. The other houses on stilts over the water. It was like a pretend life, a world away from her former one, growing up on one of the worst estates in Chelmsford.

'You gonna be all right snorkelling, Chrissy?' said

Kenny, squeezing her leg. 'You have done it before, haven't you?'

'Once,' she said. She regretted now that she hadn't practised more at the beach first, but she'd been feeling a bit merry when they'd booked the trip, and the resort's marine biologist had been very persuasive. 'I'll be all right,' she said to her husband. 'It's much easier with an instructor.' *Especially one like him*, Chrissy thought privately, admiring Pascal's slim snake hips and naked brown chest – who knew that half-wearing a wetsuit could be so sexy? She would never have admitted to Kenny just what had changed her mind, but, she'd figured, you couldn't come all the way to the Maldives and not at least give snorkelling a go.

Kenny lay down next to her and moved his hand further up her thigh. As the boat heaved beneath them, she closed her eyes and tried to imagine another twenty years of this, and she couldn't for some reason. One day at a time, she told herself. She loved Kenny, she was sure of it, and yet there was something that held her back from him sometimes, and it wasn't just his infuriatingly puppy-like nature. They might be married, but she didn't know him yet. How long did it take to really, properly *know* someone? At what stage in your relationship did your husband still have the potential to surprise you? Or betray you?

Chrissy had already taken four co-codamol this morning, for courage, she'd told herself, but now the gentle buzz was fading, to be replaced with a deep-gutted anxiety. She was sure it was nothing to do with Kenny, though. It must be her fear of the water, of the fish, of what lay beneath. It also didn't help that they were in the middle of absolutely nowhere, their tiny island as insignificant as a cork in a reservoir. She recalled the Boxing Day tsunami – hadn't that reached here? Hadn't it wiped out half the resorts? No wonder, she thought. From the boat even the island itself alarmed her now. It looked so small, insignificant, floating and fragile – just a tiny, flat, bright-green circle, ringed with white. If a rogue wave came, there would be no high ground to flee to. *They'd all die.*

'You've gone a bit pale, love,' said Kenny.

'Hmm,' said Chrissy, not trusting herself to say anything else. She leaned into him, and as he shifted to put his burly, tattooed arm around her, she tried to ignore the movement of the waves and her frantic imaginings of a giant swell sweeping across the ocean and snuffing them out, piled on top of her fear of the fish, the sharks, the snorkelling. Blimey. It hadn't occurred to her that she'd be frightened of *everything* here. Trepidation was rising in her mouth, and the taste was briny, as if she were drowning already.

At last the boat stopped, above a majestic coral garden according to Pascal, although the water looked exactly the same to Chrissy here as everywhere else. As she struggled down the near-vertical ladder from the roof, her mind was stalling and her knees were shaking, and she wished she could go back to the relative solidity of the island, have a drink.

'All right,' said Pascal, and the sexy lilt of his accent had absolutely no effect on her now. 'Please put on your masks and flippers.' He'd pulled up his wetsuit and zipped it up, and he looked smaller, lithe and slippery. As he went through the safety briefing, he kept his eyes firmly away from Chrissy, who was oozing out of her life vest, and his lack of attention made her even more nervous. When he was finished, Pascal put on his mask, stepped onto the boat's running board, gave a thumbs up, and plunged backwards into the water. The sulky English girl was the first to follow, sprawling spread-legged, her flippers awry, and then her husband jumped, and as Chrissy watched the two of them flailing in the deep, dark water, trying to adjust their masks, she realized that she could not, would not, do this.

'Go on, babe,' said Kenny. 'After you.'

'Kenny, I can't.'

'Of course you can. I'll stay with you.'

'Aren't there sharks here?'

'No, don't be daft. It's safe.'

'What if I lose everyone? What if I drift away from the boat?'

'You won't. I'll stay with you.'

'He said some fish have teeth, they might bite us.'

'No, they won't.'

'They will. He said.'

'Chrissy,' called Pascal, from the water. 'Get in.'

'No. I can't.'

'Chrissy,' he repeated. 'Come in, please.'

'You go,' Kenny said to the Chinese couple, who were standing patiently behind them. In her head Chrissy could see their faces under water already, panic-stricken, ingesting the sea. *No.* She wasn't going to do it, she didn't care what anyone said.

'Sorry, Kenny,' she said. 'You go without me. I'm happy to wait here, honest.'

Kenny looked agitated, unsure what to do.

'I'll be fine, babe,' she said. 'Please.'

Pascal beckoned them again, and he sounded impatient now. The boat's crew looked on anxiously, murmuring to each other in Maldivian.

'OK,' Kenny said. 'As long as you're sure, love. We'll get you a lesson at the beach – that's what we should have done in the first place anyway. Don't you worry.' He kissed her, causing his mask to bang into hers, and then he stepped onto the running board of the boat, and jumped.

Kenny survived. Everyone survived. Chrissy felt foolish. But that was then. Now, it was later the same afternoon, and Chrissy had bounced right back. She was currently standing at the edge of the hotel pool, ostentatiously adjusting her bikini bottoms, enjoying the glances. Her feet felt strong and rooted on the smooth hot concrete, and it made her realize just how hysterical she'd been being earlier. Fair enough, she hadn't liked being out at sea, but the island itself was solid, A-list, perfectly safe. It certainly wasn't sinking, at least not any time in the next week or so. Tsunamis only happened once in a lifetime. No-one had died of a shark attack in years. (That means someone had once, she'd said to Kenny afterwards, in self-justification.) Turtles didn't hurt you. But so what, Chrissy thought now – it was her life. She didn't have to go in the sea at all if she didn't want to. No-one could force her. The resort pool, plus the one in their bathroom, would be quite adequate for her swimming needs. And although she was embarrassed now of the fuss she'd made earlier, she really hadn't been able to help hyperventilating like that, not once Kenny had left her – and it *had* felt nice when Pascal had climbed back into the boat and held her in his slippery arms to calm her down.

The swimming pool ran parallel to the sea, and it was wide, with an infinity edge, and from this angle it looked like an integral part of the ocean. An island of tropical plants, positioned centrally for maximum visual effect, was all that seemed to exist between Chrissy and the horizon. Not only was the view gloriously azure, but, even better, there were most definitely no creatures lurking in here to bite at her ankles, carve out jagged pieces of her flesh. The sun was nicely warm on her skin. She lifted her arms above her head and stretched. She leaned over, touched her toes, gave Arnie, who was passing behind her with a tray-load of cocktails, an eyeful. She stood up again and stuck her toe in. The water was cold. But she was hot, and she needed to wash her hair anyway. Her husband was lolling at the bar on the far side of the pool, and as he swayed in the water, he reminded her of a pink blow-up toy. He really ought to wear more sun cream, she thought, and giggled. Kenny beckoned her, stretched out his brawny arms, and in his left hand he had another cocktail, for her, and it made her love him, love his forgiveness. The world was perfect, would be so forever, now that she'd found her Kenny.

Chrissy bent her knees and sprang up through her toes, into the most graceful of dives. But, as she took off, her right foot slipped and that, plus the cocktails and the pills and the trauma earlier, and perhaps the weight of her new breasts, caused her to get the angle all wrong. As the smooth plane of water slapped her in the face, smashed against her stomach, it was like a rebuke for her happiness. It knocked all the air out of her, so she couldn't catch her breath, even to panic, and as she started sinking to the bottom she could see the irony that she might end up drowning here, where it was safest . . .

Just as she was tempted to succumb, Chrissy felt a firm hand on her arm, pulling her upwards, towing her to the side. When she reached the edge, she laid her face against the lapping water, trying to breathe, quell the stinging in her cheek, ease the leaden throb in her belly. Even through her relief she felt humiliated, again. Everyone had seen. It seemed she couldn't escape being watched, and for all the wrong reasons.

'Chrissy!' Kenny said, as he finally made it over to

her, having swum across from the pool bar. 'That was the best bloody belly flop I've ever seen. Are you all right, sweetheart?'

Chrissy nodded mutely as Kenny and her rescuer hauled her out of the water and helped her onto her sun lounger. As Chrissy took in the girl's sopping clothes and recognized her from the boat trip earlier, her heart sank. 'Oh God, I'm so sorry,' she said. 'I think I owe you one.'

'No, no, it's fine.' The girl stood still for a moment, and her dress was clinging to her taut little body, and the fabric dripped dark pools which spread and opened like wounds in the concrete. Her eyes were cut-outs of the sea. 'You're welcome. Are you OK now?'

'Yeah, I'm all right, thanks. I just feel like a complete pillock – again!'

'No, of course you're not . . .'

'Look, let me get you a drink,' Chrissy said. 'It's the least I can do. I'm Chrissy, by the way.' As she stuck out her hand, she saw the other girl hesitate, for just a moment.

'OK, thanks,' she said, taking Chrissy's proffered hand. 'I'm Jemma.' She took a towel that one of the staff had brought over for her, wrapped it around herself, over the soaking sundress, and sat down on the sun lounger next to Chrissy's. As they started chatting, it seemed to Chrissy that she'd misjudged Jemma. Up close, she wasn't miserable at all – instead she was sweetly sparky, kitten-like, and her hair glowed like the tail end of sunset.

'Anyway, cheers, Jemma,' Chrissy said, clinking their glasses together, after good old Arnie had fast-tracked a couple of Mojitos. 'Nice to meet you.'

'And you,' said her new friend. 'Thanks so much for saving me.' And at the time, Chrissy thought Jemma had got it the wrong way round by accident.

58

Jemma

Chrissy and Jemma sat by the pool for a while longer, and it felt such a relief for Jemma to have someone else to talk to. After her second cocktail, she was even tempted to tell Chrissy all about her marital woes, but she stopped herself. It was nobody's business but hers and Jamie's, and even if *she'd* be quite happy to be open about the whole sorry tale, it certainly wouldn't be fair on him.

Jemma wondered where Jamie was. He'd said he was going back to the bungalow to get a long-sleeved T-shirt, but that had been ages ago now. It was fine by her, though; she was having fun at last. When her husband finally returned, his face was sour, and – or was Jemma imagining it? – faintly guilty. The only time his eyes lit up was when he was introduced to Chrissy.

'Where've you been?' Jemma asked.

'Oh, I went to the dive centre,' he said. 'I was thinking of maybe doing a fishing trip later.'

'Oh,' said Jemma. It was clear that she wasn't being invited, although she could hardly blame him. Jamie knew she hated fishing anyway, thought it was cruel.

'Look, Jemma, if you're free, why don't you go for a snorkel with Kenny,' said Chrissy. 'I'm too much of a wuss, and it would stop me feeling so guilty that I'm spoiling his fun.'

'Sure,' said Jemma. 'Is that OK with you, Jamie?'

'Fine,' Jamie said, although he didn't sound it. It was unlike him not to be charming in public, especially around someone like Chrissy. He seemed absent somehow, and yet boiling with indignation beneath the surface, and the combination was unsettling.

'Well, that's all sorted then,' said Chrissy. She lay down on her sun bed, stretched her legs and arched her back as she repositioned her bikini top, the diamond stud in her navel reflecting the sun like some kind of code – and as Jemma turned over to lie on her stomach, she caught Jamie staring at Chrissy, and his expression was inscrutable.

The next morning Jemma got out of bed and went down to the beach in her nightdress. It wasn't even light yet, but she couldn't sleep. The thought of another day here with Jamie was torture. She had cycled myriad times around the island. She had walked from their bungalow along the beach to the bar and back. She had swum in the sea and in the resort pool. She'd been on a boat trip. She had lounged in the bath, and had wallowed in their private plunge pool. She had sunbathed, for at least five minutes at a time. She had visited the gift shop, where a bottle of sun cream cost eighty dollars and the trinkets were the price of a meal out at home. She'd even made some new friends – having rescued Chrissy, been snorkelling with Kenny. She had troughed her way through the buffet, smiled at the eager chefs who waited with their ladles poised like weapons, and who were so keen to please her. She had booked a massage at the beauty spa, although she hated being touched by strangers. She'd drunk enough cocktails to make her want to throw up.

And what of Jamie? Her husband still only needed to get within two metres of her to set her nerves zip-wiring through her body, her teeth clenching and grinding until her jaw ached. If anything, the feeling of oppressive confusion was even worse here than it had been on their wedding day – as if there were a giant magnifying glass on them, refracting heat into them, burning them alive. She wanted to go home, but even the thought of the journey was torture: having to sit next to Jamie on three different flights as he went pale with fright, while she longed to be somewhere else, perhaps with someone else. *How did she feel?* It was impossible to tell, here in this parallel universe. But it was so unfair on Jamie, and the more she tried to pretend she was fine, the more bleak she felt.

There were exactly seven more days to get through, Jemma worked out, as she sat on the beach watching the sky lighten and turn pink. One hundred and sixty-eight hours. She'd definitely go snorkelling again with Kenny, no matter what Jamie said about it.

Snorkelling passed the time. It was one of the few things that helped her feel sane. She would put her head into the clear, pure water and swim with the turtles and the fish and, for a while at least, she would feel free. And then, in a week's time, she would go home, and surely put her ill-fated marriage behind her.

59

Chrissy

Kenny is such a pig, Chrissy thought fondly. He was just coming back from the buffet, and his plate was loaded with a veritable smorgasbord of delights, including various dim sum, some kind of curry, a slice of melon, a sausage, and, rather improbably, a box of Coco Pops.

'I thought I might go snorkelling with Jemma again this morning,' he said, his chair scraping as he sat down. 'You all right with that?'

'Course I am,' Chrissy replied. They were sitting on the side of the restaurant's terrace that was nearest the sea, under the palm trees. She took a sip of her tea. 'I know you prefer her to me anyway.'

Kenny looked uncertain for a second.

'Oh, Kenny, love,' Chrissy said. 'I'm joking. Course I don't mind. Besides, you know I'd rather sit by the pool and read.'

'You sure? It's just that we were talking about swimming round the island.'

'Isn't that dangerous?' said Chrissy. 'And won't it take hours?'

'Nah, it's not that far. It's just the rip we need to watch on the other side, Pascal says.'

'What about Jamie, is he going?'

'Dunno. Don't think so. He's got the hump anyway.'

'That's not very nice.'

'Well, it's true. He's a moody git. Jemma's all right, though.'

'Obviously,' said Chrissy, and a flinch of jealousy stabbed at her, right in the fleshy part of her stomach. She caught herself. It was no big deal. Just because it turned out that she hated snorkelling, it wasn't fair on Kenny to expect him not to do it either. If this went well, perhaps Jemma could entertain Kenny in the sea every morning, and she, Chrissy, could take it easy. Plus she and Kenny still had their siestas in the afternoons to look forward to. It wasn't all bad.

'You sure you'll be all right, Chrissy?' Kenny said now. 'Why don't you treat yourself to a massage or something?'

Was he trying to get rid of her, Chrissy wondered. She studied his face, looked for a sign, but there was none. The bright red of his nose made his eyes look bright and his teeth white and even.

They stared at each other, until Chrissy felt absurdly shy suddenly and dropped her gaze. She kicked him under the table, to ease the tension, and Kenny caught her foot and pressed his own bare one onto the top of it. Grains of sand dug into her skin, and she found that she enjoyed the sensation. Kenny took her hand.

'I love you, Mrs Copthorn. Remember that.'

'I will,' said Chrissy. 'Be careful.'

'I will. I promise.'

60

Jemma

Jemma stood up from the breakfast table and walked over to the buffet, where she could have anything she wanted, but found she wanted nothing. How could there be all this choice, and yet everything left her cold? It reminded her of how hard it was to find something to watch on TV now that there were hundreds of channels. She felt faintly nauseous.

'Are you all right, Jemma?' Jamie said, as he passed her at the dim sum counter. His plate was loaded already. 'Aren't you going to eat anything?'

'Um, yes, I'm just deciding,' she said. She was grateful that he was acting fairly normally today, even if she wasn't. Even though her 'period' was going on forever. Did Jamie realize the extent of how she felt, or did he just think she was having one of her neurotic spells – albeit an unusually long one – towards which he had learned to act fairly indifferently anyway? Or was he too busy enjoying the pool and the buffet and the boat trips to care?

When Jemma got back to the table, she had a single piece of pineapple on her plate. Jamie looked at her, incredulous. 'Is that all you're having?' he said.

'I'm not very hungry.'

'Are you sure you're all right?'

'What do you mean?'

'Well, you just haven't seemed yourself since the wedding.'

Jemma looked at her husband, and she didn't know what to say. The words dammed up again, behind her eyes. It seemed her mini-attempts at affection where it was safe, at the bar, by the pool, hadn't worked. *He knew.* Each night-time had been torturous for her, and surely for him too, and so breakfast was somehow the hardest to pretend over.

'It's cost us a lot of money to come here,' Jamie said. 'So can you please try to start enjoying it a bit more? You were the one who always wanted to come to the Maldives.'

'So, is that what's worrying you?' she said. 'That we're not getting our full value for money?'

'No, I don't mean it like that.'

'Well, what do you mean?' Jemma was aware she was picking a fight, because that was easier than telling him the truth.

'It's just you . . . you seem different. Maybe it's because you haven't got anything to organize here.' He smiled and took her left hand, stared at her wedding ring. She nearly asked him what he thought they should do, but then thought better of it.

'Morning,' said Kenny as he passed their table. His smile was broad but his sunburn looked worse than ever this morning. His muscly arms were blushing furiously beneath his tattoos. His nose was peeling. Jemma returned the greeting, but Jamie barely acknowledged him, which seemed odd to her. What did Jamie have against Kenny? Jemma wondered if it was because they both worked in the City, and perhaps Jamie looked down on what Kenny did. He'd muttered something about it, but Jemma hadn't understood what he was talking about and hadn't bothered asking. The City was the City, wasn't it? High-powered and awash with money. Hadn't that been at least part of Jamie's initial appeal for her?

Out of time, out of nowhere, Jemma pictured herself, drunk on champagne, kissing Jamie in front of Dan, and she felt almost as ashamed now as she had at the time. *Why* had she betrayed Dan like that? And had Jamie only played his part because it meant he had won? Perhaps she'd simply been the prize, the meaningless prize, the bird caught in the jaws of a monstrous sibling rivalry that was bigger than her, and always had been. It sounded too brutal to articulate.

Jamie finished his plateful of food and went up for more. He looked like he hated her now, and maybe that would be easier. The bed was so big, they could pile their luxuriously plumped pillows high like sandbags down the centre, and they could take up position in their respective trenches for the remainder of their time here. Plus annulment was still an option, as long as she continued to avoid her conjugal duties. It seemed that that was the important bit, as far as the law was concerned.

Jemma's mind was unplugging now and the bad stuff was in danger of swilling out, like effluence through a sewer. What had happened to her love for her husband? Where on earth had it gone? It was as if the blindfold was off at last, and it was so disconcerting she almost laughed.

'What's so funny?' Jamie said, as he came back to the table. He was scowling and his presence was like the sun going in. Bobbi, their breakfast waiter, came by with more tea, and Jemma accepted it gratefully. Like all the other waiters, Bobbi was gentle and smiley and he looked after them as though they were family, which seemed to be part of the Maldivian way. Jemma thanked him, and as he moved away she wanted to beg him to stay, to sit down with them, not leave her there with her husband.

'Nothing.'

'Jemma. We need to talk.'

'What about?'

'About what the fuck's wrong with you.'

Jemma was shocked. This was so unlike Jamie. It wasn't an accusation as such, more a tacit admission of his incomprehension of Jemma's apparent misery at having married him, at long last. Its aggressive tone was to hide the whine of insecurity behind it. Jamie was not used to feeling unwanted.

'I don't think we should talk about it here,' Jemma said.

'Well, we need to talk about it somewhere. This is like being in purgatory.'

Jemma stayed silent, but she knew it was true. They were in purgatory, with palm trees. Jamie kept eating, and a trickle of soy sauce caught on his chin, and he didn't look like a successful banker now; he looked like a twit. A needy twit with soy sauce in his stubble, in palm-treed purgatory. Jemma giggled. It was unravelling at last, and she was glad. Jamie pushed back his chair and stood up.

'That's it,' he said. 'There's something wrong with you.' He stalked away from the table, and the abandonment was clear for everyone to see, in the broken angle of his chair. The gloves were off, and they were stranded in paradise, and Jemma had no idea what was going to happen.

61

Jemma

Chrissy repositioned Jamie's empty chair and sat down across from Jemma.

'You all right?' she asked.

Jemma decided to be honest for a change and shook her head. Bobbi glided past, proffering coffee, and when Chrissy accepted, he scurried off to fetch a clean cup.

'It's OK, babe, rows happen to us all. On me and Kenny's first holiday together, I threw a hairdryer at him.'

'You didn't?'

'Well, only in the hotel room, and it was attached to the wall, but even so. Men can be so sodding annoying at times.'

'Hmm,' Jemma said. She felt numb, yet cut free at the same time. Since Jamie had stalked off, the terrible pressure she'd felt since she'd stood at the entrance to the church had disappeared, as if a boil had been lanced. Jamie, her husband, her future. What a joke.

'I don't know what to do,' she said. Her voice sounded low and strangled, and she barely recognized it.

'What d'you mean?'

Jemma looked at this near-stranger, who was built like Jessica Rabbit. Her hair flowed over her shoulders in a river of gold. Her eyes were wide and her lips were sensuous, smeared with shine. No wonder Jamie couldn't keep his eyes off her.

'It's a disaster,' Jemma said. She spoke in barely a whisper. 'I don't know what to do.'

'Oh, love,' Chrissy said. She took Jemma's hand across the table, and her fingers were soft and her nails were long and red. 'It's all right. Come on, d'you want to go for a walk along the beach? I'll just tell Kenny.'

Chrissy got up and slunk across the terrace, past the other diners, and the throw over her bikini was so transparent she might as well have not been wearing it. When she returned, Jemma stood up, and the two women walked all of ten yards down onto the beach – and as their feet pressed virgin shapes into the sand, Jemma tried to work out what she should say to Chrissy, and just how much of the story it was safe to share.

62

Jemma

Jemma came up spluttering as the sea stung the back of her throat in its brazen, briny way. It was later that afternoon, and she and Kenny were making their attempt to snorkel around the island, but it wasn't going well. Her mask kept filling up, and no matter how much she adjusted it, it didn't seem to fit properly, although it had been fine yesterday, when Pascal had tightened it for her. Jemma took care to keep her feet up, not trample on the coral, but her legs were hard to coordinate in their flippers and she felt anxious. She wished snorkelling came more naturally to her, especially as she was such a strong swimmer – maybe the row with Jamie at breakfast had upset her more than she'd thought.

Jemma tried to quell her nerves, remind herself that what she and Kenny were doing was perfectly safe. They were never more than a hundred feet or so from the island in their circumnavigation of it, and if the worst came to the worst she could always abandon snorkelling to lie on her back and kick her flippers, until she beached herself on the soft sieved sand. And as long as they stayed this side of the reef's edge she was sure there was virtually no chance of either of them drifting off or drowning.

Kenny seemed to be suffering none of these practical problems, and he was patient and attentive whenever Jemma needed to stop and sort out her mask. When he spotted a giant turtle, he even came back for her and took her hand, so she could swim alongside him as the creature swooped and skimmed below them, seemingly happy to share his magical home with these gawky landlubbers, for a few minutes at least. Gradually, Jemma felt her breath beginning to ease, the loud, hollow sound of her heartbeat becoming more rhythmic as she found herself focusing on the simple wonders of this secret city under the sea. And as she gazed in awe at the collage of coral, the lounge lizard turtle, the bright flashes of the fishes, at last her worries about her mask and going home and her marriage to Jamie slipped away with the cool slipstream of the tide, and she was a mermaid, an enchantress, and she was happy.

Jemma's watery reverie was ripped apart by Kenny first yowling, and then splashing and flipping so violently that Jemma thought he might be having a heart attack. Her mask flooded again, and she yanked it off. She was coughing and choking as she looked around in panic, trying to work out their location. They were on the island's wild side, nowhere near either safety pier, and suddenly the land mass didn't seem nearly so small any more. Kenny was a few feet away from her, flailing and screaming still. She started shrieking for someone to come, but there were no bungalows here and no-one could hear her. She swam over to Kenny and tried to grab his arm, but he beat her off, and the terror in his eyes was bottomless. He was still howling with agony and thrashing about in the water, and all Jemma could think of were sharks, and fins, and mutilation. Her mind was flipping over, and her mouth was full of sea and salt, and her stomach had dropped through itself, like a broken lift. She needed to stay calm.

Suddenly Kenny grunted, and stopped kicking and screaming. But when Jemma looked behind him, the sea was tinged with pink, and the stain swirled and turned as it grew bigger. She screeched in terror as she looked again for a fin, but the water was smooth now, unbroken. She took Kenny's arm, and he let her this time, and somehow she towed him all the way to the shore, where he managed to drag himself up the sand and collapse amongst the driftwood, spent. There was an angry red chunk hacked out of his lower left leg. She'd expected worse.

'Little fucker wouldn't let go,' Kenny was saying now.

'What on earth happened?'

'A fish bit me. It wouldn't let go.'

A sudden desire to giggle hit Jemma, at the absurdity of it, and then she remembered Chrissy on the boat, refusing to go in the water. How there was anxious talk amongst the locals of fish with teeth. Jemma wondered if that was what had happened. She was just so thankful Kenny still had both legs, was conscious, wasn't dead, that she wanted to lie on her back and howl with laughter – but there was no time; he was bleeding. She took off her lifejacket and rash vest, wrung out the vest and wrapped it around Kenny's leg to try to stem the flow. His face was white beneath the sunburn. She glanced around. It looked like there was a rough path through the bush a little way along the beach.

'Will you be OK?' she asked. 'I'm going to go and get help.'

'Ugh,' was all Kenny managed, but she was relieved to see some colour beginning to return to his cheeks.

'I won't be long,' she said. She put her lifejacket back on to cover herself up and ran through the thick, unkempt jungle. In normal circumstances the lack of path-sweeping here would have been unbearable for her feet, but she ignored the pain. The track came out at the back of a block that she'd never seen before. It was built of corrugated iron, and there was a row of plastic bins, and instead of being neat and pristine and perfect, it was a bit depressing.

'Hello,' she yelled. 'Help!'

Soon enough, a man appeared from around the side of the building, looking as though he'd just woken up.

'My friend has been bitten. Is there a doctor?'

'I'll ring, ma'am. Where is he?'

'On the beach, through there.'

'OK. Give me a minute, ma'am.'

All Jemma could think was that he'd called her ma'am, even in a crisis. *How polite.* Another man appeared, and it was the one she'd run over on her bike a couple of days previously, and she blushed that here she was again, compromised. When the three of them got to the beach, Kenny was sitting up, and he seemed much better now – in fact, more than a little embarrassed. The two men helped Kenny stand up and hop through to the clearing, where Moosa was already waiting with the buggy – and Jemma had never been so relieved to see her butler, nor to be sped along the sandy paths through the jungly trees, back to the safety of the resort.

63

Chrissy

Poor, poor Kenny, Chrissy thought. She didn't like to say she told him so, but now it was clear that he was fine, she was tempted. She *knew* she'd heard right that day on the boat, about bad-tempered fish with teeth like rats, and it seemed her refusal to enter the water hadn't been as irrational as everyone made out. They certainly didn't tell you about triggerfish in the brochures, that was for sure.

Kenny had just been discharged from the sanatorium and was propped up on the daybed, a bright white bandage wrapped around his injured leg. The sky streaked and striped as they watched it, and the wind blew softly and warmly, like a lover's breath. The atmosphere between them was a little more serene than usual, as Kenny was obliged to sit still for a change, and Chrissy was glad of it.

'The little bastard just wouldn't let go,' Kenny was saying now. He couldn't hide the tinge of humiliation in his voice.

'How big was it?'

'Oh, you know . . .' He stretched his arms outwards, to the width of his shoulders.

'Nooo?' said Chrissy.

'Honest, babe. I saw it eyeballing us, and it looked evil, but I didn't think it would bloody attack me. How did I know we'd intruded into its nesting area? It should have put fucking signs up.'

Chrissy giggled and sipped her beer. She was drinking it out of the can, and it was ice-cold and fizzy, and it made a nice change from cocktails.

'Well, just thank Christ you're all right,' she said. 'Apparently if they get hold of your face they can rip it off.' Kenny looked a little queasy, so she changed the subject. 'Anyway, what d'you want to do for dinner tonight?' she said. 'Shall we get room service?'

'No, let's go out. We can get Hassan to bring the buggy. What about the restaurant on the water? I'm not bloody walking up and down to the buffet tonight.'

'That'll be nice,' she said.

'Shall we ask Jemma and Jamie?' Kenny said. 'I think I should buy them dinner, after me putting her through that.'

Chrissy felt faintly cross, and she wasn't sure why. Perhaps it was the fact that Kenny and Jemma seemed to have hit it off so well – and now they had this additional bond between them. Jemma had been there for Kenny in a crisis, had acted heroically, had *rescued him*, when Chrissy wouldn't even set foot in the ocean. In fact, Jemma had rescued both of them now, and it peeved Chrissy a little, although she knew that it shouldn't. She told herself not to be so insecure.

'Sure,' she said.

'Great, I'll give them a ring,' said Kenny. He heaved himself up from the daybed and hopped into the bungalow to use the resort phone. Chrissy remained on the terrace, watching the last of the pink disappear from the sky, as if it was being painted away by a giant invisible brush dipped in deep indigo. A huge bat swooped over silently, and the world grew slow, and the waves lapped speechlessly, and she was at the end of the earth, and it was heavenly.

64

Jemma

I love Chrissy and Kenny, Jemma thought as she came off the phone. They were turning out to be her absolute saviours on this honeymoon from hell. Chrissy might look like someone off a reality TV show, but she was smart and sassy and fun, and Kenny was a giant teddy bear, albeit one with a nasty chunk out of his leg right now. It was so nice of them to have invited her and Jamie for dinner, and it was a relief not to be spending the evening with just her husband again — assuming she could persuade him, of course. It was quite a turn-around in their social fortunes, seeing as she hadn't been able to face even speaking to anyone before yesterday, let alone have dinner with them — but what had there been to say? *Hi, I'm Jemma, I'm here for my honeymoon, and I wish I wasn't. I think I've made an enormous mistake. I haven't a clue what I'm doing here.* None of those statements would have hit the mark as polite introductory chat. But Jemma had felt sorry for Chrissy on the boat, and she'd known her fear hadn't been just attention seeking, no matter what Jamie had said. And as for the belly flop incident, that must have really hurt — and at least Chrissy was able to laugh at herself. Kenny was great, too, Jemma thought, having dealt with his own aquatic disaster with equal good humour. She admired people like Kenny – he seemed to have such a simple way of thinking, a willingness to just go for it, and a raw courage that Jamie didn't have and never would. Perhaps that was why Kenny was a successful trader – he was obviously a born gambler at heart. He'd even taken a gamble on marriage from what Chrissy had said, and Jemma respected Kenny's ability to make up his mind, know what he wanted. He was so unlike Jamie in that respect, and Jemma couldn't help but wonder whether she would have become so fixated on marriage if it hadn't been something Jamie so clearly *hadn't* wanted? Was that why she'd wanted to marry him? Was she really that ornery? The questions, of course, were academic. She'd done it.

And so. And so. Jemma only had herself to blame. She had faced her feelings too late, at the threshold of a beautiful church, and since that moment all she'd been doing was harbouring the germs of her discontent, inside her heart, to breed and incubate and multiply. She had no idea how she and Jamie would spend the remainder of their time here, how they would get through it. The minutes were passing so slowly, as if the world was winding down, the earth turning ever slower, and their lives were gradually stultifying. Here they were, trapped together on a tiny island, stranded with a handful of strangers, and they were so far away from real life they might as well be on the moon. There was no poverty, no crime, no old or sick people, no children to make a racket – only charming, ever-pleasing resort staff in brown-and-gold shirts. There was nothing here but serenity and beauty. Or so they tried to tell you.

It seemed that meeting Chrissy and Kenny had released Jemma from her faux-romantic stupor. It was all a sham. Everyone here was pretending in a way – and perhaps real romance was found elsewhere. That inaugural kiss. A walk in the park. The very first twenty-four-hour date. By the time anyone got to the commitment levels required to fork out for a holiday like this, all spontaneity had vanished, and it became a challenge to be romantic *enough*. She could see it in the faces of her fellow holidaymakers, that they too were exhausted by it. It was like a never-ending Valentine's Day meal, and Jemma hated those at the best of times. But now that she and Jamie had an outlet, and other people to talk to, maybe they could reach an uneasy, unspoken ceasefire for a bit.

The sun was edging towards the horizon as Jemma walked across the sand to the sea. She had time for one last quick snorkel before dinner, and she'd be sure to stay in the shallows right by the shore, where she knew it was safe. She was pretty certain there were no trig-gerfish here – or maybe she just didn't want to acknowledge that there might be, wasn't prepared to forego the pleasure. As she sank into the water, she thought again how extraordinary the sea was in the

Maldives, how it literally teemed with colour and life. It was like another world under the surface, one free of stress and tension, where the fish undulated and darted and shimmered past, and the coral bloomed bulbously. The noise of the Earth was muffled in her ears, and her physical focus was on her echoey breath, the miracle of her body, this magical other world. Jamie had gone to the dive centre, yet again, and without him around Jemma felt better. She was happy in her own bit of sea, with just the fish for company. And at least for now it seemed that she and her husband had reached some kind of unspoken compromise. They'd just take each day as it came, here on their island of disintegrating dreams, and they *would not* talk about the future. The future, and whatever it would bring them, would have to wait.

65

Jemma

When Jemma and Jamie first joined Chrissy and Kenny at the white-clothed table, Jemma could tell immediately that Chrissy wasn't happy. Jamie sat down and glowered, as if he too were jealous of her and Kenny's earlier adventure. And although Jemma couldn't help how Jamie felt, it wasn't fair to be spoiling Kenny and Chrissy's honeymoon too, and she wondered whether they should make their excuses and leave. It was awkward.

The four of them were sitting outside, at a table over the water. The dark had descended oppressively tonight, and the air felt thick and chocolatey. The restaurant's pontoon was lit with sparkly lights which twinkled against the flat black of the sea. The waves lapped calmly beneath them. Chrissy had her hair piled on top of her head, and her eyes were made up like a cat's, and she was wearing a soft grey top that covered her up for a change. She looked stunning. She suited a more pared-back look, Jemma thought – until she noticed that the bottom half of Chrissy's outfit was tight silver hot pants and stilettos, which in Jemma's opinion rather ruined it.

Jamie was sitting next to Chrissy, across from Jemma, and he seemed to be finding it hard not to take a sideways look at her. His neck appeared stiff and his mouth was a thin straight line. What was even more surprising was that he'd shaved off his stubble, for the first time in months, and he looked so much better without it. Jemma couldn't believe she'd once loved his facial hair, especially now it was gone.

'Shall we have some champagne?' said Kenny now. 'Celebrate the fact I'm still alive?'

'Ha,' Jemma said. She paused. 'I must admit you had me worried, though. But you were certainly going to go down fighting!' Jemma winked at Chrissy, tried to show her that she meant well.

Chrissy smiled back and seemed to get it. But on the other hand, Jemma thought, she also knew that Jemma wasn't getting on with her own husband. It wasn't beyond the realms of possibility that Jemma would try to steal someone else's. Chrissy didn't know her, after all, didn't know what she was capable of. Jemma should never have confided in Chrissy, of course, but it had felt like such a relief after her and Jamie's row over breakfast, to get the words out, rescue her sanity. And although Kenny was attractive, in that all-male way, he wasn't her type at all. He was too well-built. He wore too much gold. Chrissy didn't have anything to worry about.

The waiter appeared with the champagne, and they all held their breath as the golden liquid frothed into the crystal glasses. Jemma craved a glass to calm her nerves – her anxiety seemed to have settled into her stomach, making her feel sick almost all the time. She yearned to feel the foam in her throat, the chill thrill of the bubbles, to take away the tang of salt still lodged there, the raw memory of Kenny's accident. It seemed she was floating in a hazardous sea of unmanaged emotions, but the champagne would lead her to dry land, would help guide her home, she was sure of it.

'Cheers,' Jemma said. They clinked glasses, although Jamie's and hers didn't quite touch, and then she tilted her head back, and it felt so good, and she never wanted it to end . . . and when she finally put down her glass, Chrissy was staring at her, looking stern . . . and then she grinned, and Jemma grinned back, and they were friends again.

66

Jemma

Jemma was drunk. Three sautéed king prawns and a monkfish curry obviously weren't sustenance enough after her earlier exertions with Kenny, and of course the lack of an adequate breakfast. Jamie still had the hump, which was undoubtedly her fault. Despite their attempt at cordiality, it had all started up again when she'd made some kind of inappropriate comment about his mother, something to do with the *Wizard of Oz* from what she could remember. Chrissy had slipped her a couple of unknown pills under the table to help calm her down, and at least they seemed to have worked for now. Jemma glanced at Jamie and gave him what she thought was a conciliatory look, but he just scowled at her.

Fair enough, Jemma thought. She smiled angelically as the waiter deposited a trio of chocolate mousses in front of her, on a long, thin plate, but the look of them turned her stomach. Kenny had left a while ago, on the pretext that his leg was sore, but possibly really because Chrissy had been insisting that he shouldn't have any more alcohol on top of the antibiotics. Their butler had brought the golf buggy all the way along the pontoon to the restaurant, and as Kenny had been driven off, he'd been waving heroically, royally, whilst Chrissy and Jemma had blown theatrical kisses at him.

Dear Kenny, Jemma thought now. What a guy.

'Jemma,' said Jamie, as Jemma drained her champagne flute. 'I think you've had enough.'

'Yeah, you could say that,' Jemma said. She felt a sharp kick under the table. 'Owww.' She stared at Chrissy, hurt. 'What did you do that for?'

'I think maybe you ought to get her home, Jamie,' Chrissy said.

'I don't want to go home with him,' Jemma said, leaning forward, towards Chrissy. She could hear the coquettishness in her voice. 'I want to stay here with you.'

'Jemma,' said Jamie, and even she could tell his patience was being stretched, perhaps further than ever before. His tone was not quite threatening. 'Don't cause a scene.'

Jemma looked around. The restaurant was three-quarters-empty. They were the only group left outside, and they were far out over the water. No-one could hear them.

'Jamie,' she said, and she was surprised at herself. It was as if the words that were about to come out of her mouth were random, from a lucky dip perhaps. 'Why don't we just admit that we've made a mistake coming here?'

'Be quiet, Jemma,' he said. He raked his fingers through his hair, his expression desperate.

'Shall we get the bill?' said Chrissy, frantically beckoning the waiter.

'The thing is, Chrissy,' continued Jemma now, airily. 'I used to be in love with his brother, you know.'

'Shut *up*, Jemma,' Jamie said. He stood up, tried to help her to her feet. 'I think you've said quite enough.'

'Oh, I disagree,' Jemma said, shaking him off. 'I don't think I've said nearly enough. Jamie didn't want to marry me for years, did you, darling? And then he changed his mind. Now why would he do that?'

'Jemma,' said Jamie.

'Don't "Jemma" me! You never wanted to marry me, did you? I wish I'd listened to your brother now.' Her voice rose. She sat forward and waggled her finger at Jamie. 'I wish I'd bloody married *him* instead.'

Chrissy gasped, and even through her drunkenness, Jemma knew she'd gone too far.

'Sorry,' she said, to no-one in particular. Her head was beginning to feel as though it had been run over by a truck. She didn't feel at all herself.

'Yeah, right,' said Jamie. 'Get lost, Jemma. You've made your feelings clear.' And with that he stood up, muttered an apology to Chrissy, turned around, and left.

When Chrissy and Jemma finally got up from the table, having stayed for another bottle of champagne, Jemma's mood had brightened. At least she'd done it at last. She'd put them both out of their misery. She and Chrissy wrapped their arms around each other and waved their goodbyes beatifically to the waiters, who smiled uncertainly. All the staff were so lovely here, Jemma thought. Moosa, Bobbi, Arnie, Chati. Kyle, their waiter tonight. They were all so lovely, and Jemma loved them all. She waved again, and even blew a kiss at Kyle, who looked mortified, and then she and Chrissy staggered along the starry boardwalk and down to the beach, allegedly on their way to the bar. But once they reached the sand, Jemma's legs wobbled, and then she stumbled, and the next thing she knew, she was lying on her back gasping, and then so was Chrissy, and they were giggling like teenagers as they looked up at the stars, which were brighter now, and they were spinning and swirling in a vortex of love and beauty, just for them, and Jemma forgot everything. She forgot Jamie and triggerfishes and sharks and sexy marine biologists and disgruntled brothers and muscly wide boys and attentive waiters and smiley chefs and Chinese power couples. She even forgot the terrible things she'd said to her husband. All she thought about was being here on the beach, now, and it was such a relief. And so, as she and Chrissy held hands in the warm night air, staring up at the miracle-sky, at last, at long last, Jemma felt like she was in paradise.

67

Jemma

It was later, though how much so Jemma did not know. The restaurant was in darkness now, and she and Chrissy were alone with just the moon and the stars and the mellow sounds of the sea. Jemma's head had stopped spinning so giddily, and the sand was cool and soft under her back. The night was breathless. She felt a sharp nudge in her ribs.

'Are you awake, Jemma?' said Chrissy. 'Come on, shall we go?'

'Where?' Jemma said.

'Home. It's too late to go to the bar now.'

Jemma didn't want to go home. She didn't want to go back to her bungalow in the palm groves, with the hand-carved furniture, and the beautiful thatched roof, and the fancy bathroom, and the discreet surround-sound music system, and the well-stocked minibar, and the new husband in the silk-sheeted bed. She wanted to stay here with Chrissy. Jemma felt like a child who'd got the wrong present at Christmas for the first time ever, and whose faith has been cruelly shaken. She sat up and started to cry. They were the tears of a drunk – flamboyant noisy sobs – but Chrissy didn't mind, and as she held Jemma close, Jemma could smell the coconut scent of her hair, and she wanted to stay there forever.

'I wish he wasn't here,' Jemma sobbed.

'I know, I know. It's a crap situation.'

'No, I wish he'd just fuck off, disappear. I wish I could get rid of him, not have to see him again. He's never loved me anyway,' and as Jemma said it she knew it was true, and it was a revelation. Jemma wondered why Jamie had gone through with it. Yet he'd seemed so happy on the day. *Hadn't he?* Or had he been faking it too? But however it had happened, right now she and Jamie were trapped here on this island together, like caged, embittered tigers, and she had no idea how it was destined to end.

Jemma turned to look at Chrissy, and she wasn't sure of the expression in the other girl's eyes. What was she thinking? The moonlight was too flighty tonight to be certain.

'I know, babe,' Chrissy replied, at last. 'It must be so hard for you both.' Her mood lightened, and she rummaged in her handbag for a blister pack of pills. 'Come on, love, have another one of these, and then let's get you home.'

Chrissy stood up and pulled Jemma to her feet, and Jemma felt so woozy, disconnected somehow . . .

And now she and Chrissy were outside Jemma's bungalow, although Jemma couldn't remember a single step of the walk along the beach to get there . . .

And now Jemma was running flat-out towards the sea, and at first the water was warm like an embrace, and then it was scary, so scary . . .

And then the lights of the world flicked off, and Chrissy was gone.

Inside the bungalow it was pitch-black. The stars must have hidden out behind the gathering clouds, as if shy, or scared of what they would witness. There was no more moonlight. Jemma couldn't see a thing when she came round, and her head felt like it had been split in two — yet she knew immediately that the room didn't feel right. She patted her hand across the bed, and it was so wide she couldn't reach right across, but it was damp, and she already knew what was absent. It was the absence of breath, and it terrified her. She imagined Jamie lying beside her, dead, and she was too scared to turn on the light. She pictured the blood-soaked sheets, the drench spreading, reaching all the way to her side of the mammoth mattress. She was being mad, preposterous. She couldn't bear it. So what if she woke him up?

'Jamie,' she whispered. *'Jamie.'* The silence was in the very bones of the building. *'Jamie!'*

She fumbled with the bedside light, and although she dreaded what it would unveil, she turned it on anyway — and the nightmare vanished, and all she could see were sandy white sheets, and what was once a love heart made out of petals laid across their centre, demolished.

There was no dead body. There was no husband.

68

Chrissy

Chrissy felt relieved to finally fall into bed with Kenny, although he wasn't quite so happy about it, seeing as she accidentally booted his bad leg. She was wrecked, but slightly less so than Jemma had been – she was obviously far more used to having alcohol in industrial quantities on top of the odd pill or two. She wondered whether she should have made sure Jemma got into the bungalow OK, but she hadn't wanted to risk running into Jamie – Chrissy had had quite enough of their toxic relationship for one evening, and didn't want to have to adjudicate another screaming match. Instead, she'd just said her farewells on the beach and had left Jemma to it. It was only a twenty yard stumble up the path, Chrissy thought, as her mind was drifting away. Surely Jemma could manage that.

Chrissy slept deeply. Sometime during the night she found herself dreaming of a giant rat swimming around a boat, its tail whipping backwards and forwards, before belly flopping into a bright-red swimming pool where, baring its vicious brown teeth, it chased her across the water and bit into her leg, at which point she screamed so loudly she woke herself up. As she opened her eyes, she saw Kenny rocking in pain, and it seemed that she'd booted his injured leg again, but even so, he stroked her hair while her heart rate slowed, and then she got on top of him, the safest position injury-wise, and soon enough all was well again.

It was nearly dawn and Chrissy was cold. The throb in her head was growing ever stronger as the memories of last night flooded in. What a car crash of an evening. The only good thing to come out of it was that she'd realized she'd been being neurotic about Jemma and Kenny – it had been clear over dinner that there was nothing between them. Jemma was definitely a bit odd, though. It seemed you could never be quite sure what you would get, when she would snap. One minute she was laughing enchantingly, and the next she was acting like a demented teenager. She'd become hysterical on the beach after dinner, and it had seemed more than just drunkenness to Chrissy. It was hardly surprising, though – had Jemma *meant* what she'd said about wishing she'd married Jamie's brother? Bloody hell, Chrissy thought, it was worse than *EastEnders*.

But whatever, it was none of her business. No, this was her and Kenny's time – she didn't want their honeymoon spoiled by other people's problems. She'd be friendly enough at breakfast, say hi round the pool, but other than that she and Kenny would keep themselves

318

to themselves from now on, especially as Kenny couldn't snorkel at the moment. Yes, Chrissy had made up her mind. Enough was enough. She didn't want any trouble. Jamie and Jemma were history.

69

Jemma

Jemma's sleep was fraught and bedevilled. She waited for Jamie to come back but he didn't. She wanted him gone yet wished he'd return.

She just wanted to know where he was.

At dawn she got up, and her head pounded from champagne and cocktails and unknown pills, and she padded from the bed out to their terrace, and Jamie's mask and flippers were missing. *Of course.* He must have gone snorkelling. But when? Straight after dinner? Yet if that was the case, why hadn't he come back? Or maybe he'd gone out this morning, but if so, where had he been all night? And either way, it wasn't safe to snorkel alone, especially in darkness. Everyone knew that.

Jemma felt thick-headed and perplexed and unsure what to do with herself. It was a weird kind of edgy feeling, not helped by her monster hangover. She couldn't even remember how she'd got home. It seemed that she'd been swimming, though: the sheets were covered in sand and her skin tasted of salt. She got out of bed, put on one of the hotel robes and walked barefoot down to the beach. She looked up and down, but all she could see was a gaggle of women in saris, with brooms, far in the distance. She sat down on her beach lounger, and as she waited for them to come nearer, she watched the sea grow greeny-grey and then a glimmering silver-pink where the sun rose and smashed off its sheeny surface. But sadly, even when the women were close enough, they were too embarrassed to acknowledge Jemma. They were meant to be the invisible path fairies who came at the fringes of night, when the guests weren't looking, to rake away the leaves, add the finishing touches to heaven. Jemma approached them anyway and asked them if they'd seen her husband, but they didn't speak English, and when Jemma gesticulated with an imaginary mask and pointed out towards the water it seemed that they thought she was asking if it was safe to swim. They just shook their heads and looked down at the ground, at the leaves and twigs they were clearing, and it was hopeless. In the end, Jemma gave up and returned to her sun lounger, where she sat down and waited, for her husband to come back.

70

Late in the afternoon on yet another blank, surreal day, seven days after Jamie's disappearance and the day before she is meant to be leaving, Chrissy is lying naked on her back in her outdoor plunge pool, looking up at the navy-blue sky, her body floating under the last sliding tackles of sunshine. The breeze is warm and the pool is warmer, but she's anxious and she wishes she could feel relaxed and woozy again, like she'd used to in here. She can feel the water wrapping sleek, silky threads through her limbs, and into bare secret places, and she knows that her skin is so dark now the minuscule parts covered by her bikini are smooth and milk-like, all the better for Kenny to lap at. Her mind is zooming in and out of rhythm with the crickets, but instead of feeling wrapped up in a little medication-enhanced slice of bliss, she feels jittery, panicky almost, which isn't helped by the fact that Kenny is out kayaking. He'd said he couldn't keep sitting around waiting for something to happen, it was driving him batty – but Chrissy's worrying about her husband now, out on the water on his own, his leg still not completely better. There's a nagging, tawdry regret hanging over their honeymoon, and it isn't just that someone might be dead, or even that

Chrissy might yet be implicated. It had seemed like a perfectly good idea, hooking up with Jemma and Jamie, at first – after all, there was only so much sex and conversation even she and Kenny could manage to eke out over two whole weeks in this place – but it has been a disaster. Jamie's disappearance has put a total downer on her and Kenny's honeymoon too.

Chrissy kicks her legs suddenly, viciously, and water drenches over the pool's infinity sides, to be instantly replenished. No matter how hard she kicks, the water keeps coming. It's hopeless. There's just too much water here in the middle of this sodding ocean, Chrissy thinks – it would be no wonder if it turns out that Jamie really has drowned. But if he has, what does that mean for Jemma? *Has* she had something to do with it? Chrissy still can't decide whether to tell the police how Jemma had blurted out that she wished her husband would disappear – on the very night he vanished. *Surely* she hadn't meant it.

Chrissy doesn't know what to do. Finally, she stops kicking and dips under the water, tilts her head back to smooth her long, silky hair, and then she stands up and hauls herself out of the water. She puts on a robe and pads the few steps out to the beach to watch the sunset, and thinks again about Jamie and Jemma, tries to work out what exactly had been going on between them. She'd felt sorry for them at first. They might have been pale and good-looking, but there had been no hot lust radiating off them, like there is off her and Kenny, where no matter how much Chrissy swims or showers, she can't clear her nostrils of the smell of him. And although she and Kenny annoy the hell out of each other at times, she's certain she's found her prince at last – or, at least, she had been up until the night Jamie went missing. Chrissy is perceptive, and she knows Kenny is hiding something. He's been acting strangely ever since that night. But what? She tries to shove her thoughts elsewhere. *Of course* Kenny has had nothing to do with it. But then, why do the police keep on interviewing him? And why won't he tell her what they're asking him?

Chrissy gets up from the beach lounger, wanders down to the water, sticks one shapely toe in, which is quite far enough for her. A baby shark is frolicking in the shallows, and there's no way she'll get any closer to that little sucker. Again, she tries to work out what had been going on between Jemma and Jamie. Chrissy had been wary of them even before that last evening. Sure, people had rows, but how could you be on *honeymoon* and be that unremittingly miserable? Chrissy prays that Jamie isn't dead, that he has managed to abscond somehow, perhaps aided by the impossibly attractive Pascal. They knew each other, after all, through Pascal's sister, who Jamie was having an affair with, apparently. If the rumours were true, Jamie had even rung her from his honeymoon bungalow, the tosser.

The baby shark has long disappeared and Chrissy gets brave, goes in up to her ankles as she continues trying to work it out. *Would* Jamie have been having an affair, though, even before he got married? Chrissy knows some men do, but she wouldn't have thought it of Jamie somehow. She just hadn't got that vibe from him, and she can normally spot the shaggers a mile off. Yet from the pictures Chrissy has seen online, Camille is stunning in that understated French way, and she certainly seems to be upset enough. But maybe it's all some elaborate plot to get the insurance money or something, and the three of them are in on it. Plus Jamie must have been always down at the dive centre for some reason, and Pascal is the one person on this island who could have offered practical help – he had access to all the boats and the kayaks. Or else, Chrissy thinks, perhaps it wasn't even that pre-planned. Maybe it was simply that Jamie had had enough after Jemma's outburst at dinner and had buggered off. But if that was the case, why wouldn't he have just left on a seaplane in the morning? And why hasn't he turned up anywhere since? Why has he never been seen again?

Chrissy's thoughts keep going round and round the possible explanations, before finally returning to Jemma. She frowns as she watches the sun spread out into the sky, making one final stand, yet still bleeding to death. There's something about her, and Chrissy can't work it out. What *is* it? What Chrissy does know, though, is never to judge someone at face value. She has watched and seen all sorts over the years, and she knows what to look out for. So Chrissy might not trust

Jemma, but she *likes* her, despite the unpredictable edge she has, the strange air of vulnerability – and as company on holiday, she and Jamie had seemed fine. But just how wrong Chrissy has been, and what impact it might yet have on her and Kenny – and, more pertinently, what role Kenny has in all this – is yet to be determined.

71

There is a different energy in the bright, airy interview room today, and at last the impasse is about to be broken. I can feel it. I dread what it means.

I'm sitting across from the police, and the greenness of the trees outside is as brilliant and life-affirming as ever, yet there is little pretence of optimism from anyone today. There are three of them for a change – the two British officers, who are still dressed like they're on holiday, and one of the Maldivians, who looks immaculate and menacing in his uniform. My dad is with me, thank goodness, so I don't feel quite so ganged up on.

'Well, Jemma,' says the round-faced one, Neil, after the usual formalities. He and I are on first-name terms these days. 'As you know, the local search has unfortunately had to be called off . . .' He tails off, presumably not wanting to spell out the fact that it seems they've given up on finding my husband alive.

'So, what's the next stage?' Dad asks, perhaps to fill the silence.

'We will be returning to the UK to continue some further lines of enquiry.' Neil's voice is reedy, as though he's coming down with something, which is a shame. Who'd have thought you could catch a cold in the Maldives?

'Do you have any definite leads?' Dad asks, when I still haven't said anything, and the air has grown hazy with the unsaid.

'Well, there's the mask and snorkel we found at the beginning, which leads to one possibility . . .' He doesn't bother articulating what it is. We all know what he means. He doesn't proffer any other theories, but by the way he's looking at me, I can tell he's read the latest tabloid exposés. They have unearthed a picture of me on Facebook now, at a fancy dress party, and I look like a prostitute. They've even dug out an ex-boyfriend I once threw my phone at, who has given a somewhat exaggerated interview about the extent of my mood swings and supposedly violent tendencies. It feels like the net is closing in on me.

'So, what happens now?' asks Dad. It seems he's doing all the talking on our side of the table, and I'm grateful to him.

The quiet one, Bob, the one with the penetrating gaze, looks at me as if we've been in the middle of playing a game, Scrabble perhaps, and he's caught me cheating.

'Well, that's up to you and your daughter, Mr Brady,' he says. 'There doesn't seem to be a great deal of point waiting on the island for any longer.'

'Are you saying you're assuming my husband's . . . *dead*?' I have found my voice at last, and suddenly I need to know.

'No, that's not what I'm saying at all. I'm just saying that the lines of enquiry can be continued in the UK.'

'Is it to do with Jamie's separate bank account?' I ask.

'We don't know, Mrs Armstrong. We can't say anything more to you at this stage.'

'What about Pascal? Is he still being investigated?'

'I'm afraid we can't tell you.'

'But I'm Jamie's wife!' I scream. 'Either you think he's dead, or you don't!' The days of soporific waiting have caught up with me, and it feels like every single muscle in my body is flexing and pulsing, and I just cannot stay still any longer. I leap up from my seat, and the chair scrapes back and topples over.

'Where the hell is he?' I yell. 'Do you think he's dead, *or don't you*? Or do you think he's absconded? You must have some idea. *Why can't you just tell me?*'

No-one speaks, so I carry on ranting, whilst stomping back and forth across the floor as best I can in my Havaianas. My mind is exploding with potential scenarios. 'Or what if he's been *murdered*, by someone on the island?' I'm aware that I'm hysterical, clutching at straws. 'Are you looking into *that* as a possibility?'

'Jemma, love, calm down,' says Dad. He sounds worried, as though he thinks I might be having a breakdown, and frankly I can hardly blame him.

'Mrs Armstrong,' says Bob, who I'm quite clearly not on first-name terms with. 'We can't tell you anything more at this stage, I'm afraid. However, it's extremely unlikely that remaining on the island will affect the outcome.'

'So that's it, is it?' It seems I can't stop shouting, and my hands curl into balls, and I am a monster. I am a monster, in white shorts and a pretty pink top, with cute pixie hair and dimples in my cheeks. I am sweet little Jemma, who is chock-full of rage, and *about what*, and who still has the occasional stroppy bent. There's been the odd smashed plate, a few fingernails in a foot. Feisty, Jamie called me. Right now, even I'm unsure what I'm capable of.

Dad gets up and comes towards me, but I shoot him a look, and he backs off.

'So that's *IT,* is it?' I repeat. 'I'm just meant to go home from *my honeymoon* without *my husband*, and carry on as if nothing's happened!' I feel slightly disingenuous at this point, seeing as I hadn't wanted to marry Jamie, or be on honeymoon with him, and until a few minutes ago had been *desperate* to go home, but I don't care. It has gone past that point. I think I might be being thrown a lifeline, but I'm not sure.

No-one says anything. Dad picks up my overturned chair, as if he needs something to do, and sits down on it, looking at his sandals. He never did know how to handle me when I was having a tantrum.

'What about Jamie's mother and brother?' Dad asks quietly now.

'Yes, we'll be telling them next that we're leaving,' says Neil. 'They're free to leave whenever they want to.'

'Of course they are!' I pipe up. '*They're* not under suspicion, *are they*?' Why am I doing this? Why am I falling apart now? This will not be helping.

'Please Jemma,' says Bob, the quiet one, his tone

perversely softening. He seems a bit more human, at last. Maybe he's wanted me to have a meltdown all along, to show that I care. 'Please calm down. It's not a matter of suspicion. It's just that they weren't here when Jamie went missing.'

I come and sit back down at last and flop my arms onto the table. I bury my head into them and then I sob and sob. The noise is so loud the Maldivian officer, in his pressed uniform and shiny boots, goes over and closes the window, which is his only contribution to the proceedings so far. Dad pats my back gently, and I can tell he's almost at the end of his tether too.

'I'm sorry we can't say anything more concrete at the moment,' Bob says. He seems to be thawing by the minute.

'That's OK.' I sit up, and if I'd been wearing sleeves, I would have wiped my nose on the left one. Instead I sniff a load of phlegm into my nostrils and then swallow. 'I'm sorry for my outburst,' I say.

'That's all right,' says Bob. Is it Check, or Checkmate? Or Stalemate? Or Ceasefire? I haven't a clue. 'We'll stay in touch,' he says, and then Dad and I stand up, and we leave the room.

72

Dad comes over to my bungalow to help me pack. I rip my clothes off their hangers and throw them into my suitcase, taking perverse pleasure in mixing clean with dirty, causing laundering carnage, as if there's no point having nice things any more. Dad deals with Jamie's stuff for me, but it's when I look into the empty wardrobes that it hits me. We are going home without him. The abandonment feels so brutal. We are taking Jamie's suitcase, as if he is coming with us, but he's not.

Moosa brings the buggy to collect us and we can barely look at each other, and he no longer bothers to disguise the fact that he thinks I'm responsible somehow. The journey is made in sullen silence. When we get to the pontoon, the manager is there waiting for us, and I vaguely wonder who checked out for me. He looks delighted to be seeing the back of me – it seems the old adage that there's no such thing as bad publicity doesn't apply to honeymoon hotels.

The police have already left, and Dan and Veronica haven't come to see me off, thank goodness. There's merely a smattering of holidaymakers, plus a few of the staff loitering, too. There's Chrissy, of course, and the love-struck American couple, and Leena, and Bobbi, and Chati. Dear Chati, the only person here apart from Dad who has kept me sane. I go along the line, saying my goodbyes. I hug Chrissy, and it's forced, and I can't face asking where Kenny is. The staff hold out their hands politely, and I mumble my thanks and keep my eyes downcast, but when I come to Chati, I ignore his attempt at a handshake and impulsively put my arms around him in gratitude, and his body feels strange somehow, as if it's recoiling, and it's clear I've made an error. It seems you're not meant to cuddle the staff here, and it's yet another nail in the coffin of my reputation. It all feels so awkward, and I'm glad to get on the dhoni that takes me out to the seaplane. But even though the water is glassy today, by the time I've got off the boat and clambered into the fuselage I feel as though I'm going to throw up. Dad takes one look at my face and asks for a sick bag for me, and I long to tell him that I think I might be pregnant, but I don't want to make things any worse for him. He looks green enough himself as it is, and the situation is almost farcical.

The plane is even more cramped and basic than I remember. I put in my squishy yellow earplugs and stare out of the window, try to absent myself, attempt to outwit the nausea. The engines roar, and we are off, skimming across the water, zooming through the blue air, and Dad is gripping my hand, his fear of aviation magnified a hundredfold in this contraption, and when I look down I see nothing but teal sea, dotted with green-and-white circles. I screw up my eyes, as if I might spot Jamie, but of course it's impossible, and after a while I give up, close my eyes, let the fierce thrum of the plane take over, let it try to quiet the voice in my brain that is whispering over and over that this is my fault, and that I did it.

73

Getting on the long-haul flight home is devastating. I find I miss Jamie now that I've finally left the Maldives – miss *him,* the person, rather than praying for the safe return of the husband I wish I'd never married. Leaving the island without him makes the end of our abortive marriage unequivocal. It means I've left Dan too, of course, and I've no idea what will happen next on that front, and even thinking that thought makes me feel enraged and treacherous. I cannot stop weeping. People keep staring at me in my seat, but I don't care. I'm probably expected to cry anyway. Dad puts his hand over mine sometimes, and it's comforting. I am a circus animal, and he is my keeper.

When we land at Heathrow and come through Security, the journalistic presence is even more vast and feral than I expected. Flashbulbs go off in my face, and jolly coarse-toned men are calling at me, 'Jemma, over 'ere', 'Jemma, my darlin'', but there are American accents too, and Spanish, and Japanese. It is scary and overwhelming, and I stare at the floor as Dad tries to protect me, but he's just my dad and he's appalled too. Getting through the scrum and into a taxi almost finishes us off, and I sit in the back, feeling nauseous and tense, and it's clear that in the Maldives I have been in a bubble. What start will my baby, if there is one, have here? It almost makes me wish I was back on the island, but not quite.

Dad and I have already discussed that I'm going home with him for the moment. I can't face going back to the flat, especially as it's Jamie's. Sasha has offered for me to stay with her and Martin, but she has enough on her plate. Dad and Kay are brilliant about it though – after all, this is a bona fide crisis, like after Mum died. I'm pretty sure they know that I hadn't wanted to go through with the wedding. Dad was the one who had to propel me down the aisle, after all, and he tells Kay everything. They don't ask, thank goodness. I can't think about that now.

I mustn't think about Dan either, not until I know what has happened to Jamie. He suspects me anyway. He lives with Lydia. His behaviour has been confusing at best, unforgivable at worst. I can't decide how I feel about him. There is a very thin line between love and hate, it seems.

Work has given me an indefinite sabbatical, which is good of them. Kay keeps the front curtains closed, just until the photographers give up, whenever that might be, and I stay indoors, feeling as trapped as I was on the island. Eventually, Kay and Dad go back to work and I spend the days cuddling Alfie, the cat, and watching rubbish telly. I don't feel up to doing anything else, especially as the press coverage has become ever more febrile. The latest is that my supposedly neglectful mother died of alcoholism, and it breaks my heart both how it makes her look, and how little the truth matters. I want to open the front door and yell that she died of *asthma*, and that she did her best, and even if she had been an alcoholic that wouldn't have made me a murderer anyway, but of course I don't. One of the couples at the resort has given an interview, and it's all about how Jamie and I appeared to hate each other: how I stormed off from breakfast, was drunk and staggering at dinner the night he disappeared, how I seemed so cold and remote, considering my husband had vanished. The picture of Dan and me hugging is reprinted in every story, the fact that we were once lovers gone over and over like it's a crime, and it seems the circumstantial evidence against me is mounting. But surely they wouldn't arrest me without a body – or would they? I start praying in earnest, as that's all I can do now.

It's the first weekend since I got home and Sasha has come round to see me, and she is the best friend ever. Yet even she'd stared me in the eyes after she'd hugged me, and I can tell she knows I'm lying about something, but she can't work out what. I'm sure she's guessed that it's something to do with Dan, but I'm glad she hasn't asked. I don't want to tell her what happened the night before my wedding. I don't want to compromise her.

Dad and Kay are discreetly busying themselves in the garden, and Sasha and I are in the lounge watching *Come*

Dine With Me. It makes me laugh, and laughter is important. It feels like laughter is what's keeping me going.

'All right, Jemma,' Sasha says at last, as the ad break comes on. She swipes at her fringe, reveals her eyes, which are unmade-up for a change. 'What the fuck is going on?'

'Nothing.'

'Don't lie to me, Jemma.'

I stare at my best friend, and so desperately want to confide in her, but I mustn't. I have to swallow the truth, until it eats me alive, from the inside.

'Sasha, I swear. Jamie just disappeared. I think the only answer is that he must have . . . He must have drowned.'

'You didn't want to marry him, did you?'

I pause. 'What d'you mean?'

'Oh, come on, Jem. I could tell in the toilets straight after the service. You were in pieces. But what was I meant to say? I was your sodding bridesmaid.'

My mouth feels dry, and the temptation to divert Sasha from her line of questioning feels so overwhelming that I can't stop myself.

'I'm pregnant,' I say.

'You're *what*?' Sasha goes white. 'Oh my God.'

'I know.'

I can see it in Sasha's eyes, how much trouble she thinks I'm in. Perhaps she's imagining the baby I'm carrying might be born in prison if I'm not careful. I know I have. Nightmare piles upon nightmare. I turn up the television.

341

'Are you sure?'

'Yes, I've taken a test.'

'How do you feel?'

I laugh. 'Oh, great. Really great.' And then I swing my legs off the sofa, rush to the toilet and throw up.

It's the following Monday and I'm watching TV, as usual. Kay has made an appointment for me at her doctor's surgery for later this afternoon and I dread leaving the house, but she says I have to get myself checked out, especially as I've been vomiting so much. I know I need to make some sort of start towards a new way of living, but I feel so drained and despairing that I assume that this is what my baby needs for now. Peace and quiet. Marmite toast. Ginger biscuits. Cups of tea. *A father.* I wonder at Dan, at what he said to me the night before my wedding. *Could he do the job?* I can feel my bones chill inside of me, at even the thought. I turn up the TV.

When the phone cuts through the televisual dinner party hubbub, I answer it on the third ring, in case it's news of Jamie. It is, but it's soon apparent it's not remotely the kind I was hoping for. Chrissy's on the other end of the line, and I don't know how she got Dad's number. She's in snotty tears, and I take a while to realize what she's saying. And then, when I understand, I just can't believe it, and I have to make her repeat it. I'm silent as I haul myself up from the couch, walk across to the fireplace, stare at myself in the polished overmantel mirror. All the while, Chrissy continues sobbing down the phone, but I can't compute how to manage her distress. I don't recognize myself, the expression on my face, the person it seems I've become. *Does this make me officially a widow?* I find myself wondering what Chrissy looks like right now, what clothes she's wearing in the depths of this English winter – I've only ever seen her do skimpy. I imagine tight leggings, Ugg boots, a big sweatshirt. My eyes fill, without warning, for Jamie.

'Hello? Jemma?' Chrissy says, for the umpteenth time.

At last I force myself back to what she's told me, and try to find the right words for both our situations, but really, what can I say? How on earth am I supposed to respond to Chrissy's anguished revelation that Kenny, her Kenny, has been arrested, on suspicion of the murder of my husband? It is devastating news, yet at the same time feels like some kind of sick prank. When I finally put down the receiver I'm almost as stunned as on the morning I admitted to myself that Jamie was missing. His disappearance had been merely a concept before then, a *possibility*, as I'd gazed out at the sea for long, wasteful hours, as I'd cycled around the island calling his name. It had only seemed real once Chrissy and I had told beautiful, smiley Leena on Reception, and the rescue boat had been launched, and it had become official.

But now it seems Jamie's official disappearance is even more than that. Now it's an official murder investigation, even though there is still no body. (I notice that I too think in terms of bodies now, like the police do, and it saddens me. It seems Jamie, the person, has already slipped beyond the horizon of my memories.) I go back to the couch, grab Alfie and squeeze him to me, but I must have done it too hard, as he hisses and struggles away. I find I miss the contact of having someone to cuddle. I know I should tell Dad, so we can update the lawyer he's hired, just in case, but I can't bear for the world to know yet. I need time to process what Chrissy has told me. I also need to try to work out what she's likely to divulge about me and Jamie now. Her call was a warning, I know that much.

I think I must be in shock. As I venture into the kitchen to make myself a mug of tea, my whole body is shaking. While I wait for the gleaming kettle to boil, I stare out of the window into the garden. Although it's still winter-worn and desolate-looking, it's a relief after the vibrant jungle growth of the Maldives, and I swear I will never go to a tropical island again, as long as I live. Heaven has officially turned to hell.

A bird hops across the lawn, looking fearful. I do my best to refocus. From what I could make out from Chrissy's quasi-hysterical phone call, it seems the key fact in all this is that Kenny was heavily involved in spread-betting – and although I have heard of that, I have no idea what it is, or how it actually works. I want to Google it, but I can't face going upstairs to get my iPad, which is on charge next to my single bed – that's how spacey and wiped out I'm feeling. But somehow it seems spread-betting has something to do with Kenny's job, and indirectly Jamie's too, as well as with money laundering, and I really am so confused I don't know what to think. Chrissy told me through her sobs that one of the police's theories is that Kenny drowned Jamie and he floated out to sea, and that's why there's no body, but I just can't believe it. Why would Kenny need to do that? He and Jamie didn't even know each other. And Kenny was in bed, in his bungalow all night, Chrissy swears he was. Their butler took him there in a golf buggy. He'd had a bite taken out of his leg by a vicious territorial fish. He could barely walk.

But what about later, after Chrissy and I had gone to bed? Had Chrissy been as comatose as I was? If so, where was Kenny then? Where was Jamie? I don't want to remember any part of that evening, my hysterics on the beach, the ugliness of my scene with my husband just before he stormed out of the restaurant. Is that any way to behave on honeymoon, drunkenly yelling that I wish I'd married his *brother*? Had either of us realized it in that moment, that that was our swansong? And, more to the point, who'd heard?

The sun leaks into the garden for a second, and then the clouds crowd around it again and it is gone. The kettle boils at last and I fill up my mug. Totteridge is a long way from the Maldives. Jamie is a long way from me. But is he dead? Who knows?

I go to the fridge and get out the milk, which Kay always decants into a blue-and-white stripy jug. The words are sinking in now, and they make me want to weep. It was easier thinking that perhaps Jamie had done it deliberately, and that he was a bastard – but an alive one. Even the prospect of him drowning had been better than this. But the thought that he might have been *murdered* is too hard to digest. *Poor Jamie.* He hadn't deserved that.

As I squeeze the life out of the teabag and slop in too much milk, I remember how unfriendly Kenny had seemed by the pool, that first morning after Jamie had vanished. How weird and aloof he'd been since. Maybe he does have a dark side after all. *Perhaps he really is capable of murdering someone.* Something else occurs to me as I take my first sip of the strong, hot tea, although I'm not at all proud of it. My thought is this: perhaps the latest development in this unfathomable mystery is not entirely unwelcome, as at last it takes the focus of suspicion off me.

74

The international media go mad at the news of Kenny's arrest, as predicted, and the missing groom story soon returns to all the front pages. But in a way my apparent innocence seems to be a disappointment to everyone. Instead of it being a bitter, years-long fraternal love triangle with a fire-haired harlot at the centre of it, now it seems it's just a common-or-garden story of City corruption and greed. That's fine with me, though, as long as I'm off the hook. It's a relief. I've got a baby to think about.

Life – at least this dysfunctional, in-between version of it – carries on. After a while, the media begin to disperse again. Sasha visits regularly. Work sends flowers. Even Donna and Greg call round, which is nice of them. Dan doesn't phone me, and I'm glad. I see Kay's GP and she sends me to the hospital for a scan and they tell me I'm eleven weeks pregnant and that everything's fine, despite how much I drank on my honeymoon, before I suspected. It's only when I see the heartbeat that it hits me. My baby's heart is beating. It seems its father's is not. I miss him.

So here I am. I'm married. I'm pregnant. I don't know where my husband is. I feel sick all the time and

I don't know if it's the pregnancy hormones, or the ominous feeling I have, that is still growing and growing, like my baby. I feel such ambivalence, and this isn't how it was meant to be. I'd been so keen to get on with getting pregnant as soon as we were married – nagging Jamie that I was thirty-four now, that it might take some time. A honeymoon baby had felt like the best-case scenario to me once. Now it feels like the cruellest of ironies. And yet, in another way, it's my saviour. I have to keep going, for my baby, if nothing else.

The phone rings early one morning, and I am in bed, my head swimming, and even the noise scares the life out of me – but it's just my boss, who asks me how I am, and when I want to come back, and I daren't tell him yet that I'm having a baby. He's so nice, and he doesn't seem to believe any of the crap that has been written about me in the press, although I can tell that he's secretly excited by his proximity to such drama, such infamy. He tells me there's an amazing project coming up in Manchester, and it's as if he's realized that the thought of going overseas right now is beyond me. I'm grateful to him. I tell him that I'll think about it, and that I'll call him in a few days, and when I hang up, I feel a semblance of normality at last, as if perhaps there is a route back to real life, after all. And then I go downstairs and watch five episodes of *Come Dine With Me* in a row, and one of the hosts makes a marvellous Maldivian curry, which wins him the show, and soon

I'll have watched all the episodes available on catch-up. Just as I'm wondering apathetically what series I should get into next, the phone rings again, and it is my taciturn policeman friend Bob, and he wants me to come in to see him, immediately.

75

For my first police interview back in England, I have my solicitor with me, who is a nice enough woman but the type who makes it clear that her time is both valuable and expensive, so I really shouldn't waste it. Bob is with someone different today, too – Lara – and Lara doesn't sound like a police officer's name to me, but I assume she must be one. It's weird to see Bob here, in the dull grey interview room, wearing long trousers. He gets straight to the point. Apparently Kenny has told them that not only did his wife witness an ugly argument between me and Jamie at the restaurant (which is OK, Bob and Neil and I went through a version of that in the Maldives), but that later, on the beach, I told her that I wished Jamie would 'just fuck off, disappear'. Those were the exact words he quoted. And then, Bob says, to top all that, at around twelve forty-five on the morning of Jamie's disappearance, Kenny claims he heard a commotion outside his bungalow, and when he got up to look out from the terrace, he saw me and Jamie fighting in the sea.

'Oh,' I say.

Bob doesn't say anything. My solicitor is furious, I can tell. She doesn't like to be wrong-footed.

'Do you have anything to say?' Lara says.

'Well, he would say that, wouldn't he?' I'm aware that someone famous said that once, and I sound impertinent, although I don't mean to be.

'Mrs Armstrong,' says Bob. First name terms are well and truly over. 'This is not a joke.'

'Can we take five minutes?' asks Jennifer, my solicitor.

'Sure,' says Bob. He and Lara get up and wait outside the door. I can't think what to say to Jennifer, compromised as I am in this horrible little room. I don't know why I didn't tell her. But I honestly hadn't remembered the fight with my husband, at first. I'd been so out of it on the night Jamie went missing, and I dread to think what pills Chrissy had given me. I honestly thought to begin with that the bed was damp and covered in sand because I'd been swimming with *Chrissy*. I'd only remembered the rest as the result of a nightmare a couple of nights before I left the island – and I still genuinely hadn't been sure if it had truly happened. And even when the memories had gradually started to come back, they'd been hazy still and poorly defined, like an old, smudged pencil sketch, so it hadn't seemed worth mentioning to the police, not at such a late stage – especially as it seemed no-one had witnessed it.

I certainly recall that night well enough now, though – maybe it was the way Bob was glaring at me. *Jamie meeting me as I came in from the beach. Words exchanged about where the hell I'd been, what the fuck I'd been doing. Me racing across the sand, into the ocean. Jamie coming after me, catching me. Us fighting in the sea. Me being under the surface, my lungs bursting, my eyes bulging in horror . . . And then Jamie stopping suddenly, storming out of the water and away along the beach, into the darkness.* That's how I remember it, anyway.

Kenny's story, of course, is different from that. In Kenny's version of that dastardly night, it is I who comes out of the sea, who rises victorious, leaving Jamie alone and dead in the ocean, never to be seen again. That's what Kenny claims he saw. And now I don't know, I honestly don't know, if Jamie came out, or if he didn't. No wonder Kenny seemed so hostile towards me the next morning, when I'd seen him and Chrissy by the pool. Maybe he truly thinks I did it.

I long to ask Kenny what he saw, but he wouldn't tell the truth anyway, not now his own neck's on the line. But what I can't understand is why he didn't tell the police any of this before. Had he been trying to protect me? Or had he just not wanted to get involved? I assume it's the latter, now it seems clear that he had something else rather damning to hide. I still haven't a clue what spread-betting is, but money laundering is fairly self-explanatory, and from what I've gathered, it seems that Kenny is pretty adept at it.

Oh shit shit shit. I don't know how much Dad's paying Jennifer, with her smart Jaeger suits and school-prefect ways, but she'd better be good. Right now, she's dealing with a mysteriously vanished husband, a wife who, it transpires, has been inexcusably economical with the truth, and a crooked witness to a watery fight between the pair of them, which coincidentally was the last time the husband was seen.

I have no idea how this will pan out. There are no other witnesses. Chrissy had passed out. The Muslim couple in the next bungalow along were asleep with the doors shut and the air conditioning on full blast. The fourth bungalow in the cluster was empty. The rest of the island was sleeping, too far away to hear anyway. But without a body, or a verified sighting, somewhere in South America perhaps, how does anyone know whether or not a crime has even been committed? And if it ever came down to it – which, alarmingly, seems more and more likely, given the way Jennifer's glowering right now – how on earth would a jury decide whether it's me, or Kenny, who is telling the truth?

76

Two further weeks pass before the unthinkable happens and I'm arrested. I know as soon as they call me, to ask me to come in again. When I return to the same interview room, in a police station in Colindale, even Bob has a defeated air about him, as though he's disappointed in me, which isn't helping anything. The first thing I worry about is my baby. *What will happen to my baby?* My second thought is, *why the hell did I admit to the police that Jamie and I had a fight in the sea?* If I hadn't confessed to it, it would have been Kenny's word against mine. And if truth be told, I'm still not one hundred per cent sure what the outcome of the fight was anyway. All I'm completely certain of is that I woke up in bed alone – sandy and salty and feeling like death. Perhaps I just *imagined* Jamie walking out of the sea, in a case of wishful thinking. Maybe he really did drown, there in the still black water outside our bungalow. But if so, *did I do it?* I know I was a better swimmer than him, but surely I couldn't have been strong enough to drown him, even if I'd wanted to. It would have been an accident – it couldn't possibly have been murder. I am lost for words. Thank God for Jennifer, who has recovered her poise, and at least has her wits about her once more. She interjects now, in her cut-glass tones.

'Well, how would that explain the flippers?'

'I beg your pardon?' says Bob. He's wearing a jumper today, over a checked blue shirt. I'm in all grey.

'If Mr Copthorn says that Jamie chased Jemma down into the sea, then how would Jamie have been wearing his snorkel and flippers? His flippers were missing, weren't they?'

I look at Jennifer, dumbfounded. I hadn't even thought of that. I wonder if the police have.

Bob is too experienced to be caught out in such an obvious way. 'Yes, well, we've had to conclude that the mask may have been planted.'

'Planted?' I say. 'Who would do that?'

Jennifer looks at me witheringly, and I realize they mean me. This is getting beyond ridiculous. I find myself longing for Jamie, for him to knock some sense into them, and the realization jolts me. I miss him, properly miss him now I'm away from that hideous island, and it's heartbreaking. I'm having his baby – and I find I'm glad that there will be a piece of Jamie left, whatever may transpire in the future.

The rest of the interview passes in a blur of incomprehension, but at least at the end Bob says I can go, and it seems Jennifer has had the wherewithal to get me bail. I think being pregnant may have helped, so I suppose that's one thing to be thankful for. No-one's told me exactly why Kenny wasn't ever charged with anything to do with my husband, but from what I can gather the long tentacles of the money-laundering scandal in which he is mired are sadly not long enough to reach across and tie him in any provable way to Jamie, or his firm, after all. Obviously I don't want Jamie to be dead, and I don't want an innocent man to go to jail for murder, but, and feel free to call me callous, I'd much rather Kenny went than me.

There's been no further news on the police's absconding theory either. Pascal hasn't been arrested, but he has a clear link to Jamie. And Jamie was always down at the dive centre – perhaps they were plotting something together. Pascal has no alibi, after all – he could have done it. Why can't they investigate that potential avenue further, I think, before they jump to conclusions? A further possibility flickers into my strung-out mind, and it's that there's been a shed-load of media coverage, and the public are baying, and the police need a resolution, and I am the most credible suspect they have left. Accidental drowning is surely far too prosaic an outcome to the case after all this. Perhaps it's no wonder they've arrested me.

When I'm finally released, Dad's waiting to take me home, and I sit in the car and say nothing. I feel too numb. It's almost as if the story has become so non-sensical my mind is shutting down from it, refusing to absorb any more. All I know is that I can't think of the future right now. Its possibilities are too hellish. When we arrive back at Dad's, I go straight upstairs, take off my interview clothes, put on the tracksuit I've lived in for days, go down into the lounge and slouch on the sofa with Alfie. I know I look awful.

'Jemma, love,' Dad says. 'Are you hungry?'

I nod, although I'm not, and I almost miss Chati, who always seemed able to tempt me. Jamie was a good cook, too. Sadly, Dad's culinary efforts don't quite hit the mark, although of course I'd never tell him that.

Dad sits down on the chair opposite me. 'Jemma, love, I'm worried about you.'

There's nothing I can say to make him feel better. He takes my hand. 'I'm sorry your mum's not here for you.'

I don't know how to respond. What can either of us do about that? Perhaps there's no point in being mad any more and, besides, Dad has more than made up for being a historically crap parent in the last few weeks. He kisses my forehead and stands up and leaves the room. Fifteen minutes later he comes back with a bowl of soup and some cheese on toast, and although the food might not be to the gourmet standard of my honeymoon resort, it's enough that my dad is trying, and that he loves me, despite everything.

77

Sasha comes round again the next day, and I'm concerned about her. I can tell by the look in her eyes, her despair that I've got myself into this mess, that she's blaming herself. Sasha is one of those people who loves the romance of consequence, of the 'If I hadn't done X, then Y would never have happened' theory of the present. In Sasha's world, her fake email to my disastrous online-date, Dan, which kick-started this whole sorry sequence of events, renders Jamie's supposed death and my arrest for his murder entirely her fault. I tell her not to be silly, but she's insisting on cancelling her beach wedding in Barbados and moving it to Caterham, and hopes I'll still be bridesmaid. The fact that I might be in jail by then anyway occurs to her too late, she's already said it, and she starts crying again. I hold her hand as she sobs, and tell her over and over that it's not her fault. Whatever I do I mustn't let this ruin her life too.

Over the weeks following my arrest, I continue to find it hard to know how to feel, even when the worst happens, and I'm officially charged with my husband's murder. It's as if I've gone beyond grief and disbelief to numbness. The days slip by, and my mind grows more and more somnolent, and my body fills outwards . . .

and when my baby kicks for the first time it should be a joyful moment, but it is laced with sadness. What start am I giving this child? What hope does he have? Where is his father? Who will bring him up, if his mother goes to jail? What on earth have I done?

Kay and Dad do their best, and my baby keeps on growing, and the weeks roll by – and then at last the status quo is broken. A date has been set, and the only good piece of news is that it's in December. *Small mercies*. At least my trial, for the murder of my husband, is three months after I'm due to give birth to his baby.

78

In a sunny corner of a large, bucolic garden near Chelten-
ham, Dan is digging a hole. It's for a rectangular fish pond,
and he really has to put his back into it, and although he
enjoys manual labour, he no longer likes digging trenches.
It makes him think of his brother, who, as far as anyone
still knows, may or may not be dead, but, assuming he is,
has never had a funeral. The ghastly scenario is a cancer
that has crept into the corner of his heart and eaten away
at the happy life he has tried so hard to build for himself.

And yet it was never meant to have been like this.
His brother's wedding was supposed to have been the
full stop to his past. It was meant to have been the time
he properly said goodbye to his love for a girl who long
ago had betrayed him. It was meant to have been a time
for forgiveness.

Dan stops and wipes his brow. The sun has a strength
to it that should be uplifting, but isn't. Instead, Dan
feels deeply saddened as he remembers past events all
over again. He'd been phlegmatic about seeing her at
the wedding rehearsal. No, not even phlegmatic —
completely fine. They'd run into each other at a couple of
family events over the previous few years. He was
happy with Lydia. It was all in the past.

It had been a foul-weathered evening, and the church had been gloomy. He pictures Jemma now, running in from the rain, completely drenched, and it reminds him of the first time he ever saw her. She'd always had a raw kind of energy that made people look at her. A neurotic glow, he'd called it. He remembers watching her race over to Jamie and throw her arms around him, in an ostentatious apology for being late for the rehearsal. Jamie laughing and saying it was fine, as long as she didn't repeat it on the day itself. Her smiling entrancingly at the vicar, getting away with it. The *jealousy* that had struck him, deep in his bones. The sudden desire to rip his little brother's throat out. It was just as bad as the time he'd seen them kissing in his parents' house. What had been stronger in both of those moments, six years apart? Dan's possessiveness of Jemma? Or his resentment of his brother? He still isn't sure. He can barely admit to himself the extent of his desire for revenge. He's tried so hard to suppress his feelings over the intervening years, but it seems he has failed.

As Dan carries on digging, the hole he's in getting bigger and bigger, he recalls Jemma's gaze moving away from Jamie and falling briefly on him, and the fact she was finally over him had been obvious, and it had angered him further. He'd *hated* her and Jamie in that moment, almost wished them both dead.

Dan groans as he flings another shovel-load of dirt over his shoulder. The earth is black and rich, so full of potential. The sun is too hot on his back. He wonders vaguely whether Jemma will be found guilty of his brother's murder. The case against her is almost entirely circumstantial – a trial by media, in his opinion – but it has been relentless and brutal and utterly destructive for all of them. *Was* she capable of killing someone, though? Dan honestly doesn't know. And would it ultimately prove to be his fault, for ruining their happiness, just as they had once ruined his? What kind of Armageddon had one little phone call unleashed?

Dan puts down his shovel, as if in surrender, and lies prone in the trench, which is just long enough to fit him now. He lies still and closes his eyes and imagines soil being flung on top of him, and the midday sun on his face is glorious, and the smell of the earth is rich, and mellow, and full of worms and maggots, like death.

79

A few months later

The police call Jamie's parents second, straight after they've let Jemma know. His mother takes the call, and when she puts down the phone her breath is jumpy and her eyes are flinty. She calls for her still-unwell husband as she lies gasping and swooning on the multi-pillowed sofa, and when Peter shuffles in, she insists that he fans her face, as she's sure she's about to pass out. Eventually, she sits up and her lips are thin and red, and her eyes are flashing with a hard-to-define emotion. What is it? What is she feeling? It's as if the path has been opened up again, the faint hope that her Jamie, her precious baby, might still be *alive,* after all this time. And yet, if it turns out that that is indeed true, that Jamie has absconded somehow, a different path might therefore be blocked. *The one that sees Jemma go to jail.* Even Veronica is appalled at her conflicting emotions, the depths of her hatred.

'That was the police,' she says, at last.

'Oh?' says Peter. He starts coughing, a little at first, and then harder, until he's hacking – taking away the attention from her as usual, she thinks crossly.

'Apparently the story is about to break, so they wanted us to know first . . .' Veronica takes a long, self-important pause. It's the most extraordinary feeling, that this is her moment, and she despises herself for it. ' . . . Another tourist has gone missing in the Maldives.'

'Oh.'

'Another honeymooner. Another man.'

'Oh.'

'On the same island.' Veronica starts weeping.

'Ohhh,' says Peter, but she can tell that this last one has a note of understanding in it, rather than being a filler to hopefully appease rather than antagonize her.

'It's too much of a coincidence,' she sobs. 'I *knew* it must have been that Pascal. I never trusted him, the slimy French snake.'

This is no time for xenophobia, Peter thinks, but he daren't say so. 'Now, come on, dear, is that what the police have said? Otherwise it's rather jumping to conclusions.'

'Well, no, they haven't said anything yet. But perhaps Pascal's running some kind of racket, helping people disappear and start new lives. How could Jamie *do* that to us?'

'We don't know that, Ronnie. We don't know anything. It might turn out to be just a terrible coincidence. We need to wait for the police to investigate it.'

'Oh, my nerves just can't stand it!' Veronica says. 'Fetch me a sherry, will you, Peter?'

Peter nods, ever obedient, but in her heightened state her husband's compliance just annoys Veronica. Why is he always so passive, she thinks. Why can't he be passionate for a change, show some emotion? Why hadn't *he* ever loved *her* the way Dan and Jamie had fawned over that dreadful girl? And now her darling boy is still missing, and yet Jemma is surely off the hook. It's too much.

Veronica lets out a low, guttural wail that turns into a growled, 'Hurry *up*, Peter.' She needs a drink. She watches her husband take a few shaky steps towards the door, and then he wheezes again, and an expression crosses his face that she hasn't seen before . . . And now, instead of going out of the room, he turns around, walks over to his wing-backed chair and sits down decisively – and has the temerity to tell her that if she wants a drink, she can bloody well get it herself.

80

The buffet is as enticing and food-laden as ever, the cream puffs fresh, the fruit displayed in a bounteously flamboyant fashion, the sushi cut like jewels, the aromas sweet and intoxicating, but Nathalie can't stomach anything. *She* hadn't hesitated for one single second to report her husband missing – in fact, she'd run into the main restaurant and screamed the place down, so pretty much everyone had heard the moment she'd realized he was gone. But that had been twenty-four hours ago now, and since then the island has been crawling with police, seemingly dozens of them, and she's been either completely hysterical or else on the verge of it. Surely it was too much of a coincidence to expect a good outcome for Cory, not after the last disappearance here. She'd even suggested to him, once she'd realized, that they pick another island, but Cory's heart had been set on this one. He'd just laughed and told her that she was being paranoid, and besides, it was the wife who'd done it anyway. So unless *she'd* been planning on drowning *him*, her husband had quipped, he was sure that he would survive their honeymoon.

Nathalie feels light-headed again. She wonders where he could be, what could have happened. He'd said he was going for a quick walk to look for baby sharks basking in the shallows while she was blow-drying her hair before dinner, joking that she always took so long. But then he'd never come back, and when she'd run down and looked at the beach, curling emptily away in both directions, she'd known instantly. The feeling had been like a rock, wrapped in barbed wire, landing in the bottom of her stomach. Thank goodness her parents had got straight on a flight from Sydney and are here with her already. The situation is just too horrific to handle alone.

'Traditional curry, ma'am?' says the smiley, soft-eyed chef. She shakes her head, but her mother insists that she eat something, and even Nathalie isn't completely averse – she hasn't eaten a thing since she realized Cory was gone, and the food *is* delicious. Mrs Jarvis nods in thanks and says that she'll have some too. Mother and daughter head back to their white-clothed table, which is in the far corner, shaded by palm trees, the view exquisite. Their waiter, Bobbi, appears discreetly and pulls out the chairs for them, rearranges their linen napkins across their laps. Once they are settled her mother does her best to cajole her, but it seems Nathalie has no appetite after all. She can't bear the eyes on her, the thrum of the search boats, the grotesque atmosphere of suppressed excitement. She can't bear the feeling of doom, gathering in the pit of her belly. She longs for Cory, who she has been with since high school, who is her best friend in the world. And so as

Nathalie picks at her plate, she can't help but break down again – and to hide her endless tears, she turns and stares out to the blinking blue sea, and she searches hopelessly for her brand-new husband, out there in the soft, slack waves.

81

Pascal Anais sits sullenly across from two Maldivian policemen. They are the same officers who'd managed the initial investigation into the baffling disappearance of Jamie Armstrong, although the interview isn't taking place in the sanatorium this time. Instead they're all crammed into the small office behind Reception, cooped up with whirring printers and photocopiers that make the air-conditioned air feel hot and full of static. Pascal is furious with himself. He *knew* he should have quit his job and left the island after the police had departed nine months ago. It seems he'd been right about it being too risky to remain.

The police officers are as smartly uniformed as ever, but they have a noticeably brighter air than they'd had by the end of the original investigation, when they'd been upstaged by those British police who, in Pascal's opinion, seemed just as keen to get a tan as solve any potential crimes. Pascal feels ganged up on today, and he's still in his wetsuit, and he doesn't know how many more times he'll have to say that he really doesn't know where Jamie is, or this new man, whatever he's called. Why do they have to keep picking on *him*? Do they really think he runs an international smuggling ring from a small thatch-roofed building on the south side of an island that you could fit into the middle of the Seine? It's a ridiculous suggestion.

Pascal wishes he'd never got involved with Jamie now, then perhaps none of this would ever have happened. *Mon dieu.* All he'd done was sort out a deal on a honeymoon, as a favour to his sister, but no matter how many times Pascal tells that to the police, they refuse to believe him. And now this other guy has gone missing too, and Pascal doesn't even know who he is, yet the police insist on insinuating that he's involved somehow. It's as if there's a magic sinkhole, somewhere on this atrocious island, which husbands fall into. Pascal folds his arms and scowls as the police try again.

'So, where were you on the evening that Mr Faustino disappeared?'

Pascal huffs. 'I told you. In my room. I was tired.'

'Did you speak to anyone?'

'No.'

'Did anyone see you go into your room?'

'I don't know. I wasn't looking.' Pascal feels trapped, enraged, and he longs to just get up, walk out of this whirring, clattering room. Don't these clowns know how exhausting it is, taking bored, rich tourists out to see the same fish, the same reefs, day after day? Constantly having to balance flirting with the wives with not pissing off the husbands. Often, after he's showered and eaten, he just stays in his room and watches a movie, gets away from everyone.

Pascal sighs. Whatever happens, as soon as he can, he's going to go back to Thailand, where people are normal. Staying on this tiny island has stultified him, turned him ever so slightly crazy, and it isn't worth it, no matter how good the pay might be. He's had enough. The police have nothing on him. They can't force him to stay and sit through this ludicrous charade.

'Can I go now?' Pascal says. The policemen look surprised. They turn and glance at each other, shrug their shoulders.

'Do you have anything more to add?' the sinister-looking officer asks.

'*Non*,' Pascal says. '*Rien.*'

'I beg your pardon?'

'Nothing. I have nothing to say.'

The two policemen look at each other again. Pascal holds his breath.

'OK,' the smaller one says. 'You are free to go. For now.' He clicks off the tape recorder.

'*D'accord, poulets.*'

'I beg your pardon?'

'I said, thank you,' says Pascal, and he stands up and stomps barefoot out of the office.

82

Nine months earlier

Jamie lurched out of the sea and ran along the dark, cool beach, stumbling and retching. *Oh my God.* What had just happened? What the *fuck* had he and Jemma been thinking? Physically fighting in the sea, in the dark, off their faces – they could so easily have drowned.

Jamie hared his way across the sand and around the tip of the island, away from the bungalows, until finally he began to slow his pace as his breath caught up with him. Just before the beach bar, he slunk away into the patch of jungle that crossed the north-east side of the island, where the sand became pebbly and it was scratchy underfoot. He stopped completely now, and bent over for a moment, panting. Thank *fuck* he'd come to his senses and let her go, but bloody hell, it had been way too close for comfort. But what on earth had been the matter with her? Despite all the times she'd gone for him before, like a wild cat, he'd never thought she would actually try to *kill* him.

And yet maybe it wasn't all that surprising, Jamie thought now. Ever since their wedding day, Jemma had been acting like she fucking hated him, would barely come near him, certainly wouldn't sleep with him, and on their *honeymoon* too. He'd known all along that she was lying about her period, but short of forcing her, what else could he have done, apart from try to make the best of a bad situation.

Jamie sank down onto the sandy ground, his head between his legs, trying to work it out. None of it made any sense. Had she meant it when she'd said in the restaurant that she wished that she'd married *his brother*? Had there been something going on between Jemma and Dan behind his back – perhaps even on the night before the wedding? He and Jemma had stuck to tradition and been apart that night – and it would explain Jemma's apparent gigantic change of heart. *Surely not?* If it were true, Jamie would *kill* Dan. Literally pulverize him.

Jamie's hypotheses continued to crawl through his brain, like maggots. He just couldn't work it out. If Jemma *was* having an affair with Dan, why would she have gone to all the trouble of marrying him, Jamie? She had many faults, for sure, but he was pretty certain being a deceitful bitch wasn't one of them. Yet what had made her so suddenly hostile? Jamie had willed himself not to react tonight, to walk away from dinner with his head held high, but he'd been drunk, and overwrought, and utterly demeaned. He'd even tried calling Camille when he'd got back to the bungalow to ask her what to do. Camille had been so great to him when Jemma had delivered her marriage ultimatum, had even talked him into proposing – not that he dared tell

Jemma that, of course, just in case she took it the wrong way. But Camille was married anyway; there was no need for Jemma to be jealous. Or maybe marriage didn't count for anything in Jemma's book, if her attitude to being a newly-wed was anything to go by. The whole situation was a joke.

Jamie didn't know what to do, who else he could confide in. He felt too humiliated to talk to any of his mates, and there was no way he could let his family know what was going on – his mother hated Jemma enough as it was.

Slowly, Jamie's mind turned a corner, to a new realization. Perhaps this was all his fault anyway, for stealing Jemma off Dan in the first place. Maybe it had never been destined to end well. But there had been something about Jemma that had got to Jamie the moment he'd set eyes on her. And true, he'd behaved badly in the beginning, should never have humiliated Dan so publicly by snogging his girlfriend, and at a family party to boot, but he'd tried his best to make amends. He'd begged Dan to forgive Jemma, to take her back, but Dan had refused, like the pig-headed sulker he'd always been. Sometimes Jamie didn't know what Dan's fucking problem was.

Jamie started to shiver. He wondered what he could do to rescue his marriage – or was it really set to be over before it began? He'd been so happy about getting married, despite having dragged his feet for so long beforehand – but it was never because he hadn't loved her. It had just been that hardly any of his friends were married yet, and he hadn't seen the point of rocking the boat, and Jemma had stopped mentioning it, anyway – and so he'd thought she was cool with it too. He hadn't realized how unhappy it had made her. Her ultimatum had shaken him, and he'd been shocked at how much he'd missed her in the week they'd been apart. He'd missed the way things were never predictable with Jemma, how she was never dull like his other girlfriends had been. Maybe crazy was how he liked his women. They'd totally blown it now, though, that was for sure. Nearly drowning each other was not the way to build bridges.

Jamie put his head on his knees and groaned. He'd tried so hard to make this honeymoon perfect, had brought Jemma to the place of her dreams, to a resort so luxurious it had cost an absolute fortune, even with the discount Pascal had got them. Perhaps he should have told Jemma about that, but she was still so paranoid about Camille he hadn't wanted to infect their honeymoon with any link to his ex-boss. However, a lie was a lie – maybe Jemma had picked up on it somehow and that was why she'd become so hostile. Or perhaps she'd found out about his new bank account – but he hadn't dared tell her how much this place was, even at the reduced rate, and so it had been easier to just put some money away each month without her knowing. It would have just spoiled it for her.

Jamie heard a tremor behind him and turned, but saw nothing. The jungle was black and impenetrable.

Only the warm breeze, the sandy ground beneath him, gave a clue to his whereabouts. He'd rarely felt so alone, as if he was at the edge of the world. He tried to decide what to do next. The irony was that, even after his and Jemma's row at the restaurant, Jamie had been sitting on the terrace, waiting for Jemma to come home, so he could *apologize* for his part in the argument. But when she'd come lurching up the beach with Chrissy, laughing as though she hadn't a care in the world, it had infuriated him. And then when she'd seen him and instantly turned on her heel and raced back down towards the water, as though she couldn't bear to even breathe the same air as him, *of course* he'd gone after her. And when she'd run straight into the sea, the nutcase, he'd gone in too – but only because she was clearly paralytic, and he'd been worried about her alone in the water.

Jamie could hardly bear to remember the next bit. How he'd easily caught up with her, even though she was usually a better swimmer than him. Jemma lashing out at him, trying to push him under, telling him over and over that she *hated* him, that she wished she'd never married him. Fighting her off, holding her down. Her coming up gasping and choking once he'd released her, and then attacking him all over again. He felt sick at the memory.

Jamie got to his feet. His heart was still hammering, although his breath was finally beginning to regulate. He shook his head, as if to free it of the images circling through his brain, and started walking again, his wet clothes unpleasant against his skin now. He needed to check on her. Hopefully she was safely out of the water by now and had gone to bed. As Jamie kept walking, again he tried to make sense of how he and Jemma had got to this last dismal point in their relationship. He couldn't work it out. But however it had happened, it seemed that everything, absolutely everything, was fucked up. His marriage. His honeymoon. His life.

What the hell was he going to do?

Jamie looked down through the trees to the beach. It was quiet, and dark, and the sea gleamed blackly. A flash of plankton lit up the surface and it was mesmerizing. The air was hot and perfumed. He imagined taking a kayak out into the waves, chasing the glow, seeing where it led him. Escaping from all this, to a little secret island perhaps. Maybe that's what he should do. It was possible. The water would be calm, and huge, and lapping, and liberating . . .

And he was being an idiot.

Jamie sighed and turned away, and started to follow the path across the island to home. He might have been being a coward before, but he wouldn't be one now. He needed to go and face the music, sort things out with her. Perhaps he just needed to ask her outright, find out what she was so unhappy about. And if confronting it meant that their marriage was over before it began, at least they'd both know. It was the paralysis, the pretence, on their supposedly perfect honeymoon, that had been driving them both mad. Yet despite everything, he loved her still. And she loved him, he was sure of i—

The thud landed right in the middle of the back of Jamie's head, and it was dull, and satisfying, and entirely effective, and Jamie's redemptive thought process was never quite completed, and after just a few seconds his poor tortured mind was quieted forever, which, considering what happened next, was probably just as well.

83

In Gloucestershire, a million miles from the Maldives, it is pouring with rain. It's Saturday, late-afternoon, and Dan is at home, alone. Lydia has gone to her mother's, again, and he's feeling fairly bereft, but he's been like that for months now. He still feels so guilty about his little brother, who had been a thorn in Dan's side from the moment he'd sprung out of their mother's womb. And although it was true that Dan had wanted revenge on Jamie, he hadn't wanted all this to happen. Dan keeps going over and over the call that he'd made to Jemma, the night before her wedding. He can still remember it word for word. It still makes him feel terrible.

'Hello?' She'd sounded sleepy, content.

'Hi, Jemma.'

'Hello? Is that *Dan*? What are you calling me for?'

'Jemma, I just wanted you to know something . . . I still love you.'

'*What?*'

'I still love you, Jemma.'

'Dan . . . What the fuck? What the *fuck*?' He remembers the bewilderment in her voice, swiftly rising to rage. 'What the hell are you calling me for? I'm getting *married* tomorrow. You're insane.'

'Perhaps, but I wanted you to know how I feel.'

'*No*, Dan. I can only assume that you must be drunk or something, because this is *really* not on. I will pretend this conversation never happened. Go away. Leave me alone.' And with that, she'd slammed down the phone.

Dan had felt satisfied. He'd known the damage was done, and he'd revelled in it. He couldn't let them have a completely perfect day, could he? The pair of them had deserved it. But then when Jemma had rung him distraught the day after the wedding, saying that she'd made a mistake marrying Jamie, Dan had been rattled, and he'd realized that maybe he'd gone too far. In the end, he'd just begged her to go on her honeymoon, as he certainly hadn't wanted her back. Not after she'd spent years with his brother.

And now? Now Dan feels chock-full of regret, as if he is drowning in it. Yes, he may have always resented Jamie. Yes, it was true his love for Jemma had turned to hate – but he had never intended for all *this* to happen. He still hopes that one day his brother might turn up, come back, especially now someone else has gone missing too. Improbable as it sounds, perhaps both men have absconded somehow. Frankly, nothing would surprise him at this point.

In the end, it is a call from his poor, broken father that alerts Dan to the latest theory. Dan checks the news on his phone, but he just can't believe it. He flees into his garden, despite the weather, and stands in the deluge, his face turned to the sky. He needs some fresh air in his lungs, to try to breathe out the stench permeating his body. Rain is driving into his eyes but he doesn't care. He feels the need to weep, and this is the best he can manage for now.

Soon Dan's stomach inevitably starts to turn, and he vomits into the flower bed. The story is too disturbing to contemplate, but he supposes it might just be true. After a few minutes, he wipes his mouth, turns around and heads back into the kitchen. He stands at the sink and puts his mouth under the tap, rinses out the bile, dries his face on a tea towel. Muddy footprints trail across the pale-grey tiles. Water drips off his hair. Dan goes into the lounge and checks the iPad this time, just in case his father had been lying, just in case he, Dan, has imagined it.

No. The headlines carry the normal gleeful tone the tabloids usually reserve for these situations:

Honeymoon horror:
Chef cooks bridegroom and feeds to bride.

Mohammed Chatala, a chef at the luxury Seabreeze resort on Baadhoo Island in the Maldives, has been accused of murdering Cory Faustino, 30, of Sydney, Australia, and adding his flesh to dishes that he then served to guests at the seven-star honeymoon resort, including Mr Faustino's own wife, Nathalie, 30.

Police are currently looking into the link between this disappearance and that of Jamie Armstrong, 35, of Islington, London, who went missing on the same island nine months ago.

Before this latest development, Mr Armstrong's wife Jemma, 34, who has recently given birth to their son, was on bail, awaiting trial for the murder of her husband.

Dan throws down his iPad and sinks to the floor, his head in his hands, where he rocks back and forth, in disgust, and horror, and shame.

84

Chati is sitting quietly at the back of the little red sea-plane, which is preparing for take-off. There are four Maldivian police officers on board too, right at the front, as well as the pilot and co-pilot. Chati is in leg chains and hand-cuffs, which are really quite unnecessary, but he supposes he can't blame them. They don't understand.

Chati is well aware that he'd been playing a dangerous game, doing it again, and he wonders now whether he might even have *wanted* to get caught, otherwise surely he wouldn't have done it. Or maybe his cannibalistic tendencies, once indulged, had become too strong to deny. Well, he thinks, at least he's killed two birds with one stone, as the charges against Jemma will be dropped now. He'd been horrified that his vainglorious attempt to free her from her miserable marriage had resulted in her being accused of her husband's murder. That hadn't been the plan at all – but, there again, he hadn't known until afterwards that she'd had such a complicated history with the brother. It had been unbearable watching Jemma suffer as the net closed in on her, and all he could do was bring her meals, try to show her that he believed in her, was looking out for her, even if no-one else was. They'd become such good friends. He'd missed her so much when she'd left.

Chati hears the roar of the engines starting up, and in a moment he will be leaving this island forever. It saddens him in a way. He'd enjoyed his job at first, had taken pleasure in flashing his widest, friendliest smile at the prettiest guests from his position behind the serving counter, doling out culinary comfort with a flourish. But after a while, he'd become lonely, and he'd been on the island too long, with nowhere else to go. So at least coming up with his plan had given him something to think about, work towards. He'd thought of everything. The place deep in the jungle where he'd spent hours sawing up the body, and where no-one had been able to hear him. The neat packages of meat he'd put in the industrial-sized freezer, ready for use in the dishes he'd so carefully planned. The bones and fat and unwanted flesh that he'd taken out in a boat the next day, in his time off between shifts, and fed to the fish. Other bits and pieces of Jamie that had gone out in the refuse tugs, along with the rest of the island's rubbish. The clothes that he'd cut up and burnt on the beach, while preparing a romantic barbecue. And all executed before it had occurred to anyone that it might be anything other than an accidental drowning. It was like one of those magic tricks, where you divert attention from the scene of the deception. It had been so simple. A mask and snorkel washing up on the beach on the wild side of the island.

The missing flippers being dumped with all the others at the dive centre, as no records were kept of who'd been loaned which pairs, and Jemma would never have been able to identify them.

Chati feels devastated as he thinks of Jemma, broken-hearted that he'll never see her again. There had been something so special about her. Up until now, he's been getting his fix of her through watching clips of the news stories on YouTube, but he doubts he'll have access to the Internet where he's going. She was so beautiful, and so sad. Chati had been drawn to her from the very moment she'd run into him on her bike in the bushes, when he'd been out there finalizing arrangements. And as soon as he'd realized how unhappy she was with her husband, he'd known that she was the one – or rather, that Jamie was. And she'd been so kind to him when he'd delivered her meals each day, and he'd derived such a deep satisfaction when he'd seen how happy he'd made her, under such stressful circumstances.

Dear, sweet, brave Jemma, Chati thinks now. Look at how she'd lugged a fish-bitten hulk of a man to shore and then had sprinted to find help. Had sprinted to find *him*. It had been their destiny, surely? Her lovely face had made his heart warm with hope, and he'd known then that he was ready. It had been almost too easy. By far the worst part had been having to watch, helpless, from the edge of the beach as his sweetheart nearly drowned – but when he'd finally watched her rise from the sea like a mermaid, her slender form lit up by the moonbeams, he'd been on the verge of ecstasy.

As the plane takes off, Chati looks down at the brilliantly freakish seascape, his home for so many years, and tries to think what might happen to him now. He knows it will be nothing but bad – but that's the price you pay, he thinks, when you love someone. He and Jemma had shared such a special bond, and he'd never ever forget her. And at least he'd always know that she would be OK now, that he'd done the right thing by her – that both times he'd killed a man, he'd ultimately ended up saving her.

85

I've known for eleven unimaginable days, and although I still pray it's not true, I know it almost certainly is. It's evening, and I'm sitting alone on a sofa in one of the furthest corners of North London, weak with dread. Dad and Kay are in the kitchen, attempting to make me something I might feel able to eat, and I know I have to try, if not for them, then for my baby. Although I do my best not to let them, my thoughts turn yet again to Chati, dear, kind Chati, who had fed me, looked after me, nurtured me. Had he really *murdered* Jamie, and then chopped him up and fed him to me, his despairing bride, for the best part of a week? I hadn't thought things could get any worse. My head floats and spins, again. The nausea rises, again, although of course I am no longer pregnant.

And yet I can't stop thinking about it. Somehow, processing my feelings for Jamie's murderer feels important to me. I am almost as horrified by my erstwhile friendship with Chati as I am by what he has done. How had I not felt his evil? How had I thought he was sweet, that his wide, gleaming smile was one of benevolence? The irony is that I was drawn to Chati, not just because of his gentleness, his assiduousness in looking after me, but because he was the only one who seemed wholeheartedly to believe in me. And yet *of course he was*. He was the only one who knew the truth.

But just how deluded was I? Shouldn't I have realized how inappropriate it was, when he started staying to watch me eat? Shouldn't I have guessed something was wrong? If I'd thought to mention it to the resort, or the police, *might I even have saved the next man?* And then I tell myself not to be fanciful, that never in my wildest dreams could I have imagined the truth. That it's not my fault.

Kay comes in with a tray, and she places it in front of me, and then she sits down next to me, just the right distance away to make me feel safe, but not too close for me to feel threatened. There are triangles of Marmite toast, with the crusts cut off, and I can eat those. There is an apple, and I know that will be fine too. A handful of crisps is beyond my limits for the moment, but that's OK. Kay smiles at me encouragingly, and I press her hand gently, and we both know I'll get there. I have to, for my son. I have no choice.

'Hello?' Gabriel is squawking in the background, so it's hard to hear, but my phone has told me who it is, of course. And although I dread doing it, I know I need to confront this, and sooner rather than later. I need to purge everything, for my baby's sake.

'Jemma, it's Dan.'

'I know.' I walk over to Gabriel's carry-cot, by the window behind the ever-closed curtains.

'Look, I'm so sorry,' he says.

'Thanks.'

'D'you think that's what happened to Jamie too?'

I pause, gently wipe Gabriel's nose. He is so tiny, and perfect. Dan's line of questioning is brutal, in front of my son, but how can it be anything but? Brutal is probably best. I blanch, suddenly, at the thought of it all over again, and lean heavily against the window.

'Have the police contacted you?' says Dan now.

'Yes.'

'Are they going to drop the charges against you?'

'I don't know.' They have, but I don't feel like telling him. It's none of his business.

'Jemma?'

'Yes.'

'I'm sorry.'

'Oh.' I can't even bear to ask what he's specifically referring to. There are so many options. 'And?' I say now to Dan, who is silent, and I know I sound rude, but, really, what does he expect?

'Are you all right?'

'Yes. No. I'm coping, but this is . . .' I can't think of a word that even begins to reflect how bad it is, and I'm relieved when Kay pokes her head around the door to see if I need rescuing. Again, I wonder how I would have coped without my step-mother these past months. She's a world away from Veronica, who barely even acknowledged me when she and Peter came to see me after the birth, and instead just cooed over Gabriel. I have given up on my mother-in-law ever doing anything other than hating me, even though she's Gabriel's grandmother and we are bound to each other forever.

'That's good to hear,' says Dan.

'Hmm,' I say. I wish he'd just go away.

'Jemma,' says Dan. He tries again. 'I'm sorry about what happened between us.'

His statement makes me draw in my breath, and I'm dimly surprised my mind finds the energy to respond. But as the words settle in the air somewhere between us – me in London, him in Gloucestershire, I presume – it occurs to me all over again that, if Dan had forgiven me all those years ago, maybe I would have ended up married to him, instead of to Jamie. Which would have meant that I would never have married Jamie at all, of course, never gone on honeymoon with him, never flown to that particular island, never met Chati . . .

But it gets worse than that. I *had* married Jamie. And I'd adored him – until Dan had rung me up out of the blue and told me that he still loved me. Still I wonder at that phone call, at Dan's motivations – the *night* before my wedding. What had he really hoped to achieve? Did he do it just to destabilize me, fuck up Jamie's and my chances of happiness? That's certainly how it looks to me now. And maybe Chati would never have picked Jamie if we hadn't been so miserable together. I hadn't thought of it like that before, that it might be Dan's fault, whichever way you look at it.

'Dan, it's not OK,' I say. 'It will never be OK. Jamie's dead.' My throat tightens around the last word in that sentence.

The silence is painful, but I don't care.

'I just . . . I just wanted you to know how sorry I am,' he says, again.

'OK. You've told me.' I can't bring myself to forgive him. My heart doesn't stretch that far.

'All right,' says Dan. 'Look . . . keep me posted, will you?'

'OK,' I say, although I know that I won't. He sounds close to tears but I don't care. My voice is so quiet. 'Bye, Dan.' When he has gone, I stare at the phone and decide I won't talk to him ever again. His guilt is not my problem. I need to survive.

The cooing is dulcet. I turn and gaze at my miraculous son, give him a little smile, before dropping my head in despair and grief for Dan's brother, Gabriel's father, my husband. I say a prayer for Jamie, who I feel so devastated for now, and who I'd loved so much once. I find myself wondering whether we'd have got through it, recovered from our disastrous honeymoon, and it kills me that I'll never know. And then I stand up and pick up Gabriel, who gurgles with contentment, and I take him out into the garden, and I stand on the cold winter grass and look up into the wide, wondrous sky, to see if we can see his daddy out there, somewhere in the stars.

What makes Emily Coleman wake up one morning and walk right out of her life?

No-one has ever guessed her secret.
Will you?

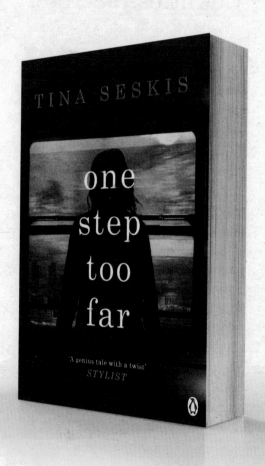

TINA SESKIS

one
step
too
far

'A genius tale with a twist'
STYLIST

Available now

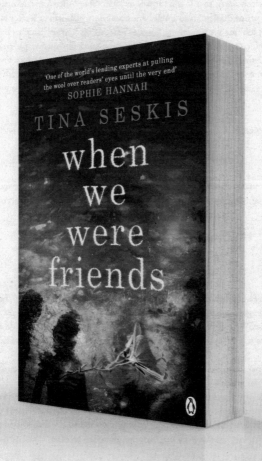

He just wanted a decent book to read …

Not too much to ask, is it? It was in 1935 when Allen Lane, Managing Director of Bodley Head Publishers, stood on a platform at Exeter railway station looking for something good to read on his journey back to London. His choice was limited to popular magazines and poor-quality paperbacks – the same choice faced every day by the vast majority of readers, few of whom could afford hardbacks. Lane's disappointment and subsequent anger at the range of books generally available led him to found a company – and change the world.

'We believed in the existence in this country of a vast reading public for intelligent books at a low price, and staked everything on it'
Sir Allen Lane, 1902–1970, founder of Penguin Books

The quality paperback had arrived – and not just in bookshops. Lane was adamant that his Penguins should appear in chain stores and tobacconists, and should cost no more than a packet of cigarettes.

Reading habits (and cigarette prices) have changed since 1935, but Penguin still believes in publishing the best books for everybody to enjoy. We still believe that good design costs no more than bad design, and we still believe that quality books published passionately and responsibly make the world a better place.

So wherever you see the little bird – whether it's on a piece of prize-winning literary fiction or a celebrity autobiography, political tour de force or historical masterpiece, a serial-killer thriller, reference book, world classic or a piece of pure escapism – you can bet that it represents the very best that the genre has to offer.

Whatever you like to read – trust Penguin.